D1395962

ALSO BY JOHN COREY WHALEY

WHERE THINGS COME BACK

JoHN CoREY WHALEY

NoGGIN

SIMON & SCHUSTER

**FOR MOM AND DAD,
WHO ALWAYS HELP ME KEEP MY HEAD ON STRAIGHT.**

First published in Great Britain in 2014 by Simon and Schuster UK Ltd
A CBS COMPANY

Simon & Schuster UK Ltd
1st Floor
222 Gray's Inn Road
London WC1X 8HB

Originally published in the USA in 2014 by Atheneum Books for Young Readers
an imprint of Simon & Schuster Children's Publishing Division,
1230 Avenue of Americas, New York, BY 10020

www.simonandschuster.co.uk

A CIP catalogue record for this book
is available from the British Library.

PB ISBN: 978-1-47112-289-7
Ebook ISBN: 978-1-47112-290-3

1 3 5 7 9 10 8 6 4 2

Printed and bound by CPI Group (UK) Ltd, Croydon, CR0 4YY

"It is just an illusion here on Earth that one moment follows another one, like beads on a string, and that once a moment is gone, it is gone forever."

—Kurt Vonnegut Jr., *Slaughterhouse-Five*

CHAPTER ONE

ADVANCED STUDIES IN CRANIAL REANIMATION

Listen—I was alive once and then I wasn't. Simple as that. Now I'm alive again. The in-between part is still a little fuzzy, but I can tell you that, at some point or another, my head got chopped off and shoved into a freezer in Denver, Colorado.

You might have done it too. The dying part, I mean. Or the choosing-to-die part, anyway. They say we're the only species on the planet with the knowledge of our own impending doom. It's just that some of us feel that doom a lot sooner than expected. Trust me when I tell you that everything can go from fine and dandy to dark and depressing faster than you can say "acute lymphoblastic leukemia."

The old me got so sick so fast that no one really had time to do anything but talk about how sick he got and how fast he got that way. And the chemo and the radiation and the bone marrow transplants didn't do anything but make him sicker faster and with much more ferocity than before.

They say you can't die more than once. I would strongly disagree. But this isn't a story about the old me dying. No one wants to hear about how I told my parents, my best friend, Kyle, and my girlfriend, Cate, that I was choosing to give up. That's a story I don't want to tell. What I do want to tell you, though, is a story about how I suddenly found myself waking up in a hospital room with my throat sore, dry and burning, like someone had shoved an entire bag of vinegar-soaked cotton balls down it. I want to tell you about how I was moving my fingers and wiggling my toes and how the doctors and nurses standing around me were so impressed with this. I'm not sure why blinking my eyes earned a round of applause and why it mattered that I was peeing into a bag, but to these people, it was like they were witnessing a true miracle. Some of the nurses were even crying.

I want to tell you a story about how you can suddenly wake up to find yourself living a life you were never supposed to live. It could happen to you, just like it happened to me, and you could try to get back the life you think you deserve to be living. Just like I did.

They told me I couldn't talk, said it was too early to try that just yet. I didn't know why, but I listened anyway. My mom and dad walked in, and she cried big tears and he went in to touch my face, and the nurse asked him to wait, asked him to please step aside until they were sure everything was working okay.

They gave me a small white board and a marker and told me to write my name. I did. Travis Ray Coates. They asked me to write down where I live. I did. Kansas City, Missouri. They asked me to write down my school. I did. Springside High. They asked me to write down the year. I did. Then the room got suddenly quiet, and even though it was bright and clean and I could smell medicine and bleach, I knew something was wrong.

This is when they told me that they'd done it. They'd gone through with the whole cranial hibernation and reanimation thing. They'd actually gone and cut my head off. I was so sure they'd put me under and changed their minds and that I'd gone through all that paperwork for nothing. But then my mom held up a mirror, and I saw that my head was shaved nearly bald and that my neck had bandages wrapped all around it. I looked pretty rough—my lips were purple and cracked, my cheeks were flushed, and my eyes were big and glazed over. Drugged, my eyes were drugged.

I'm going to tell you the truth here and say that I never, not once, not even for a tiny second, thought this crazy shit would work. And I never thought they did either. My parents, I mean. But I looked up at their wet eyes and felt their hands on my hands, and I knew right then that they were as happy as any two people had ever been. Their dead son lying on a bed in front of them, silent but with a beat in his chest again. Mary Shelley's nightmare come true, right there in a hospital in Denver.

Hospitals. I knew hospitals. I knew them like most kids know their own homes, know their neighborhoods, and know which yards to avoid and which ones it's safe to leave your bike in. I knew a nurse was only allowed to give you extra pain meds if a doctor had signed off on it first but that getting extra Jell-O only took a few smiles and maybe a joke or two, maybe a flash of the dimples. And like a factory, a hospital has its own rhythm, sounds from every room that collide in the air and echo down into your ears and repeat themselves, even in the night-time, when the world wants so bad to appear silent and quiet and peaceful. Beeps, footsteps, the tearing of plastic, spinning wheels on carts, *Wheel of Fortune* on the neighbor's TV. These were the sounds I died to, and these were the ones that welcomed me back. A world so noisy you have to lean up a bit to hear the familiar doctor as he tries to speak over it all, and just as you were starting to get used to the light, you have to close your eyes to hear him. A world that looks almost exactly the same as the one you closed your eyes to before, so much the same that you think about laughing because you got so close to being done with it all. Until you finally hear the doctor as he speaks a little louder this time.

"Welcome back, Travis Coates."

CHAPTER TWO

WELCOME BACK, TRAVIS COATES

When Dr. Lloyd Saranson from the Saranson Center for Life Preservation showed up at my house, I was puking in the guest bathroom with my dad sitting on the edge of the tub and patting my back. By that point I'd been sick for almost a year, seen every cancer specialist in the tri-state area, and given up all hope of survival.

Then this guy walks in and insists on pulling me out of my deathbed long enough to pitch us the craziest shit in history. And we listened because that's what desperate people do. They listen to anything you have to say to them.

"Travis," he said. "I want to save your life."

"Back of the line, buddy. No cutting." I looked to my parents with a grin, but they were either too tired or too sad to laugh.

"And how do you plan to do this?" Dad asked.

"Are you familiar with cryogenics?" Dr. Saranson asked with a serious tone.

"All right. Thanks for stopping by," Mom said, standing up and signaling for the door.

"Mrs. Coates, I wish you'd just hear me out for a few minutes. Please."

"Doctor, we've really been through a lot and—"

"Mom," I interrupted her. "Please don't take this away from me."

"Fine, go on," she said, sitting back down.

"Travis," he said. "Your body is done on this earth. We all know that. It's a sad state of affairs, but there's just no way we can change that."

"Try harder, doc. You're losing us here," I said.

"Right. That's to say, with what I'm proposing to you, that all doesn't matter anymore."

"Why's that?" I asked, looking to my parents, who were on the verge of launching from their seats and attacking him.

"Well, because in the future there'll be different ways for you to . . . exist."

"The future," I said. This wasn't something I'd given too much thought lately.

"Exactly. The future. Imagine, Travis, that you could simply fall asleep in this life and wake up in a new one someday."

"How far into the future?" I asked. In my mind I was

seeing my spaceship folding down into a suitcase like George Jetson's.

"With our latest breakthroughs we're hoping to develop the means to reanimate our first patients within a decade or two."

"You're serious, aren't you?" Dad asked.

"Quite serious, Mr. Coates."

"Has anyone else volunteered for this?" I asked.

"You'd be our seventeenth patient."

"So cryogenics," Dad said. "You want to freeze Travis with the hope of bringing him back someday?"

"Not exactly," he said. "As I was saying, Travis's body is done on this earth."

"Oh my God," Mom said quietly, this look of terror and disgust washing over her face.

"My head?" I pointed to it when I spoke, like the surgeon needed that. "You want to freeze *just* my *head?*"

"It's the only part of you not riddled with cancer cells."

This guy, he talked like he'd been there with us the whole time—with this familiarity and casualness that most strangers never used around "the dying kid." I liked it a lot, actually.

"So you knock me out and freeze my head, and I'm supposed to wake up in the future without a body and just roll with it?"

"Actually, there are several options for your hypothetical future recovery scenario, should we proceed any further."

*Options for My Hypothetical Future Recovery
Scenario (Abridged)*
1) Full-body regeneration through stem
   cell implantation into controlled
   fluid environment
2) Transplantation of full cranial
   structure onto robotic apparatus
3) Transplantation of full cranial
   structure onto donor body
4) Neuro-uploading into donor body
   and brain

*Personal Reactions to Options for My
Hypothetical Future Recovery Scenario
(Abridged)*
1) Gross
2) ROBOT ARMS!!!
3) Well, that's not happening
4) Say whaaaat?

After Dr. Saranson left that day, Mom and Dad started
laughing, which would've been really nice for a change
had I not secretly decided that I was going to volunteer
whether they liked it or not. I was tired of dying, and I
figured since this was the best idea I'd heard in months,
and didn't involve radiation or weeks of vomiting, then
I may as well go for it. I saw it like this: I was going to
die either way. Why shouldn't I be able to just fall asleep

with this slight (okay—completely impossible but still slight) possibility of my return instead of continuing on this never-ending torture fest of having everyone I love watch me slowly fade away? Maybe I'd never really get to come back, but damn it, once that idea got into my skull, there was no letting it go.

My parents took a little less convincing than I'd thought. They loved me. I was dying. This was a way for me to not be dying anymore. It was weird how simple it all became once the decision was made. I never thought knowing my actual expiration date would make a difference, but it did. It made a difference to us all. The few people who got to know we were doing it had a hard time understanding why, but in the end I think maybe they all needed the relief of letting go just as much as I did. So I let go. We let go. And then I came back. Holy shit, I came back.

It was good being back for just about as long as it took for my parents and Dr. Saranson to explain that I was attached to someone else's body. Then they had to go ahead and sedate me again because I kept clawing at my neck and ripping out my IV. The next time I woke up, my wrists and ankles had been restrained with cushiony little straps, and the looks on my parents' faces had worn a bit, like they'd forgotten how to sleep. These looks were much closer to the way I'd remembered them.

After a few days passed, and by the time I was finally allowed to speak, I was ready to have things explained more thoroughly and able to promise them that I wouldn't freak out and try to separate myself from my new body. You know, just your everyday sort of situation.

"The good news, Travis, is that you're back," Dr. Saranson began. "You're completely healthy, and now you'll get to live your life the way you were supposed to."

"And the bad news?" My voice was scratchy, raspy even.

"It isn't bad news, so much as it's a little strange and will take some getting used to."

"The body, you mean?"

"Yes. *Your* body, Travis. It belongs to you now."

"Where'd it come from?"

"A donor. A sixteen-year-old young man, like yourself, who we couldn't quite save."

"What happened to him?"

"Brain tumor," Dad said quietly.

"He knew this would happen. He wanted to save someone else's life, and that's why you're here."

"His family? Do they know about me?"

"They do. It's up to them to make contact. You know, if that's something they might want in the future. Nice people. Didn't want what Jeremy did to be a secret. They were proud of him."

"But you'll decide if you ever want to meet them or not," Dad added.

"Jeremy?" I asked.

"Yes. Jeremy Pratt," Dr. Saranson said. "Good kid."

"How long was I gone?"

"Five years last month," Mom said.

"Five years?" I asked, stunned.

"Science moved a lot faster than we could've predicted," Dr. Saranson said with a smile.

"Well, I knew you guys couldn't have aged *that* well over twenty years or something," I joked.

"Hey now," Dad said. "Don't be so sure about that."

"Are . . . are there others?" I asked.

"There's one other. A man named Lawrence Ramsey from Cleveland. We brought him back six months ago, and he is already enjoying his life again."

"He was in a Ford truck commercial last week," Dad said, rolling his eyes.

"And you know, Travis, there's probably going to be a point when you'll need someone to talk to—someone who knows a little bit about what you're going through. I'd say Lawrence would be up for that when you're ready."

"Okay. I'm not sure I'm ready for anything right now, though."

"Right. Of course. Your situation is a unique one, and it's possible and very likely that things are going to be pretty weird for a while. But you'll go back home and go back to life as normal."

"The way it was before you got sick," Mom said.

"Yes. You'll get back home, you'll go to school, you'll

make new friends. It won't be the easiest thing in the world, but you'll prove it can be done, right?"

That's when it hit me that Cate and Kyle wouldn't be Cate and Kyle anymore. They'd be these older versions of themselves that I'd have to learn about and get used to. They'd have forgotten things about me by now, especially things about the healthy version of me. They watched me die and then kept on living. I wondered if they had it in them to try again.

And *new* friends? I didn't want *new* friends. I had plenty of friends. I had a girlfriend. I had a best friend. Cate Conroy was probably sitting by the phone at her house on Twelve Oaks Road waiting to hear if I was okay or not, and Kyle Hagler was most likely on his way to her house so they could drive to the airport and get to me as soon as possible.

But they wouldn't let me just call her. I kept asking when I could call her, when I'd be able to see her, when she'd be there, and my parents just kept looking at each other like they were in a contest to see which one could go the longest without being helpful. Then Mom finally tells me some bullshit about how Cate probably needs more time to "process" all that's going on. Time to process? I mean, I was the one with the stranger's legs and arms and, let me remind you, private parts. I figured if I could process things so quickly, then why couldn't she?

"Can I just call her? I know she's waiting for me to call her."

"Travis," Mom whispered, "I have to tell you something."

"Okay."

"It's Cate, Travis." She was speaking in this calm, almost weak voice, like she was on the verge of being completely speechless.

"Cate? Is there something wrong? Did something happen?"

"She's engaged." She immediately covered her face with her hands and started crying.

I wasn't quite ready for that. This new body wouldn't react the way it should have reacted. I could barely make myself do anything at all; instead I just sat there in the sad quiet of the room. I mustered just enough energy to slump down a little in the bed and let out a kind of whimper that made me sound less like a human and more like a dying animal.

Cate was engaged. My girlfriend had a boyfriend. More than that, she was going to marry someone I'd never met. Maybe he was better than I was. I bet he even had his own body. I'd told her I'd come back for her, and even though I hadn't really believed it myself, I'd thought surely she'd believed me. I'd thought she'd wait. Why hadn't she waited for me? Why couldn't it be that I came back to life and now every little piece could fall perfectly back into its place?

But neither Kyle nor Cate ever showed up. I kept expecting it, though, every single day. I couldn't figure it out. Nothing about them not being there made any sense to me. They had *just* been there. They had *just* seen me. I had *just* seen them. I had said good-bye to them and I had closed my eyes. I had opened them and nothing. No word from either of the two people I wanted to be seeing more than anyone. Were they so different now? If it was really five years into the future, could that be all it took to change them? I mean, what's the point of getting another chance at life if everything's going to be so different that I can't stand it?

Then one night after I'd begged my parents to go to the hotel and get some rest, this nurse came in and asked if I needed anything. She was kind, and you could see that in her face and hear it in her voice.

"No, thanks," I said.

"This all must be very strange for you, huh?"

"You have no idea."

"I was there, you know."

"Where?"

"Here, I mean." She sat down in the chair by the window and looked over toward me. "When you were here before."

"You can say it," I said. "Go on. You were here when they took my head off."

"Yes. You had this little smile. It was the most surprising thing. There we were, the entire staff, watching this surgery that none of us could believe was happening. And you were so young. It was different with the other

14

ones. You were just so young that I held my breath the whole time."

"Did you think it would work? Did you really think it was even a possibility?"

"I stayed," she said, standing up. "Some of the others transferred out after that, after what we did to you."

"Why'd you stay?"

"I needed to see it," she said. "I didn't know if it would work, but I knew if it did, then I had to be here for it, if I could."

"Ta-da." I raised my new arms slowly into the air.

"I know you're sad. Confused and probably in shock. But you don't get to come back for no reason."

"Sorry?"

"You've just been handed the keys to the kingdom, Travis. Don't waste a second of it feeling sorry for yourself."

The next day I asked to see the nurse again, and they told me she'd quit a few weeks before, that she'd resigned and moved away somewhere. Then I wondered if I'd just dreamed the whole thing up. They say you can only dream about people you've seen—either in real life or on television—that we don't have the power to create new faces in our minds, but that we recycle the thousands and thousands of faces subconsciously stored in our memories. So maybe I'd seen her five years before, in that operating room, just as they'd put me under. Maybe I'd seen her and seen her kindness, and that was all my brain had needed from her. Maybe I was remembering her now to bridge the gap. Maybe the past me and present me could find a way to coexist, keys to the kingdom in hand.

Kansas City looked pretty much the same overall, save for these strange electronic billboards all over and a new gigantic building downtown that looked like two side-by-side shiny metallic spaceships half submerged into the earth and slanted upward.

"Kaufman Center for the Performing Arts," Dad explained on our drive home from the airport. "They have concerts, plays, you know, that sort of thing."

"It looks so strange there."

"A few people got all in an uproar about it looking so modern, but they eventually settled down."

"It looks like it came from outer space."

"Yeah," he said. "It is pretty alien, I guess. But I love it. I think it's interesting."

Our house was the same in all the obvious ways, same curtains in the living room, same couch, same dining table, though it had a new centerpiece. The television was much larger and flatter than the one I remembered, no doubt something my dad had waited in a ridiculously long line for on some Thanksgiving weekend since I'd left. My first thought upon seeing it was the hope that maybe they'd put the old, still rather large TV in my bedroom.

I couldn't help noticing how walking up the stairs felt different. All the same family photos still hung on the wall, ascending up to the top. But it used to be that I couldn't see my whole face in the frames. They were just high enough so I'd see the top of my head. Now, with Jeremy Pratt's body holding me up, I was taller and I could see all the way down to the scar on my neck in every single reflection. It'd been a while since I'd taken this walk. I'd been carried up a few times after I got sick, until they decided that moving me down to the guest room made more sense, right around the time we all concluded that this thing wasn't going to go away. The hallway bathroom was terribly white and shiny clean, like it had always been, but with new towels and an automatic hand soap dispenser by the sink. I immediately stopped to use it, my parents looking on from the doorway.

"Is this a common thing now?" I asked, pulling my hand back and then placing it underneath again, and then doing that again until green soap was almost pouring over the sides, completely covering my entire palm.

"It's catching on," Mom said. "It's better for germs, I think."

"I can get behind that," I said, rinsing off my hands and wondering if this was it. Was this the furthest we'd come in five years? Where were the jetpacks? The hoverboards? If they could bring me back from the dead, why wasn't a robot greeting me at every door and asking what I needed?

Then we got to my bedroom and nothing was the same. I should say that the old TV from the living room *was* there, but nothing else looked familiar at all. There was a bed I'd never slept in, there was a dresser that hadn't held my clothes, and there was a desk where I'd never done my homework. Even the walls were different, not the green-and-white-and-maroon plaid wallpaper that had always made my friends so jealous. No, this was a light gray–colored IKEA nightmare, and I was expected to live with it.

"What happened?" I was barely able to ask.

"Travis, it's been so long," Mom said.

"Did you throw everything away?"

"It was just too hard to look at it every day. You understand?"

"We'll go shopping this week," Dad said. "We'll get you whatever you want to make it feel like home again. Okay?"

"I'm so sorry, Travis." Mom turned to walk down the hallway and into their bedroom, closing the door.

"Sorry," I said, sitting on the edge of the bed.

"This is weird for all of us," Dad said. "So weird but so amazing, too. She's just sensitive. I know you haven't forgotten that." He chuckled a bit.

"It's okay," I said. "The room, I mean. I guess I understand."

"We can make this work, huh?" he asked, looking around us at the empty, unwelcoming space.

"When did you guys know I was coming back?" I asked him.

"About two weeks before they did it," he said. "Didn't have too much time to prepare."

"She gonna be okay?"

"She'll be fine," he said. "Let's get you some dinner. You hungry?"

The kitchen smelled the same as always, like clean clothes and vanilla with just a little touch of something else—citrus, maybe—like someone was always standing around the corner peeling an orange and doing laundry.

"Eggs okay?" Dad opened the fridge.

"Sure. No cheese, though, please."

"I remember."

My dad's hair had started to gray on the sides and around his temples, but his face didn't look all that much older. He wore new glasses, black plastic frames, that looked surprisingly modern for him, I thought. I was taller than him now too, which was weird. Still is weird.

"How's work?"

"Good. You wouldn't believe how much stuff has happened since you've been away."

My dad was an executive at the largest arcade chain in the country, Arnie's Arcade, Inc. Which meant two things: 1) My dad had a job that is much cooler than all other dads' and 2) I got to hang out at the arcade all the time, even on school nights. If you've never been to Arnie's, then you're missing out. The whole idea of Arnie's is for kids to feel like they've stepped back into what Dad calls the "golden age" of video arcades. Each Arnie's looks like it's been there since before anyone inside the place was ever born. And they're full of all these classic games that can't be found in any other arcades in the country. My dad's boss, Arnold "Arnie" Tedeski, won a bunch of video game competitions back in the '80s. He was pretty famous, or so my dad tells me. Kyle and I practically lived at the Arnie's in Springside up until I got sick.

Ah, Springside. I should tell you about Springside. Springside is a neighborhood in the Country Club District of Kansas City. This district is the largest contiguous planned community in the United States, and if you're black or Jewish, you weren't allowed to live there until 1948. Also, you probably still don't live there because you're pissed off about it. Needless to say, there's a lot of snobby white people in Springside. My mom refused to send me to private school not because we couldn't afford it, but because she hated the one she'd attended as a child. It was fine, though. What my school lacked in snobbery and tacky striped ties, it more than made up for in people like Kyle and Cate. And neither of them would've ever survived in a place like Springside. But we've got shopping! Lots of shopping and parks and an Arnie's Arcade right here in Whiteside. Sorry, *Spring*side. Mostly, though, I spent my time with Kyle or Cate, and it didn't really matter what neighborhood we were in or what any of the people there thought about anything or anyone.

"Do you remember anything about being gone?" Dad slid a plate of scrambled eggs across the counter toward me.

"Not a thing. I remember closing my eyes and I remember opening them. And now this."

"Your mother used to ask me if I thought you were dreaming."

My dad started to cry as soon as he'd gotten that last sentence out. He gripped the sides of the counter with both hands and held his head down, shaking it. It looked like he was about to apologize, you know, for showing emotion, but he stopped himself and it was quiet for a while longer.

"We're so happy you're home, Travis."

"Me too."

Before bed I walked up to my parents' room and knocked on the door. My mom said to come in, and I found her lying there with puffy eyes. She'd already put on her pajamas, black ones with little red hearts all over. She sat up and smiled a little as I walked to the other side of the bed and sat down next to her.

"Well, Sharon Coates." I held an invisible microphone up in front of her. "Your only son's just come back from the dead—what do you have to say?"

She paused, looked over at me the way she used to in

church when I'd try to make her laugh during the sermon, and smiled, shaking her head.

"Go on, Sharon. Tell us what you're thinking about."

"I'm thinking about how I must be the only mother in the world who has ever gotten to have this conversation."

"Maybe Lawrence Ramsey's mom did," I said.

"Maybe," Mom said. "And what about you, Travis Coates? You've just been brought back to life, what are *you* thinking about?"

"I'm thinking about how long it's gonna take me to remember that everything's so different. I can't quite understand it yet, I guess."

She leaned over and hugged me, set her head down on my shoulder, and patted my back a little.

"I think we'll have to get used to a lot of things we don't understand."

She was right about that one. I didn't understand a damn thing that was going on. So how come it felt so familiar, every motion and breath and sound? How could it feel like nothing had changed at all when I wasn't me from the neck down?

CHAPTER THREE

FROM THE NECK D O W N

Healthy or sick, Jeremy Pratt's body was better than mine. I knew this because the only thing separating me from him was a straight, pink line that circumnavigated my neck. There were no stitches, though—I was told this was a thing of the past. Connecting us together, Jeremy's body and me, was a spinal cord, blood vessels, nerve endings, and this swollen scar right in the middle of my neck about halfway between my clavicle and my chin. In time it would fade to a dull, more permanent purple.

This kid was an athlete, though—I can tell you that much. He did sit-ups and push-ups and other things that I suddenly felt pressured to try to do, just to maintain this impossible physique. But not just yet. I was still getting used to standing without help and to breathing without coughing up a lung. It was like this body was taking care of me until I was ready to take care of it. There was a six-pack, a real one, and arms that looked like real man arms, like they could actually lift something without too much effort, and a chest that was much more than the almost concave skin board I'd always known.

That first night back at home, I stood in front of the mirror that now hung on the backside of my bedroom door and just stared at myself. My hair was mostly gone, but the rest of my face looked exactly the same. Green eyes, dimples, that one little brown mole on the top of my right cheek. It was sort of like my head had been photoshopped onto someone else. I took my shirt and jeans off, stood there in only a pair of boxer briefs, and looked over every inch of my new self.

Just so you know: yeah, shit got weird. Imagine most of you is suddenly someone else, and this is the first moment of privacy you've gotten. The weirdest part, I guess, wasn't seeing my new chest or stomach or legs. It wasn't turning around to see that someone else's ass was there below someone else's back. And, surprisingly, it wasn't the moment I dared to just go for it and take a good, long look at my new dick. Sure, it was weird, but it wasn't disappointing *at all*, to be quite honest. The weirdest part, truly, was realizing I'd been doing all this undressing and examining and making sure the door was locked with hands that were different from my hands, with hands that had never touched Cate or knuckle-bumped with Kyle or opened my locker at school. These were Jeremy Pratt's clever hands, and they'd fooled me into thinking they were mine.

That night in bed I couldn't stop staring at them. The palms, the fingernails, the knuckles and backsides. The skin tone was nearly the same as the rest of me, maybe a little more tan, but not so different that I thought anyone but me would notice. The nails were longer than I liked to keep mine, so I went into the bathroom and clipped them down to the skin, like the ones I'd seen every day of my life.

"You'll get used to it faster than you think, I bet," Dad said the next morning at breakfast.

"I don't believe you," I said. And I didn't. Again, I had someone else's package.

"You're taller now, you know?" Mom said.

"Taller than Dad," I said, nodding his way. "It's weird."

"Six foot one," Mom said. "You always wanted to be six feet. Well, mission accomplished."

"There has to be a better way," I said.

"You made the news this morning," Dad said.

"Second miracle patient comes back to life!" Mom added, coming up behind me and squeezing my shoulders.

"I saw."

I'd stayed up the whole night before, pretty much every night since I'd been back, flipping to different twenty-four-hour news channels to try to catch stories about me. They always said something about my return being a "miracle," and every time I heard that word or saw it spelled out on the little scroll at the bottom of the screen, I had to close my eyes and breathe in deeply. I was back, yeah. And it was ridiculous and impossible all in one. I just wasn't all that ready to call it a miracle.

"School's gonna be pretty weird," I said.

"There are lots of things that'll make it pretty weird for a while," Dad said. "But you'll manage. I know you will."

"Has anyone called for me?"

"Your grandmother. She wants to see you as soon as possible. Your aunt Cindy may drive her down next week."

"Great. Anyone else?"

"You'll have to give them some more time, Travis."

"Time. More time," I said, a bit frustrated.

"They'll show up. Wait and see."

I couldn't believe I'd been awake for nearly three weeks and hadn't heard a single thing out of Cate or Kyle. Mom and Dad kept telling me to try to understand what it must be like for them, to just try to be patient. And that only got me thinking that maybe my parents were just faking their way through all of this, that they were actually freaking out inside, their brains quietly exploding. Maybe they'd been carefully coached by Dr. Saranson and his staff. Maybe they were told to be as calm and collected as possible, at all times, for fear that too much excitement could throw me over the edge.

But I had to talk to someone. Maybe it would have to be Lawrence Ramsey. He'd be the one person on earth who could relate to what I was feeling. We were two people unstuck in time, and as much as I wanted to forget what happened to me, I knew I'd need some help. It's pretty sad when you feel like a complete stranger is the only person you can turn to.

Sure, I was *trying* to be hopeful and not waste this opportunity like the nurse said or didn't say that night at the hospital. But wasn't I always going to be *Travis, who died* to these people? No matter what I did, wouldn't they always remember the way they had to let me go? I guess it turns out you don't have to be all that dead to be a dead guy.

CHAPTER FOUR

A DEAD GUY

Before we had left Denver, Dr. Saranson had given me his card and told me to call him any time I needed anything. He had said this while firmly shaking my hand and looking me right in the eyes.

"Travis," he said, picking up the phone. "I'm so glad you called."

"Thanks."

"How are things going? You adjusting okay? Everything back to normal for you yet?"

Was he kidding me with this? Did he really think anything would ever be even close to normal for me?

"Things are okay, I guess."

"That bad, huh?" he asked, his tone changing from a higher-pitched fake professional to a "Let's cut the shit" serious.

"It's just weird, you know. Everything's pretty different."

"And every*one*'s different too, right?"

"Right."

"Did you ever hear from your friends?" he asked.

"Not a word. It's really hard to understand."

"I know it is, Travis. But if you can, try putting yourself in their shoes. They lost someone very close to them, and it took a long time to move past it, I'm sure. For you, it's been a few weeks, but for them, it's been a lifetime since seeing you, since hearing your voice."

"I guess I thought they'd be excited I was back," I said.

"You know they are, Travis. They have to be. They're just scared, I bet. We have this way of putting certain ideas out of our minds . . . we do that. Humans, I mean. We have to bury things, hopes and dreams, so deep sometimes that it takes a little while to access those things once we need them again."

"So you think they just need more time to understand that I'm really back?"

"It's not that, no," he said. "I think they just need more time to understand *why* you're back and what that means to their lives. Maybe you think that's selfish, but I'd bet you anything they've been talking to each other just about every day since you've been back and trying to figure out how to deal with this thing. You woke up from a nap and everyone was older and different, but they've stayed up a lot of nights thinking about you, Travis. They've grieved you for years and now they're being asked to un-grieve you, and, sadly, that just isn't something that very many people understand because, well, it's never been a possibility before now."

"Did Lawrence go through this too?" I asked, feeling like this wasn't the first time Dr. Saranson had had this conversation.

"He did. Yeah. But I'll let him tell you about that. I think it would be really good for you. For both of you. What do you say?"

"I think I'm ready."

"Great. I'm going to give him your number, and I bet he'll be calling you very soon."

"Thanks," I said.

"Travis?"

"Sir?"

"It's all going to work out. I promise."

"Sure it will," I said.

"And I'll see you next week, right? For your first checkup? I'm flying down on Wednesday. You can tell me all about school."

Three days before my first day back to school, Mom came into my bedroom and woke me up. I looked at my alarm clock, and since I was in that just-awake haze, it took me a second or two to figure out if it was midnight or noon.

"Lawrence Ramsey's on the phone for you," she whispered, sitting on the edge of my bed.

"What?" I sat up, squinting my eyes. It was definitely

daytime because sunlight was filtering in through the curtains and heating up the side of my face.

"Lawrence Ramsey. He's waiting for you." She held a cordless phone with one hand, her other covering the bottom of it.

"Can you give me, like, five minutes?" I said, yawning.

"What do you want me to do, Travis? Chit-chat?"

I couldn't tell if she was annoyed or amused, but I didn't care. I nodded my head and got up to use the bathroom. When I came back, she was sitting in the same spot and repeating "Yeah . . . yeah . . . uh-huh" into the receiver. She waved me over.

"Okay, Mr. Ramsey. Well, here's Travis. Yes. You too. Okay. Bye-bye."

"Hello?" I said, sitting down.

"Well, if it isn't the man of the hour!" he said.

He had a kind voice, one much less animated than his public persona used. I'd seen him in so many interviews that I knew his whole story. I knew how he lost both of his parents to cancer by the time he was out of college. I knew he met his wife ten years before by accident when he, then an air-conditioner repairman, showed up to the wrong house and she pretended her A/C was broken just to get to know him. I knew they named their twin daughters after their respective grandmothers, Francine and Delilah. And I knew that he was thirty-six years old when they told him he would die. You could ask anyone you met and they'd tell you something about the life of Lawrence Ramsey and how it was a miracle that such a "good man" had been given a second chance to be happy, that he would get to see his children grow up after all.

"Huh?"

"You're all over the place, kiddo. Letterman even made a joke about you in his monologue last night. Funny stuff."

"Am I ever going to get used to all this?"

"Well, the public's known about you for, what, a week or so? They're still hassling me and I've been back for six months. So sorry to say, but I doubt it."

The Saranson Center had officially announced my reanimation the week before, so the news had been flooded with all these stories about how I got sick and volunteered for the surgery and all. They kept showing old photos of me because, thankfully, my age allowed me a little more privacy than it had Lawrence, and they couldn't show up at our house or anything like that.

"You're lucky," he said. "Lucky you're so young. They'll probably be at your school, though. I wouldn't be surprised at all. Just be ready. Duck your head down and walk past them as fast as you can. Vultures. All of 'em."

"Okay."

"I'm sorry, Travis. I'm sure you're still feeling really overwhelmed, and here I am shooting even more crazy stuff at you."

"It's okay. Thanks for calling. Dr. Saranson said it might help us both."

"Oh yeah," he said. "We're the sole members of a very exclusive club, you and me."

"It's just all so . . ."

"Fucked up?" he said. "Excuse me. I'm sorry."

"No," I said, laughing. "You're right."

"Let me ask you something. If you don't mind."

"Go ahead."

"When you woke up and people, I dunno, maybe your mom and dad or whoever, they started saying how much they missed you. Did that make you feel weird? It made me feel so weird."

"Yes," I said, maybe a little too loudly. "So weird. I mean, I love them, but I *just* saw them."

"Right? I wake up and I see my wife standing there, and my first thought was, *Damn, how'd she find time to get her hair cut in this hospital?* And then I realize that the kids standing beside her are *my* kids. They're my kids with five years added to each of them, and I'm pretty sure I passed out from the shock. Then I come to again and she's telling me all about missing me so much, and all I can think about is how different they all look."

"I feel kind of guilty about it," I said. "I see the way my folks look at me, and I feel like I'm supposed to be acting some special way around them, like I'm supposed to be proving how grateful I am to be back when I don't even really feel like I left in the first place. And of course I'm grateful. I'm not sick anymore. I wake up and suddenly I can stand up on my own again; no one has to help me to the bathroom or feed me. I think everyone forgets that the last thing I remember is months and months of dying."

"Travis, not to freak you out or anything, but I'm probably going to cry when I get off this phone. I've waited a long time to have this conversation with someone."

"Me too, Mr. Ramsey," I said.

"No. Now, you call me Lawrence. My dad was Mr. Ramsey and he was a dickhead."

"Fair enough." I laughed.

"Well, listen, Travis. I should probably run, but I just wanted to let you know that I'm here. Any time you need to talk, just call me, okay? And maybe we'll eventually figure all this weird shit out together. And don't be fooled by that guy in the truck commercials, okay? I don't have a damn clue what I'm doing back here, but I figure I might as well make a buck or two off my fifteen minutes of fame while I can."

"Absolutely," I said. "Thanks, Lawrence. Talk soon."

"You bet, Travis."

We didn't talk long enough to discuss what it was like to be attached to a new body, but I knew we'd get to that eventually. He'd been so easy to talk to, and I could tell he felt the same way about me. Relief, I guess. I think we were both so relieved on the phone that it was hard to decide which of our million questions to ask first. Like, I wanted to know how long it took for his friends to treat him normally again. And I wanted to know if things with his wife were the same as they'd been before he left. He'd obviously had to make this whole new persona up for the media, so maybe I'd need a *Travis, the Head Kid* character to get through this too. I couldn't hide from reporters my whole life, after all. There'd be a day when I'd have to know what to say to them.

But first I had to go back to school. And I had to do it without Kyle or Cate. I wouldn't know a single person there except the teachers and the principal. I'd be stuck in high school while all my friends were off living their lives and working their jobs and going to their college classes and partying. This was all so ridiculous, and when things got this way before, the only two people I could talk to were Cate and Kyle. But now they were part of the problem. They weren't there. They weren't there when I woke up, and they wouldn't be there when I went back to school. Some people say dying alone is a fate worse than death itself. Well, they should try being alone during the living part sometimes. There's no quicker way to make you wonder why the hell you ever thought you'd want to return.

CHAPTER FIVE

THE   RETURN

The day before I went back to school, I found out that there is an urn containing my ashes hidden in the closet of the guest bedroom. I discovered this when I was in there looking for an extra blanket for my new cold-natured body.

Oh, I thought to myself. *This sure is an odd place to keep a heavy vase.*

So I brought it out to the living room and asked my parents, who were both staring at their cell phones, what was in it.

"Shit." My mom was no longer looking at her phone.

"Why would you keep a vase full of shit in the closet?"

"Travis, watch your mouth," Dad said.

"Have a seat, honey."

There is no delicate way to tell a person that he is holding a container full of the incinerated remains of his own body. Had there been a better way, I might not have accidentally dropped the urn right onto the hardwood floor, which made my mom scream and my dad immediately jump down on all fours and start sweeping the ashes into a pile with his bare hands, almost as if he were trying to save each and every molecule of my former self.

"Go get the vacuum!" Mom shouted.

"We can't use a vacuum on Travis's ashes!" he yelled back.

This is about the time I walked outside and sat down on the front steps. It was October, so it was pretty cool in Kansas City, too cool to be wearing just a T-shirt and gym shorts borrowed from my dad. I still didn't have any clothes, or much else for that matter, so my parents had planned to take me shopping later that day. I was guessing that dropping my leftovers all over the living room floor had slowed things down a bit.

Ashes. I don't know why I was so surprised. I mean, they had to do something with what was left of me after the surgery. God knows that body wasn't worth a damn to anyone. By the time Dr. Saranson offered to turn me into Frankenstein, I was barely able to sit up by myself. I spent most of my days in the downstairs guest bedroom, in a hospital bed, watching old TV shows all night and sleeping all day because of the pain meds. I'm not sure why so many people get addicted to pain pills because, at a certain point, not feeling anything becomes much more painful than the disease eating away at your cells.

So yeah. They burned that mother, stuck it in a

nice blue-and-white vase, and it's probably been on the mantel for five years, reminding everyone who visits that these people, my parents, are broken and sad. No one else got to know, by the way. Just my family and close friends. You don't want to go telling everyone that a dying kid volunteered to be decapitated and that his parents signed off on it. At least not until it all turns out well.

Now everyone knows. Travis Coates: The Second Cryogenics Survivor in History. Once I was famous for dying, in my own little way. People came to visit me and bring me flowers and pray with me and such. They came to get closure. Teachers, classmates, old ladies from church. They all came to say good-bye. Now I'm famous for living, and I can tell you this much: people expect a lot more out of you when you're not lying in a hospital bed doped out of your mind. One minute I'm dying, and the next I'm supposed to be this beacon of hope for everyone around me? This miracle kid? I knew how to die, but I wasn't so sure about being a living hero yet.

I sat there on the front steps, and just as I was about to go back inside, hoping my parents had dealt with the creepy mess without inhaling too much of it in the process, a black truck pulled into the driveway. I knew who it was before he could even cut the engine off. Kyle Hagler, my best friend, had driven straight from the future to my front door.

"Wow," he muttered after stepping out of the car. He leaned against the hood with one hand.

"Well, you look different." I walked across the yard, squinting in the afternoon sun.

"You look exactly the same," he said. "Shit. You look *exactly* the same, Travis. I mean, from, like, here up." He took one hand, flattened out, and moved it from his neck to his forehead.

"You're tall," I said. "And . . . handsome. You're *handsome*, dude."

"We're both tall now, huh?" He stepped closer, looking me up and down.

He laughed a bit, and I noticed how his smile was the only thing proving this was actually him. The old Kyle Hagler was shorter than I was, which was terribly short for our age, and a little chubby around the middle. He had a voice that was higher than you'd expect from a sixteen-year-old boy, and he wore shirts that were always a little too tight. And his blue jeans. I'm not even sure where one buys pleated blue jeans, but it was possible and he proved it every day.

But this new Kyle was about my height—my new height, that is—was dressed in nice slacks and a button-down shirt, and had a voice that immediately threw me off. It was a great voice. Powerful but not threatening. He had grown up. The slight hint of a man he'd always been was replaced with a pretty impressive new form. It was weird.

"Should we hug or something?"

I was barely able to finish my question before he

wrapped his arms around my shoulders and squeezed me into his chest. Two best friends hugging strangers' bodies that were somehow now their own. He was crying, but it was quiet enough to be appreciated and not pitied. It was the best kind of crying. He let go for a second and wiped his face with the back of one sleeve before holding me by each shoulder and sort of just staring at me for a while with this expression that I'm still convinced no other person has ever had, a combination of shock, joy, pain, and terror. It was like I could see all his memories of me projected into the air between us, rushing and swirling around and enveloping us both in a nostalgic haze.

"I missed you, man."

"I would say the same," I said. "But I just saw you, like, three weeks ago."

"Weird. It really feels that way?"

"It's like I just took a nap or something and now everything's different. Everyone's older."

"Does it hurt?" He sort of nodded toward my neck.

"Can't feel a thing. Gonna be a righteous scar, though. I guess I can live with it."

"I think you'll make do."

"They say scars give you edge," I said.

"That right? What about coming back from the dead? Think that'll get you laid?"

We went into the house, and my parents both got teary as they greeted and hugged him and immediately forced him to take a seat in the living room. I wondered if they looked at him the same way I did. I wondered if they saw the grown-up who walked in or the kid who used to practically live here.

I looked around and any evidence of the ashes was now gone. Part of me hoped they'd thrown it all away, just flushed the pile of dirt down the toilet and forgotten all about it. But the other part of me, the part that was still toggling between life and death and still very confused about how to define either, hoped that they'd hidden the ashes away somewhere safe, somewhere to be found when needed.

My parents insisted on Kyle staying for lunch, and then they ordered a pizza because my mom obviously hadn't started liking cooking any more than she had before I'd left. We set up shop at the kitchen bar, Kyle and I taking the same seats our past selves had taken most nights of the week back when we'd binge on Mike & Ikes and study for Ms. Grady's ridiculous biology exams and compare answers for Mrs. Lasetter's never-ending Algebra 1 homework assignments. I was always much better at science than math, and Kyle was the opposite, so it worked perfectly that way. We piggybacked off each other's strengths and weaknesses. That's real friendship, right?

"Tell me you'll get to go back as a junior." Kyle shoved pizza into his face.

"Sophomore. I missed way too much the first time. I don't have the credits."

"Shit. Well, I have epically bad news, then."

"What? Don't say it. Do *not* say it, Kyle."

"Lasetter."

"Damn it. Kill me now."

"Turns out that isn't so easy."

"No kidding. I can't believe she's still there. I guess I just thought hell would've opened up and taken her back by now."

"She made Audrey cry last year. Twice," he said.

"Audrey. Wow. Your little sister's in high school? Holy shit."

"Yeah. She's seventeen. She's older than you now, dude."

"This gets so much weirder every day."

"Have you seen Cate yet?" he asked. We both knew the conversation would turn to her sooner or later.

"Not yet. Maybe she doesn't know."

"Everyone knows, Travis. I talked to her last week— she's pretty freaked out."

"She is? She told you that? I know it's weird. I know. But it's *me*, Kyle. Why wouldn't she just be happy?"

"She is, Travis. Of course she is. It's just . . . well, she's been seeing this guy for a while, you know. They're engaged."

"Mom told me," I said. "You know him?"

"Met him once. We all had dinner. He's a good guy. So there's that," Kyle added.

"There *is* that."

"You gonna try to reach her?" he asked.

"Eventually. I have to, don't I? Doesn't she want to see me?"

"There's no way, no matter how long it's been or how different she is, that she wouldn't want to see you. You know that."

"And you?" I said. "Why'd it take *you* so long?"

"Scared, I guess. Your mom called before they flew to Denver, and my first thought was, *What if they bring him back and then he dies all over again?* I couldn't deal with that, Travis. Not again."

"So you decided to wait it out and see if I'd make it?"

"Well, it sounds a lot worse when you put it that way."

"I understand, I guess."

I did understand. He had been there for all of it, for every treatment and its often-violent aftermath. He'd seen my family's small glimmer of hope squashed over and over again by doctor after doctor, bad results after bad results. He'd told me once, after I'd been through another round of especially painful chemo, that he didn't understand why I had to get so sick to try to get better, why they had to keep almost killing me to save my life. He'd been so angry that day that he'd kicked a hole in the bathroom door at his house when he'd gotten home.

Kyle Hagler had been my best friend since kinder-garten, since the day a game of tag at recess had turned dangerous after Holly Jones decided she couldn't go home without a kiss from me. I was darting across the playground with her at my heels when Kyle ran up and planted one right on her lips.

"There!" he yelled. "Now go away."

"She your girlfriend now?" I asked him afterward.

"Holly Jones? She's everybody's girlfriend," he said.

Then in fifth grade Kyle and I skipped guidance class, which was just an hour every Wednesday where we had to watch movies about not doing drugs and having low self-esteem—you know the ones. We skipped class to sit behind the gym and share a pack of peanut butter crackers. This was us being pretty rebellious.

"If someone ever told me they didn't like peanut butter crackers," he said, "I'd never speak to them again."

"What if they had a peanut allergy, though?"

"Doesn't matter. Take a Benadryl, wussies."

"I don't think that's how it works," I said.

"People only say they're allergic to things because they don't like them. It's all a big scam anyway," he said.

"Yeah," I said. "I've been allergic to lettuce since I was six."

"Exactly."

I knew, by the time we were freshmen, that Kyle was allergic to girls. It wasn't in any obvious, stereotypical way, but he was my best friend and I knew him better than anyone. Around the time I started dating Cate, Kyle started acting pretty weird and apologizing for hanging out with us all the time and not having a life of his own. It was strange. Kyle had never been the type to apologize for anything.

When I was dying, I mean in those last few weeks, Kyle would come over and keep me company until really late at night and sometimes into the early morning. My parents had to work, after all, and he wanted to spend as much time with me as he could. One night we were flipping through the channels and stopped on some of that really cheesy, bad music-ridden soft-core porn on Cinemax.

"Ah, every dying boy's dream come true," I said.

"Travis," he said, oddly quiet and reserved.

"Yeah?"

"Can I tell you something?"

"This movie doesn't do a thing for you, right?" I said.

"Not a thing," he said, a sour look on his face.

"And did you think I would give a shit about that?"

"Not really. But no one else knows, okay?"

"Well, I'd say your secret's safe with me, but that's sort of a given," I joked.

"I'm serious, Travis. I wouldn't even be telling you if . . ."

"If I weren't about to be curtains?"

"Sorry."

"Don't be. I understand. Secrets will kill you, you know?"

"You're a good friend, Travis. Really."

"Hey, hey. All right. I don't care if you're gay, but you don't have to go spreading it with all this sappy shit."

When this new Kyle, sitting in my kitchen and telling

jokes about all of his former teachers and my soon-to-be-yet-again-current ones, nonchalantly said "my girlfriend," I suddenly felt like my head had found a way to slightly float just above my new body, barely connected. My parents had been drifting in and out of the room all evening, almost incapable of staying away from us, of seeing us the way we used to be. I nearly blurted out and interrupted him to ask "Girlfriend? Why would you have a girlfriend?" But I caught myself and let him keep going. Maybe he just wasn't sure if my parents knew about him. Maybe he was just using "girlfriend" as a code for "boyfriend" or "partner" or whatever. He mentioned her again, said she'd been in one of his college English classes. I wanted to know what the hell was going on here. I wanted to know why he was talking to me, *me*, about a girlfriend five years after he'd told me he had no interest in girls at all. I wanted to know why my best friend was pretending to be someone he wasn't and why everyone was letting this happen.

When he eventually had to leave and after my mom had hugged him enough to embarrass us both, I walked him outside. I thought this would be my chance to get the truth out of him. I couldn't let him leave with this huge thing hovering over us.

"Kyle, man. You . . . umm . . . said you had a girlfriend?"

"Yeah. Valerie. She's cool. You'll have to meet her soon."

"*Valerie?*"

"Yeah, Travis. Valerie. I'm actually on my way to see her now. Running a little late."

And then I realized I was the only one he'd ever told. There were no secret codes here, no hidden meanings behind his words to protect people like my parents from the truth. The truth was that he was still lying to everyone, including himself. His secret died with me on the operating table, and now it was back staring him right square in the face, scar and all.

CHAPTER SIX

SCAR AND ALL

Kyle eventually had to go, and I was never brave enough to confront him about his identity crisis. Maybe you can be gay and then not be gay a few years later. I wasn't sure. That didn't really sound right to me, though. But I'd been asleep for half a decade and was starting high school all over again the next day, so I didn't have much time to figure it all out for him. Plus, who was I to disappear and then show back up all these years later and start calling people out on their problems?

There are certain things that change with time, things like the skyline of your city, the size and shape of the cars beside you on the road, and even how people are wearing their blue jeans, really tight on their calves. But other things, things like your parents, don't really change at all. And I knew this immediately when my mom and dad started arguing over where to go shopping.

"The place with all the fancy stores? Do we really need to go there?" Dad asked.

"That's the one. They have everything. It's a nice evening—we can take our time, get some fresh air walking around, and do a little shopping." Mom was ready for his dissent.

"Anywhere's fine, really," I said. "I just need some jeans and a shirt or two."

"No, Travis. You're not going to keep wearing the same outfit I bought you in Denver. School's about to start, and you're getting whatever you want today, no arguments." Mom was using the visor mirror of my dad's car to put on her mascara, something she'd done since I could remember.

"Sharon, if there were something he wanted, he'd tell us, don't you think?"

She ignored him, opting instead to continue talking to me and asking me what size pants I thought I needed now.

"I dunno," I said.

"I'm thinking thirty-two thirty-four. You look a little bigger now. More filled out, I mean."

"You guys didn't save *any* of my old clothes?"

"No, honey. We gave most of them to your cousins. You know, Chase and Chad. The twins."

"Wow," I said. "They're old now, I guess."

"Fourteen last month."

"They're even worse now," Dad chimed in.

"Ray," Mom said. "They're nice boys." She sounded like she was trying to convince herself, too.

"Travis, believe me. They're holy terrors," Dad said.

"They're . . . unique." Mom slapped Dad on the arm, her smile unable to be stopped.

"Yes, Travis. They are unique. In that same way that serial killers are unique."

"And now they've got all my clothes. Great," I said, laughing.

By the time we found parking and were finally walking down the sidewalk, it was turning dark out and the lights from the insides of the large-windowed stores stretched at least halfway into the streets. For whatever reason, this made me remember going there with Cate and Kyle during one of my last healthy days. We had walked around, drunk coffee, and mostly played in the Apple Store while our phones recharged. Kyle had pretended to flirt with some girl at the Genius Bar, and Cate and I had made out by the iPods. It had been awesome, just a simple afternoon before everything got bad.

Several people noticed me before my parents and I even made it inside the store. They knew me from somewhere—that's what their expressions said, at least. I even saw some kid snap a photo of me with her phone and run over to her friend and start whispering into her ear.

Mom kept piling clothes on me—T-shirts, jeans, pants, hoodies—everything she saw, basically. It was like we hadn't really stopped moving from the moment we walked through the door to the time we'd made it to the dressing room. I could barely see over the clothes in my arms.

"These are pretty tight," I said, walking out to model a pair of jeans for my mom.

"It's the style."

"I don't understand. I can hardly move."

"Do you want to try a bigger size?"

I tried the bigger size, and even though they were easier to button, they still hugged me all weird around the thighs.

"Are these girl jeans, Mom?"

"No, Travis. I told you. It's what everyone wears now. Girls *and* boys."

"We can just take him over to J. Crew and get him some more grown-up clothes, don't you think?" Dad suggested. He was bobbing his head to the shop's loud techno music while people all around us stared on in horror.

"He's not a grown-up, Ray. He's sixteen. He's not going to school dressed like an accountant."

"Yeah, Dad. I'll go to school dressed in tight pants like a girl or I won't go at all."

He laughed, threw his hands up, and walked out of the dressing room area and into the store.

We finally found some jeans that fit better, that didn't make me feel as exposed and all-around disgusting, and a pile of T-shirts and sweaters that I thought looked pretty good, but only because of my new body.

"You look *so* handsome, Travis. I mean, you're, like, hot," Mom said.

"Never ever say anything like that again."

"I'm sorry, but you just don't know. Seeing you like this, standing up strong, your hair starting to grow out. I'm just . . . this is so great, Travis."

She hugged me, right there outside the crowded dressing room in front of all these strangers, and she had tears in her eyes when she pulled away. I forgave her for this. I let her have this moment because she'd earned the right to do all these things the day she let me go into that operating room and say good-bye to the world.

"Okay, wait right here. I want you to try one more thing."

A few minutes later, once I was back in my own clothes again, she knocked on the door and handed me several turtlenecks and a couple of scarves. I gave her a look that would, I hoped, tell her these were not about to go onto my body, in style or not.

"Honey, I just think maybe you want to consider finding ways to . . . to not *accentuate* your neck, you know?" She had this look on her face like she knew she'd said something wrong.

"You want me to cover my scar every day?"

"No. No. I just want you to try these out and see what you think. And if you like them, wouldn't it be easier that way? Not calling attention to yourself?"

"Mom, everyone at school is gonna know who I am the

second I walk through the door. Do you think it matters?
Do you think they give a shit about my neck?"

"Travis. I'm not trying to . . . I just . . . Can you try
them for me?"

I tried them on. All four turtlenecks. And I looked
like a 1970s pimp. I let her buy me the scarves as a con-
solation and so we could just get the hell out of there and
get some dinner.

"I like that jacket," Dad said as we sat down to eat in a
little Italian place down the block.

"Me too. Thanks, guys."

"You don't have to wear the scarves, Travis," Mom said.

"Unless your neck's cold," Dad added.

"No, I like them."

And I did like them, but I didn't so much like the idea
of them. I didn't like the idea that I had to pretend to be
something I wasn't, to try to blend in despite the fact that
my face had been cycling on national news for a week
and I'd already been recognized several times that day. To
tell you the truth, I didn't so much mind getting noticed.
Maybe I could show up at Springside High the next day
and be more popular than old Travis ever had the chance
to be. Instant celebrity surely had plenty of perks, even in
a place like high school.

CHAPTER SEVEN

A PLACE LIKE HIGH SCHOOL

Going back to school was something I never thought I'd have to deal with. By the time I elected to be a science experiment in Denver, I'd been out for about nine months, including summer break. My teachers sent me assignments for a while, back in the January before I left. Some of them even put little *Get well soon* notes inside, but I didn't really see the point of doing anything, and I guess that eventually became everyone else's attitude because the assignments stopped and my parents quit asking me about them.

I never really liked school the first time around. I didn't hate it. I wasn't bullied or anything. I had plenty of friends and I got along with most of my teachers— the ones who weren't Mrs. Lasetter, that is—and even though I wasn't all that great at things like math, I studied enough to make okay grades. I just never liked being there. I used to lie in bed every school night I can remember and be filled with this massive dread that I had to wake up and do it all over again. If it weren't for Cate and Kyle, I don't think I'd have tried as hard as I did. I used to think about how easy it would've been to turn into one of those dropouts who has to get a shitty job somewhere around town and never grows up.

But that dread, that dislike, it had *nothing* on how I felt the morning of my fateful return to Springside High. Of course, I'd never had to walk into school with photographers and news cameras lining the sidewalk out front either. It wasn't enough that I was about to enter a school full of complete strangers, but I had to do it as the famous miracle boy everyone's been seeing on TV.

"They can't go inside," Mom said to me. We were sitting in her car in the roundabout drop-off zone in front of the school and watching the dozens of reporters waiting for me to show up. There were curious students standing all around them, and I saw a few smiling for the cameras as they walked past.

"Shit," I said.

"Travis." Dad turned around from the passenger seat and looked at me. "Give them a few days and they won't care anymore."

"You think?"

"I know," he said with confidence. "Just duck your head down, don't say anything, and walk inside. If you don't give them anything to use, they'll go away."

"Be boring," Mom added, a smirk on her face.

It was loud. With the countless reporters yelling questions and the other kids looking on from their little huddled groups, it was such a chaotic and stressful scene. I was wearing one of the scarves Mom had bought me because it was cold enough and because I thought maybe she'd been right. I wasn't ready for the kind of attention these people wanted to give me. The whole time I was burrowing through the crowd, all I could do was imagine a zoomed-in photograph of my neck on national television.

The school secretary couldn't stop giving me that look, that "I can't believe it's really you that I'm talking to right now" look when she printed out my class schedule in the main office. I also caught her staring down at my neck. She wanted to notice an inconsistency in the skin tones, to gossip about the freak science-experiment kid who had just walked onto campus. Even though I was embarrassed and felt like I'd just run through a battlefield, I thought about lowering the scarf to give her a quick glimpse of it. It wasn't going away, after all.

Before I could do that, though, Principal Carson ran in and put an arm around my shoulders. She smelled exactly the same as always, like Irish Spring soap.

"Travis Coates! What an outstanding kid!"

"Hi."

"Travis, what you've done. Your story, it's just . . . it's so inspiring for us all."

Then Principal Carson was crying these little tears and wiping them away with the back of her left hand. Her fingernails were shiny red, and she was wearing a ring that looked to me like she didn't even need this job. Maybe she's for real, I thought. Maybe she loves kids that much.

"We should get a picture, no?" She perked up, still wiping tears and snorting as she breathed in.

"Really?" I asked. But I knew Principal Carson was for real when the secretary stood up and pointed her cell phone toward us.

Then Principal Carson waved her arms out to invite everyone standing around in the office—the staff, a few random students, and a PE teacher—to join us. Maybe they'd planned the whole thing because it didn't take long before I was sandwiched between them and forcing a smile for the camera.

"I'm probably late for class," I said, attempting a move for the door.

"I'll walk you, sweetie," Principal Carson said.

There was clapping when we stepped into Mrs. Lasetter's geometry class. Even that battle-ax was standing behind her desk and smiling as kids started getting up to pat me on the back, shake my hand, and hold their phones up in front of us to snap quick photos. I was sweating now, nervous with all the eyes on me and all the attention. This was harder than I'd thought, and it made High School Round One seem so easy. Back then I could hide away and talk to the handful of people I chose and then go home. This was just getting ridiculous. I managed to say "Thanks" over their collective noise, and I took a seat in the front corner of the room. As soon as I sat down, I felt like everyone was looking at me, staring at my head and wondering if it were at all possible for it to fly right off or roll down one of my arms. Principal Carson was still standing at the front of the room, and she held one hand up to signal for silence.

"Boys and girls, I hope you understand the privilege that has been bestowed upon you. You all get to witness one of the greatest miracles of modern science right here at Springside High. What an amazing day!"

And then more clapping and even a few cheers rang out from the students. I closed my eyes and clinched my fists while forcing a smile. I wasn't prepared for this, and it was becoming pretty overwhelming. Then one kid from the back yelled, "NOGGIN!" like he was trying to start a group chant with it, but the whole room fell super quiet instead.

"Hatton!" Mrs. Lasetter barked. "Apologize! Now!"

"Sorry."

I turned around to see a skinny kid with glasses and blond, almost white hair slumping down in his desk. He looked at me with this sincere regret on his face.

"No." I stood up. "It's fine. I like it."

"You like what?" Lasetter asked. She'd always hated me, and I could already see it coming back. I thought about succumbing to that look she gave me, the one that had always made even the most defiant students lower their heads in shame. But I was back, and even though I just wanted to run away and hide, defying her was the best moment of my new life.

"*Noggin*. It has a nice ring to it."

"He was being rude."

"But I liked it. What's your name again? Hatton?"

He perked up and nodded his head. He was smiling now but still looking over at Lasetter with a cautious expression, unsure if he'd be punished for going along with me.

"I always wanted a nickname. Thanks."

"How do you like that, kids? What a *fantastic* attitude this young man has! And after all he's been through!" Principal Carson clasped her hands together and sighed deeply.

"Speech!" one kid shouted from the back of the room.

I looked up at Mrs. Lasetter, and she was clenching her jaw so hard she'd have to take an aspirin later.

"SPEECH! SPEECH! SPEECH!" they all started shouting.

Then Principal Carson looked at me, looked right down at me and into my eyes, and I knew I had to do it. As much as I just wanted to be boring, like Mom said, I knew they weren't going to let me. I mean, it couldn't be that bad, right? So I stood up, waited for them all to settle down, wiped sweat from my forehead with the back of one arm, and spoke.

"It's good to be back here," I began. "It seems like just yesterday I was walking these halls, even though it was with a different set of legs and all."

And they laughed. Thank God they laughed. There were even a few "awesome"s whispered from the back.

"I just hope I haven't forgotten everything I learned five years ago. It would be a shame if I can't keep ahead."

Nothing. Not one murmur of a chuckle.

"Get it?" I asked. "A*head?*" I pointed to my skull.

They laughed again, even harder this time. And it could've been that they just didn't know what else to do, but it didn't matter. I realized, in that moment, that maybe I could do this. I could be this new person. Lawrence Ramsey had done it. Hell, I saw him in a luxury car commercial just the day before. He was cashing in on this whole "Miracle of Modern Science" gig, and he'd only been conscious for a few months longer than I had. But as comfortable as it felt right at first, while they were laughing and looking at me with this strange excitement, it still wasn't right. It only took me a few seconds to snap out of it and remember that the last time I was in that classroom, I'd just been diagnosed with a deadly illness and my best friend had been sitting right beside me.

After I sat back down and Mrs. Lasetter continued writing notes on the board for a while, the bell rang to dismiss class, and my new fellow students lined up to shake my hand on the way out. Principal Carson had stepped back in and stood proudly beside me, even once leaning down and whispering into my ear something I'll never forget.

"I've never seen that woman get so mad. Well done, young man."

The last kid in line was Hatton, who opted for a high five in place of a handshake and said I was already the coolest guy he'd ever met.

"I was supposed to be boring today," I said.

"No way, man. Noggin," he said proudly. "Superstar."

The rest of my classes that first day back were filled with similar reactions from my new classmates. And photos. My God, the photos never stopped. I couldn't even walk down the hallway without people running right up to me, sometimes not even speaking, and holding a phone out in front of us just long enough to take a picture. Then they just walked away like nothing ever happened. Celebrity is weird.

At lunch my usual table, where Cate, Kyle, and I had always sat, was full of strangers, so I took a seat at an empty one in the far back corner. I ate quietly, just sort of scanning the large cafeteria to see if I noticed anyone. All these people had been just little kids in elementary school when I was here before. It was odd to think that maybe I'd seen them then, playing around in their yards or shopping with their parents at the mall. And that's when I saw Audrey Hagler, who used to be Kyle's twelve-year-old littler sister with a pink bedroom and an obsession with Disney princess movies, but was now something very different. She was beautiful, with that long brown hair and just the right amount of makeup on. Seeing her like this made it easier to believe that Kyle needed time to grow into his looks. That was how it worked in this family, it seemed. I couldn't stop staring at her and I wanted to go say hello but didn't want to embarrass myself in a roomful of strangers either.

"Do you know her?" Hatton asked when he walked up.

"I did."

"Geez. Even dead people know Audrey Hagler. Go figure."

"Her brother's my best friend."

"Oh. Cool. Can I sit here?"

"Sure."

He sat right beside me, and we both stared across the room at Audrey together. It was something I imagine looked pretty strange to the rest of the kids around us, but we didn't care, neither of us. That much was obvious. Hatton didn't strike me as someone who cared what anyone thought of him, and I was a guy with someone else's body attached to me and a very noticeable scar around my neck to remind everyone of that fact, so I sure didn't care either.

"Everyone's been talking about you all day," he said.

"Has the nickname caught on yet?"

"Not as well as I'd like. But I'm working on it," he said, his mouth full of food.

"It's weird, you know. She looks so different. Grown-up, I mean. But her face, the nose and eyes, they're the same."

"Trippy," he said. "See anyone else you recognize?"

"Just teachers. I can't believe I have to take Lasetter's class again."

"A fate worse than death. Sorry. Was that okay to say?"

"Of course. And closer to the truth than you'd think."

"She's coming over here, dude."

I looked up to see Audrey headed straight for us with pretty much the whole room staring my way.

"Travis?" she said, smiling. Her smile was exactly the same.

"Audrey?" I asked. "Hi."

"Get up!"

I got up, Hatton still seated beside me, and Audrey reached over the table and hugged my neck. She did the same thing everyone else had been doing, where she pulled back slightly and looked me up and down, starting at the neck, then down to the shoes, then back up again.

"I can't believe this," she said. "Kyle called me yesterday and he was so happy. He could *not* shut up about you. No one can, really."

"He really grew up," I said, not knowing what else to say.

"We all did, I guess." She laughed.

"That you *did*," Hatton said from his seat.

"Huh?" she asked.

"Hi." He stood up. "I'm Hatton Sharpe. I'm Travis's new friend."

"Hey." She gave him a suspicious stare and then turned back to me.

"Anyway. Let me know if you need anything around here, okay? I'm junior-class president."

"Cool. Thanks," I said like an idiot.

"Travis Coates. Wow." She shook her head and walked off.

"She loves you," Hatton said as I sat back down.

"No, she doesn't."

"She does. I can tell. I'm very astute about these things."

"Hatton, she's my best friend's little sister. That's wrong and all kinds of gross, and I don't even know where to begin explaining to you how weird this is."

"You're a modern-day Casanova, you know. You're a hero. All the women in this school want you."

"I have a girlfriend."

"Oh. Already?"

"No. I mean yeah. From before."

"She waited for you?"

"She kind of has a fiancé. But still."

"Oh. Okay."

"I know," I said. "It's complicated. I haven't seen her since I've been back."

"Can I ask you something?" Hatton leaned in a little closer, his chest hovering right above his lunch tray. "Did you guys ever . . . you know . . . *do it?*"

"Are you asking if I ever had sex with my girlfriend? I met you, like, two hours ago. Is there something wrong with you? Are you the school pervert?"

"Maybe. But did you?" He raised one eyebrow. I probably should've gotten up and walked away, but there was something so sincere about the way he'd asked it, the way he talked to me in this familiar, comfortable tone like we'd been friends our whole lives.

"No," I said. "We kind of ran out of time."

"Shit," he said quietly. "So I bet it's pretty hard picturing her with some other guy, then. That sucks so bad."

"It isn't ideal, Hatton," I said as the bell rang.

"What's your next class?" he said, standing up.

"Chemistry. You?"

"Chemistry. Awesome."

Speaking of chemistry—yeah, Cate and I wanted to have sex. We were teenagers who loved each other and one of us was dying, so we had plenty of talks about if and when we should try it out. But, like I told Hatton, we just never got the chance to go all the way. We tried, though. One night when my parents had gone to this charity thing for my dad's work, Cate came over and we turned out all the lights, and she lit some candles and put on some music and everything that we thought was supposed to accompany sex. I'd had an okay week and it'd been a while since my last round of chemo, so we figured I'd have enough strength to . . . you know . . .

And this is what happened:

Cate: *I'm going to take my clothes off, but I need you to close your eyes. Okay? You can take yours off too.*

Me: *Okay.*

Cate, now under the covers: *Okay. All done.*

Me: *I need help.*

Cate, lifting the covers: *Doesn't look like it to me, champ.*

Me: *No, I mean, I can't get my boxers off.*

Cate, crawling under the covers: *Okay. There. Got 'em.*

Me: *If I weren't dying of so much else, the embarrassment would be killing me.*

Cate, back beside me, her bare shoulder touching mine: *I love you, Travis.*

Me: *Ditto.*

Cate, crying.

Me, wrapping my arms around her and falling asleep.

I was glad I met Hatton on the first day back. He was funny in that unintentional way where he mostly just said more of the truth than anyone else around, at least when he wasn't making things up to flirt with girls. In chemistry I watched him tap a cute girl on the shoulder and tell her she was the only person he ever dreamed about. She looked disgusted, and I nodded my head in affirmation to try to help. Then she gave us both the finger and never turned around again.

At the end of the day Mom picked me up and had this look on her face that asked a million questions all at the same time. So I answered them as efficiently as possible to ease her mind.

"School was good. I made a new friend. He's hilarious. And I saw Audrey Hagler, and she is so different and grown-up now. But also the same. It's weird, but I can make it work. I like my new clothes, too—thanks, Mom."

And she smiled so big, even though she was sort of crying. I wondered if she'd ever smile again without crying, or if this had become her default setting. Maybe I wasn't the only one who needed a reset button. I turned on the radio and pretended not to see it. That's what she wanted anyway. She didn't like getting attention like that, which is something I really loved about her.

"Any word from Cate?" I asked as we turned onto our street.

"No, sweetie."

"Sucks."

"Maybe she'll be ready soon."

"I want it all to go back, you know. All of it." I looked out the window, my forehead pressing up against the glass.

"You may want to think about that a little longer before saying it again, Travis."

But I had thought about it. It's all I could think about since I'd woken up. And, to be honest, I couldn't really see all that much difference between the life where I was dying and the one where everyone had become a stranger. Some of my happiest moments were in those few months leading up to the surgery, so maybe this wasn't right. All those hours in the hospital that I spent thinking about whether or not this crazy procedure would work, whether or not I'd get to come back, and it hadn't even once occurred to me that it could happen this way. I thought if I woke up at all, it would be in a hundred years to a brand-new world full of new people. But instead there I was stuck in this mutated version of my old life where everyone had grown-up just enough to forget about me. Or, at the very least, move on to lives I could no longer fit into. My best friend had secrets and my girlfriend had a fiancé. I came back from the dead for this? Joke's on me.

CHAPTER EIGHT

JOKE'S ON ME

She'd always been there in very small ways, I'd say. I didn't really know her before middle school, but then we had a few classes together and I eventually noticed that she was the only other kid who got my jokes, the only one who knew the exact *Saturday Night Live* reference I was making or the impression I was botching. She'd always be there laughing and, in the cutest way possible, following up whatever I'd said with something she hoped would be funnier. She was competitive in that way alone, and I realized after a while that she was only this way with me. In classrooms full of more attractive, more popular, and all around better guys, Cate Conroy would take pains to sit next to me and be my partner on projects and ask me for help on assignments. By the end of eighth grade she mentioned being tired of riding the bus every day, so I asked my mom if we could start picking her up in the mornings. Luckily, her house was on the way to school from ours.

She lived with her mom and stepdad in a very small house that was actually one half of a car repair shop. It was nicer on the inside than I'd imagined, but something about it never quite felt like a home to me. Maybe because Cate was shy about it and always made sure to tell everyone that they were saving up to buy a new place. Her stepdad, a mechanic, was a nice guy from Chicago who talked faster than an auctioneer. He was always covered in grease from his fingertips to his elbows, usually with a smudge or two on his face, and before Cate and I ever started dating, he would whisper things to me like "I'm rooting for you, buddy." And I'd always pretend not to know what he was talking about and walk away embarrassed.

I told Cate I loved her, that I was *in* love with her, outside of a movie theater in downtown Kansas City. She was supposed to say, with tears in her eyes, that she felt the same way. She was supposed to let me grab her and swoop her dramatically down to one side and kiss her like no one's ever kissed anyone else in the world. Instead she said, "Thank you, that's sweet," and hugged me good night when her mom pulled up to take her home.

The next day, after school, she showed up at my house holding a large, flat square, something wrapped in plain brown paper. She asked if we could go upstairs, and as I led her up, there was the sort of quiet between us that made every creak of our steps echo through the house. We got up to my room, and even though no one else was home, I shut the door behind me. She just stood there, holding the mystery gift, and she had this grin on her face that at least made me step away from the door and let go of the handle. I was ready to bolt, ready to run out of that room as soon as she broke my heart, so I wouldn't have to face the mortification.

"Relax," she said.

"What's that?" I asked, my voice shaky just like the rest of me. Even my chest.

"It's a present for you."

"Why?"

"Because I didn't know what to say last night."

"I'm sorry."

"Don't be sorry. Why would you be sorry for saying something like that?"

"I don't know."

"Open it," she said, handing it over.

It was a painting. But I'd known that much when she'd walked in. For starters, Cate was always painting. And also, right as she handed it to me, I saw a smudge of red on her hand. She was messy that way, never unkempt but always looking like she'd just been working on something important, something that just couldn't wait.

Something like this painting she handed me. It was us, right in the center of the canvas, sitting alone and side by side in a big empty movie theater. I had my arm around her, my feet kicked up on the seat in front of me. She even made the sneakers green and yellow. You could only see our backs. You could see her wavy blond hair hanging over the back of the seat and my short brown hair jutting just a little over the tops of my ears. There were empty black seats all around and behind us. Nearly the entire far background was a white screen with little tatters and cracks at the edges with huge red curtains on either side. It looked exactly like our theater.

"This is amazing," I said.

"Like us."

"I love it," I said.

"I love you," she said. "I do. I'm stupid and I don't like surprises and you caught me off guard. But there it is."

"Don't say it just because you feel obligated, Cate."

"I only feel obligated because it's the truth, Travis."

Cate Conroy was a good girlfriend who used to draw dragons on my arms in black Sharpie ink and send me messages of photos that I'd have to translate into words. And she made me laugh like no one else could, this hard laugh that shook my whole body and brought tears to my eyes. The best thing about it, though, was that she could be so funny, so incredibly ridiculous and goofy sometimes, but never at anyone else's expense. For that, and for a lot of other reasons, I was better when she was around me. That's how I knew I loved her so much, because not loving her didn't make any sense once I'd known what it felt like.

Before Cate I was just Travis. I was a quiet kid who

would blush easily when he got too much attention and always walked with his head down and his hands in his pockets. Usually I was sitting in class thinking about something funny to say and never being brave enough to speak up and say it. In my mind I pretended I was too mature and intelligent to clown around with my classmates, but even I knew that wasn't totally the case. I just wasn't quite sure how to be one of them. Not until she helped me figure that out. Before she was there to be my audience, to pay me attention when everyone else had given up on it, I was quite sure I'd always sort of fade into the background.

I remember the first real time we talked. It was in eighth-grade French class, and we were working on a group project. She'd been assigned to my group, along with Daniel Thompson and Marybeth Cutler. We had to choose a poem from a book the teacher had given us and then translate it into French.

"I think we should do this one," Daniel suggested, presenting us a four-line poem.

"Too easy. I want a good grade," Marybeth said, grabbing the book from him.

"She said size didn't matter," Daniel added.

To me, the moment was too funny to keep from laughing. I was turning red, I knew it, and I was trying my best to keep my mouth shut and sort of look away, like something else was on my mind. Then Cate leaned over and whispered into my ear.

"Let's hope size doesn't matter, for Daniel's sake."

And we both burst into laughter that was so loud the teacher walked over and gave us her death stare. But I couldn't stop. And neither could she. After that it didn't take us long to go from being Cate Conroy and Travis Coates to being just Cate and Travis. I'd be somewhere without her, and the first thing I'd get asked was "Where's Cate?" She said it was the same exact case when she was without me.

And now I just wanted to see her. I didn't care if she looked different. I didn't care if she had a fiancé and I didn't care if she said she didn't want to see me, because that's bullshit. I was there first, and after seeing Kyle and Audrey and all those kids at school and all my old teachers and classrooms and hallways, all I could think about was seeing and hearing and touching the one person I'd promised to come back for. We had to finish what we started. We got to do that now. No one else could say that. Well, Lawrence Ramsey could but no one else. We had to go for it. I had to go for it. Just like those doctors had done with my head and Jeremy's body, I had to take my old life and mash it together with this new one. That meant there'd probably have to be a few more scars.

She still lived in Kansas City, that much I knew. Kyle said she was working some temp job at a law firm and taking night classes to be a paralegal. All I heard, though, was that she wasn't doing art. Something wasn't right about that.

"I need you to call her for me," I said to Kyle on the phone the day after I started back at school.

"Travis, I just think if she were ready, she'd have already contacted you."

"Kyle, please. I'm trying to be cool about this, but you know it's weird that she hasn't seen me yet. It has to happen."

"And then what?"

"What do you mean?"

"Then what happens? Do you just pretend you aren't a teenager and run off with her and live happily ever after?"

"No. I don't see why we'd have to run off anywhere."

"Damn, Travis. Listen to yourself. I know it's hard, but listen. We're older now. It sucks, but it's how it is. If you show up bringing back the saddest time in her life, what will that do to her?"

"She just didn't know, man. No one knew I'd come back. I get that. I didn't know either. I thought if I woke up, it'd be so far in the future that you'd all be gone. I can't make sense of it, really. And I never gave much thought to seeing any of you again, you know? I can't just tell myself that it's all okay. It's not. I'm here. That's got to mean something."

"It means a lot. It means you're alive again and everyone in the world is happy about that. You're a freakin' miracle. But, for whatever reason, she's avoiding you and you have to find a way to respect that until she's ready. Okay? Don't pretend you don't see where I'm coming from here."

"No, we wouldn't want to go *pretending* things would we?"

"What the hell is that supposed to mean?"

"Nothing. Look, I'm sorry. Thanks. I'll figure it out. Can you just, if you talk to her, can you just tell her I want to see her? Can you do that?"

"Sure, Travis."

"Kyle?"

"Yeah?"

"Anything you want to tell me?"

"No, Travis. I gotta run. Big test tomorrow."

"Good luck, then."

"Good-bye, Travis."

CHAPTER NINE

GOOD-BYE, TRAVIS

I know I'm not supposed to be talking about dying. That's not what this is about. But, see, I sort of have to break my own rules for a bit so you'll understand what I was missing when I got back.

When we said good-bye in the hospital in Denver, Kyle had already been crying in private, so I could see the sadness in his eyes just as he grabbed my hand and pulled me toward him. I was probably just as nervous about what he would say to me as he was. I'm not a huge fan of sentimentality, and even in those last days I was finding it hard not to laugh at what others would consider very meaningful, emotional moments. I wasn't coldhearted—I was exhausted and, unlike any of them, I was relieved.

So I started laughing and crying pretty hard when he leaned down, with all seriousness, with those same sad eyes and years of shared memories floating heavy in the small space between us, and whispered: "Can I have your Xbox?"

And it was perfect.

When Kyle had left the room with me still laughing and Cate knew it was her turn, she walked in quietly and carefully slid herself into the bed with me. We just lay there for a while not saying anything. She looked up at me a few times and then closed her eyes again, tears squeezing their way out. But she knew time was running out because she suddenly popped her head up and looked at me with the most horrified expression I'd ever seen. I was about to remind her to keep breathing when she interrupted my thoughts.

"Tell me you really think you'll come back."

"I really think I'll come back."

"Bullshit," she said, almost smiling but still pale, still very careful with her motions.

"It could happen," I said. "Just as likely as anything, I'd say."

"What if I'm an old lady?"

"Then things are going to get really creepy for me."

"Shut up."

"Just promise to eat right and do lots of cardio. Don't go facelift, though. I want to see the wrinkles. I think you'd look good with wrinkles."

"Shit, Travis. This is too hard."

"Look," I said. "Kiss me. Then turn around and walk out."

Being a tough guy didn't work for me, and before I

could spit out the words, I was using my one remaining molecule of strength to sit up and grab her around the shoulders. We cried and she said things about it not being fair and she got angry so fast that it turned to sadness before I could react to it. So instead of calling me an asshole, it came out more like "Ass love you," which made us both pause for a few seconds in each other's arms.

"Yes, babe, ass love you too," I said.

"I mean, I love you."

"I know. And I love you, Cate Conroy. Can you do me a favor?"

"Yeah."

"Keep my painting safe for me? Now that they've got the house to themselves, I don't want my parents breaking it when they start partying it up every night."

"Done," she said. "You're stupid."

"Remember me this way," I said. "And I promise, when I come back, that I'll be just as stupid as ever."

"Deal."

A few minutes later she was gone. She didn't turn around or anything—there was no dramatic movie moment where she ran back in and kissed me passionately and it started raining inside or anything. She hung her head low, and she beelined out and down the hallway. I was proud of her too. I couldn't have done it that way. They would've had to pry me off her.

We'd stayed up pretty late the night before, my parents and me, because they wanted the good-bye to be short and sweet. They didn't want to upset me before my procedure, and they certainly didn't want me to question their faith in all this Frankenstein madness. I knew, though. I knew they believed this would be it and it broke what was left of my heart when they walked in, together, and stood on either side of the bed after Cate had left.

"How you feeling?" Dad asked.

"Good. Ready, I think."

"You're not scared, then?" Mom was choking up.

"I've been scared a lot," I said. "Through all of this, but not now, no. Not so much."

"We're so proud of you, Travis. You're so brave," Dad said with tears and a scratchy, broken voice.

"You guys have been better than you should've been," I said. "Can you just *know* that? Can you just try not to forget how good you were at all of this?"

"We haven't been good at anything," Mom said.

"You took care of me," I said. "Every second, my whole life."

I hugged them each good-bye, and they each kissed a cheek and left their faces next to mine for longer than I expected, long enough to feel like, in some cosmic world, we were sharing thoughts that way. We were shooting invisible little lines of sentiment and love and anguish. Then they stood there, holding hands, and they watched as my eyes began to close, as the chemicals began to tell my brain to go to sleep, to take the longest nap in history. And they told me they'd see me soon.

See, I had all these people who had to watch me leave and pretend to hope that I could come back. It was all pretend—I was pretending and they were pretending because that's what got us through it. We fake it sometimes, don't we? We go along with impossible things because we have to survive when life starts getting too dark. And, well, usually we never have to deal with the too-good-to-be-true thing actually becoming true. But when it does, I can tell you that the pretending gets a lot harder. You can find ways to be okay with dying, but you can't fake your way through living. You can't be okay with not having anything you want when it's staring you right in the face. And you can't go to sleep at night knowing you have some poor kid's body attached to you and feeling like you don't have any damn good use for it.

CHAPTER TEN

ANY DAMN GOOD USE FOR IT

We met up with Dr. Saranson at the local hospital on the Wednesday after I started school. He flew in from Denver that morning just to examine me and make sure everything was still attached properly, I guess. He actually made that joke during the appointment, and I'm not ashamed to say I laughed pretty hard. I'm a big fan of bad jokes, as I'm sure you've noticed.

"Travis," he said. "You couldn't be in better health. I'll admit I was a little worried that Jeremy's body would be weak after all he went through, but you seem to have been the right cure for that. Your head, anyway. How's your appetite?"

"He can't eat enough. We're keeping Whole Foods in business," Mom said.

"That's good. Very good. And how's school?"

"It's okay. Weird but okay."

"He's already made a new friend," Dad said.

"Hey there. That was quick. No surprise, though. Just be careful they're not in it for your fame." He chuckled to himself, staring down at his clipboard.

He eventually asked my parents to give us a few minutes, and we talked about Jeremy Pratt a little more. He said that, like me, Jeremy wasn't too scared to die when the time finally came. To me, the saddest part about Jeremy's story wasn't how he died but how he found out he was sick in the first place. Apparently, he wanted to be a professional skateboarder. So he was skateboarding with his friends one day and he kept falling down, kept losing his balance on the simplest tricks, ones he'd been doing for years. Then it was the headaches, then mood changes, and eventually nausea and vomiting. They say there's a very good chance of surviving a brain tumor if it can be removed. If it can't, you'll probably end up like Jeremy Pratt. Well, except you won't be attached to me afterward.

Dr. Saranson had a flight to catch, so we parted ways with one of his long handshakes. He was so glad I'd talked to Lawrence, but he didn't ask for too many details. I liked that about him, that he knew it wasn't his place and that he probably wouldn't be able to understand Lawrence and me anyway. He knew that no one—except his future patients, maybe—would ever understand us.

I started thinking about Jeremy a lot more after that day. It was hard not to, I guess. Just when I'd realize I hadn't thought about my situation for a while, something would happen and I'd suddenly look down at my knees or the tops of my now size twelve shoes and be thrown off course all over again. But still, it felt so right. It was so comfortable to just be moving and breathing and able to sit up and bend and jump and stand on one leg. Jeremy Pratt's body was now doing all these things that my old body had stopped doing for me, things that everyone takes for granted until they aren't there anymore. Hell, I was even impressed with my new ability to fart with such ease and so very little pain. You know things are weird when you start appreciating your farts.

"Do you skateboard?" Hatton asked at lunch after I'd told him Jeremy's story. It was my fourth day back at school, a Thursday.

"Never was any good at it."

"You should try it now."

"You think so?"

"Hell yeah. Muscle memory. You'd probably be awesome."

"I don't think that's how it works. But do you have a board?"

"No. But my little brother does."

"You have a little brother?"

"Yeah. Skylar. Bane of my existence."

After Hatton and I made a plan to test out my skateboarding skills that afternoon and sat through another excruciating chemistry slide show, I went to my favorite class of the day, which was study hall. This was usually reserved for seniors only, but they made an exception for me since I started school in October and because, well, they were probably scared if they gave me a full class load, then I'd want to die all over again.

But on that fourth day back, just as I was closing up my geometry book and prepping for my afternoon nap, the school secretary's voice blasted out over the intercom.

"Mrs. Huxley," she said. "Please send Travis Coates to the counselor's office."

"Travis," Mrs. Huxley said, never looking up from her computer. I wasn't sure she was even a real person. I'd never seen her move from that spot.

I got my stuff together and walked out. There was always something sort of creepy about walking around the halls of Springside High when everyone else was in class. You'd see a few kids here and there, but mostly you'd notice the way the floor glowed with thick coats of wax and how, no matter what part of the building you were in, it smelled like someone was popping popcorn. I think teachers survive mostly on popcorn and Diet Coke.

I waited outside the counselor's office and leafed through a few pamphlets tossed onto an old coffee table in front of me. I thought maybe if I kept looking, I might find one titled "So You've Just Come Out of Cryosleep to Find That Your Girlfriend Is Engaged and Your Best Friend Is Trapped in the Closet?" But, alas, I didn't have any luck. I *did* learn how to talk to my parents about STDs, though. So at least there's that. I actually hadn't seen Mrs. Taft, the counselor, since I'd been back. I hadn't spent too much time around her, but I always thought she was nice.

"Travis, you ready?" a surprisingly young guy in slacks and a skinny tie said, standing right in the doorway of the office. This was not Mrs. Taft.

"Uhh. Yes, sir."

I followed him into the tiny room and took a seat across from his desk. An engraved gold nameplate told me he was Philip Franklin, and I wondered if he had had a hard time growing up with two first names.

"Sorry to pull you out of class like that," he said. "I'm Philip." He extended his hand to shake mine.

"Nice to meet you," I said.

"Likewise. So how's everything going?"

"It's okay, I guess."

"Yeah? Not too overwhelmed by your classes yet?"

"Study hall helps," I said. "I should be fine."

"Good, good. So I know I wasn't here before. How do I say this . . . when *you* were here?"

"It's okay," I said, saving him. "I get what you mean."

"Thanks," he laughed. "Looks like you're getting used to people not knowing what to say, huh?"

"A little bit."

"So anyway. Principal Carson wanted me to check on you every now and then to make sure things are going okay. And to let you know that we'll do whatever we can to make this easier for you, Travis."

"Thanks."

"The press . . . have they bothered you at home or anything?"

"No. There's a cop patrolling the neighborhood for a while to make sure they leave us alone."

"That's good," he said. He looked so nervous and twitchy, like he was talking to someone really famous or something.

"Yeah. I'm not ready to talk to the press just yet. Not sure I ever will be."

"I don't blame you one bit. It must be difficult for you— to be thrown into something so much bigger than, well, being a teenager in Kansas City."

"Dad says they'll lose interest eventually."

"Probably. Something weirder will happen and they'll leave you alone."

"Yeah."

"Sorry. I didn't mean to say *weird*. Something else . . . I don't know . . . *newsworthy*."

"Mr. Franklin," I said. "I'm thinking *weird* is probably the right word here."

"And you've made some new friends this week?"

"A few."

"Mrs. Lasetter says you hit it off with Hatton Sharpe. That's good. Hatton's a good kid."

"He's funny, yeah."

"And you know Audrey Hagler, right? Her brother's a friend of yours?"

"Yes, sir. Kyle. My best friend."

"That's great. This must be so strange for you. I've got to be honest here and say I've felt a little clueless. There isn't really any research for cases like yours. I was a bit worried."

"And now?" I asked. "Still worried?"

"Not really. You seem okay, I think. Do *you* think you're okay?"

"Can I get back to you on that?"

He smiled and stood up, grabbing a set of keys out of his desk drawer.

"Before you go, Travis, I have something for you."

"Okay."

He unlocked and opened this tall, metal cabinet and brought out a brown cardboard box. He set it down in front of me, and I saw that it was full of sealed envelopes. Most were white, but some were yellow and green and even pink. A few had stickers on the front. They were all addressed to me.

"What's this?" I asked.

"I think it's fan mail," he said. "We've been getting them since you came back."

"Oh. Huh."

"We haven't opened any of them or anything. They're all yours."

I picked one up, a green one, and used my index finger to tear it open. There was a single sheet of notebook paper inside folded three times. I unfolded it, and since

Mr. Skinny Tie was just watching me the whole time, I started reading out loud.

> Dear Travis,
>
> My name is Claudia King, and I've been
> following your story on the news. I think what's
> happened to you is the most inspiring thing I've
> ever heard. I lost my son when he was a little
> boy, and I've had a hard time dealing with
> his death. I've even questioned my faith. But
> when I heard about you, I started praying again.
> I hope you have a very happy, long life.
>
> Sincerely,
> Claudia King

"Wow," Mr. Franklin said.

"I don't want these."

"I'm sorry?"

"I don't want these," I said, dropping the letter back into the box. "You have to keep them. I don't want them."

"Travis, it's really great that your story means so much to all these people."

"Throw them away. Read them yourself. Whatever. It doesn't matter. Just keep them away from me."

"Okay," he said. "I don't understand, but whatever you like."

"Are we done, Mr. Franklin? I need to go back to class."

"Sure, Travis. We'll talk soon."

I left his office as quickly as possible, and I didn't notice the shiny floors this time or the smell of popcorn or any of the other creepy, silent shit going on in the school. I couldn't think about anything except for that letter and all the other letters in that box. I felt like my head was spinning, like maybe the damn thing was about to twist right off my body, so I ducked into the first bathroom I came to and ran into one of the stalls. I leaned down over the toilet with my hands pushing against the walls on each side of me, and I don't know if it was the letters or the fact that my face was so close to a public toilet, or both, but I puked Jeremy Pratt's guts out.

Hatton's mom picked us up after school, and I didn't say anything to him about the letters or the counselor. And I definitely didn't say anything about throwing up in the bathroom because I was afraid if I thought about it too much, I'd start right up again. Thank God I was going to Hatton's house, because I obviously needed some distraction.

At Hatton's I stood in the hallway while he begged his brother, Skylar, who was twelve years old, to borrow his skateboard. The only way we could get him to lend it to us was if I agreed to let him take a picture of my scar. When I stepped into his room, he immediately started attacking me with questions.

Did it hurt? Is there a video anywhere of them chopping

off your head? Can I see it? What did you think about for five years? If you get phantom limb syndrome for your entire body, how will you even know? Is your new thing bigger or smaller than your old thing?

And I answered them with my usual enthusiasm:

No. I hope not. No. Nothing. I have no idea. None of your business, dude.

But then he got really quiet and asked about the others. Leave it to a middle schooler to be the only one brave enough to ask me about them.

"There were seventeen volunteers," I said. "Lawrence and I were the last two they tried to bring back. And the only two who woke up."

"So they just died?" he asked, his skateboard still in his hand.

"Unless maybe they were dead the whole time."

"But you weren't. That Ramsey guy wasn't," Hatton added.

"Yeah, but I think maybe something could've gone wrong five years ago when they put them under. It's just that we were lucky, I guess."

"Really lucky," Skylar said, handing me the board.

"Now let's see if I can't break a few bones to make up for it," I joked.

Before long we were outside in their driveway, staring down at the board.

"Go on, then," Hatton said.

"I'm a little nervous."

"Jeremy Pratt wouldn't be nervous."

"He's dead."

"So are you. Big deal."

I stepped up on the skateboard, my left foot forward, my right foot behind it and slanted, and I swayed back and forth for a second, bent down at the knees, just tried to get a feel for it, tried to balance myself before I started moving. I closed my eyes, let my right foot touch the smooth concrete of Hatton's driveway, and I kicked off.

And in that moment, I swear to you, gravity changed. I'm not sure if it was the height difference or the bigger feet or the fact that maybe I *wasn't* all that scared to die anymore, but I was riding that thing like I'd invented it, like I'd forged the world's first skateboard out of pure kickass in the fires of Mount Awesome. Or maybe, by some off chance, there was still a trace of Jeremy Pratt left in this body. Hatton and Skylar started clapping their hands and cheering for me, and eventually pumping their fists in the air.

"Your turn," I said, letting the board slide from under my foot and roll over toward Hatton.

"No way, José. I've still got a scar from the last time I tried."

"Ah, come on. You only live twice."

CHAPTER ELEVEN

YOUONLYLIVETWICE

I called Lawrence Ramsey again that weekend and told him about the letters. He said he was still getting them, said he thinks we'll both get them until there's more people like us—ones who wake up, anyway—and then maybe the novelty will wear off.

"The letters that call you an abomination and accuse you of being the anti-Christ aren't the worst ones. Those are mostly just funny," he said. "It's when they start saying 'miracle' and 'blessing' . . . that's when they get to you."

"Yeah," I said. "Believe me, I know."

"What're we supposed to do with that, huh?" He raised his voice a little. "What the hell are we supposed to do with ourselves if we go around thinking we're some great gift from God or the universe or whatever? Like we're special or something? Lucky. We're lucky."

"You all right?" I asked.

"I'm fine." He was still nearly shouting. "Look, Travis. It's been a long few months. Sorry. It gets frustrating, and Lord knows I haven't made it any easier on myself. But hell, it's like everyone expects us to explain how this all works. We don't have any more answers than they do."

"Less, I think."

"This helps, though. Knowing it's not just me anymore."

"Gee, thanks," I said, laughing.

"Oh, you know what I mean."

The one-month anniversary of my reanimation was the same day I decided I couldn't wait a second longer to see Cate. So I did what any resurrected teenage boy desperate to see his soul mate would do. I showed up at her parents' front door holding a bouquet of flowers from Target and wearing a tie. I knew she didn't live there anymore, but I also knew that my once future in-laws did and that I needed to do as much as I could to be back in these people's lives, whether they were ready for it or not.

I was always pretty nervous any time I was about to be reunited with someone. A lot of people, like my grandma and my aunt Cindy, just hugged me a lot and cried and blew their noses and kept asking me things about how I was feeling. And then others, like our next-door neighbors, would stare at my scar and pretend they weren't staring at it and say, "The neighborhood sure wasn't the same without you," and other meaningless things like that. Some people tried to play it very cool, like what happened to me wasn't any big deal at all. But I could see it, the silent freaking-out. Like the first time I went back to church with my mom, and people were whispering and pointing at us. I swear I even heard one lady say "unnatural" when we walked past. People don't like being confronted with things they don't understand, I guess. Just about every night there'd be someone on the news arguing over my existence and what it meant for science and religion and humanity. It was all a bit overwhelming.

So of course I was wondering how Cate's parents would react. Five years before, I'd been the love of their daughter's life. But then I went away and this new guy swooped in, and I guess what I really needed to know was that they hadn't forgotten me, that even if you're gone for as long as I was, that people who treated you like their own son would still look at you the same.

I knocked three quick times, the way I always knocked on their door, and I waited there with the flowers covering my face. I was rocking from side to side, trying not to be nervous but also crawling out of my skin a little bit.

As soon as Cate's mom opened the door, she started screaming. I hadn't even moved the flowers from my face. She knew it was me. It was one of those excited but shocked screams, like Publishers Clearing House was at the door with a check for a million dollars. She put both hands to her mouth, shook her head, and then attacked me. She still hadn't said a word, and now she was swaying us back and forth a bit with her arms wrapped all the way around me. It was less of a hug and more of a wrestling move, her head nearly tucked under my arm. The flowers didn't survive.

"Hey," I said.

"Travis Coates. My God in Heaven. Travis Coates. I love you. Do you know that?"

She stepped back and led me by the hand inside. She was wearing faded blue jeans and a pink T-shirt. The house was exactly the same—cramped, dimly lit, and with the faint smell of motor oil. It was attached to an auto repair shop, after all.

"Glen! You will not believe who it is!"

"These are for you." I handed her the squashed flowers, a few petals falling to the floor.

"Travis, you charmer. I should be giving *you* flowers."

"Why would you do that?"

"I don't know. You know what I mean. GLEN!"

"That Travis?" Glen said, rounding the corner.

It was amazing how little the two of them had changed in five years. They had the same clothes, same hairstyles, same, well, everything. I loved it. I wanted to stand there for as long as I could and listen to them talking to each other and asking me questions and just being the way they always were. For a few minutes I forgot I was living in the future, like Glen and Janice had been preserved perfectly in a time-immune bubble just waiting for me to come back.

They asked a lot of the same things that everyone asked me back then. But it wasn't uncomfortable with them—nothing ever was. Glen even walked over and started inspecting my scar, his breath hot on the side of my face as he tried to convince Janice to have a closer look.

"Glen, stop that. Leave him alone."

"You're telling me one of the *two* people on Earth to come back from the dead walks into my house and I can't even see the scar? Look at this thing. Weirdest thing I've ever seen in my life," he spouted out with great speed, like always.

"So I guess you know about Cate, huh?" Janice said, sitting across from me at their dining room table.

"Yeah."

"Gettin' married at twenty-one years old. Ridiculous," Glen said so quickly I barely caught it.

"He's a good man," Janice said. "He's got a degree, a good job, a nice place in Springside."

"He lives in Springside?"

"Yep. Cate's there too—she moved in with him a few months ago."

"How old is . . . sorry, what's his name?" I lied. I knew his name. I was trying to play less like the jealous boyfriend and more like the understanding victim. It was torture.

"Turner. He's twenty-five."

"Pretty old," I said. "What's he do?"

"He works with computers for this big company,

AdverTech. He's super smart. Got a good head on his shoulders."

She got really quiet when she realized what she'd said. She looked embarrassed, but I just started laughing and broke the tension up pretty quick. It *was* pretty funny. Glen was still shaking his head at her a few minutes later when I asked them how I could get in touch with Cate.

"You know, Travis. It's just that . . ."

"I know. I know this is hard and that she's got a different life now, but I have to see her."

"It's just not fair, is it?" Glen said. "What's happened to you."

"Oh, what do you want with a girl in her twenties anyway? You're a teenager still. You get a do-over. Have some fun." Janice reached out and slapped the side of my leg.

"Janice," Glen said. "He just got back. Take it easy."

"I should probably go."

I stood up and started heading for the door. I wanted to stay, though. I wanted to go to Cate's old room and sit down on the floor at the foot of her bed and watch her put on her makeup. I wanted to play with the metal Slinky she always kept on her nightstand and pretend to be frustrated with how long it took her to get ready, just so she'd give me that look in her mirror from across the room, the one where she raised one eyebrow and snarled a little bit with her top lip. I wanted her to be there the way she would've always been there. But she wasn't.

"Travis." Janice cornered me by the door, stood really close, and put her hand on my face.

"It's okay. I understand."

"Listen, I'll talk to her. Glen's right. It's not fair. She's different. Everyone's different, but you're not. You're just *Travis*. The sweet boy who got dealt a pretty bad hand the first go-round."

"I feel the same," I said. "Except for, you know, the obvious." I held my arms out, looked down at my body.

"Well, you're better. You're alive. Lord knows that's a big improvement from the last time I saw you. So maybe some things have changed." She lightly tapped one finger on my forehead. "But not where it matters."

CHAPTER TWELVE

WHERE IT MATTERS

They say high school is the best time of your life. Well, it wasn't the best time of either of mine. Though my first attempt at it was pretty short-lived. I was fifteen when I got sick and then, like I said before, I gave up even trying to do any of the work they sent me. All told, I had about a year and a half of high school before I had to quit, and a lot of that was bogged down with doctor's appointments and sick half days.

And the second round of high school felt unnatural in every way. I didn't know anyone and, as it turns out, I didn't know any*thing*, either. Three and a half weeks in, and I already felt like I was going to fail all my classes. All I could think about was Cate, with a healthy dose of Kyle thrown in. Why hadn't he just told everyone he was gay? He'd spent all these years not living the way he was meant to. There I was aching all over to have some sense of normalcy, to have any kind of glimpse of the life I was used to, and I couldn't understand why he'd wasted all these years, years I didn't get, living this lie. Maybe that wasn't fair, but my brain wasn't all that accustomed to fairness around that time.

"What do you think about this for a band name: A Reptile Dysfunction?" Hatton asked at lunch one day.

"I love it."

"Me too. Can you play the drums?"

"No."

"Damn. Oh well. What's wrong, man?"

"Things are just weird. I dunno."

"Yep. You're officially a member of the living once again. Things are always weird."

"Let me ask you something."

"Okay."

"Promise not to tell anyone?" I looked right into his eyes.

"Dude, who am I gonna tell? You're one of about three people who listen to me."

"Fair enough. So you know Kyle?"

"Kyle Hagler. Your best friend. Yes."

"Yes. Him. So before I died or went away or whatever we're calling it, he told me something."

"He was sleeping with Cate?" Hatton perked up, his eyes huge.

"No. Shut up. Listen."

"Sorry. Go on."

"He told me he was gay."

As soon as I said it out loud, I felt like the worst friend in history. I'd betrayed Kyle's trust. But what was I supposed to do? I wanted to help him, and I didn't think I could do that *and* get Cate back without a little help of my own.

"Oh, okay. That's cool, I mean, whatever," Hatton said.

"And, see, he said I was the only one who knew. So when I saw him the other day, for the first time, he brought up having a girlfriend. A *girl*friend. I don't get it."

"A beard."

"What?"

"He's got a beard."

"No, he doesn't. What are you talking about?"

"Travis, a *beard* is a girl who dates a gay guy to . . . you know, cover up the fact that he's a gay guy."

"Oh. I get it. *Beard*. Yeah, he's got a beard. Shit."

"Have you seen her yet?" he asked.

"No."

"I bet she's ugly. If she's beautiful, then he's not gay anymore. It wore off."

"Can that happen?"

"I dunno. Probably not. I just know that my uncle Jimmy had a wife when I was a kid, and then one day Mom tells me he's getting a divorce, and then he showed up to Thanksgiving dinner with my *new uncle Terry* and everyone just rolled with it."

"Awesome."

"Yeah. And kind of sad, I guess."

"For sure. I just feel like I should help him or something."

"You mean like, *sexually?*" Hatton smirked.

"No. Good Lord. I just need him to know that it doesn't matter. Right?"

"Have you ever been gay, Travis? Of course it matters. Don't be stupid, man."

"Well, I know it matters, but not to like, the *good* people, you know?"

"I was watching this show the other night," Hatton began. "On CNN. It was this roundtable of experts— a scientist, a surgeon, a couple of politicians. And they were talking all about you and Lawrence Ramsey."

"Oh yeah? What's new?"

"And the reporter guy, you know the one with the weird name? He was asking them if they thought it was right. Not if they thought it was good for science or anything like that, but on a *personal* level, if they thought that bringing people back from the dead or whatever was right. If they thought it was okay."

"What'd they say?" I asked.

"Well, the scientist and the surgeon sort of had a hard time answering it without getting technical. One said he was devoted to saving lives and that he looked at this as a medical breakthrough or whatever. And the other, she agreed with him and said she thinks we'd all jump at the opportunity if it meant we could spend more time with our loved ones. But the politicians, they were different."

"Republicans?" I asked, rolling my eyes.

"One was a Democrat, actually. And you know what he said?"

"What?"

"He said despite all the arguments and all the evidence and even seeing you and Lawrence Ramsey alive and healthy, he just can't seem to wrap his head around the idea of it. Said it still feels like one step too far to him and he just can't get over it."

"Why are you telling me this, Hatton?"

"Because I think you and Kyle might have a lot more in common than you realize."

"You think so?"

"Yeah. I mean, you're both living these lives you didn't choose to live with a world full of people telling you what that's supposed to mean. It's messed up."

"Damn. I hadn't really thought about it that way," I said.

I called Kyle after school and invited him over for dinner. He said he needed to study, but I told him it was really important and that I was going through a hard time and needed to talk. Maybe I was being dramatic, but I thought it was okay to guilt my best friend into spending time with me since I'd been, you know, preoccupied for so long. When he got to the house, we played video games for a while before sitting down to dinner with my parents. Dad told us about this new interactive dance game at Arnie's that was supposed to "blow our minds" but, if I'm being honest, sounded pretty lame.

"I think it sounds amazing, Mr. Coates," Kyle said.

"Well, you two should go by there sometime soon. What do you think, Travis? Might help you feel a little more at home again?" Dad nudged me with his elbow.

"Yeah. We'll do that soon," I said.

But I was too distracted by my mission to really add much more to the conversation than that. And my parents wouldn't leave us alone long enough for me to talk to Kyle about his secret, or anything for that matter. They were like this for a while after I got back, just clingy and too involved. I probably would've appreciated it more had it not felt like I just spent the last several months stuck in that house with them. By the time we finished dinner and they shut up, Kyle had to go home and study.

"I'll walk you out," I said, following behind him.

He was inside his truck with the window down by the time I went for it and just asked him what I'd wanted to ask him all night.

"Kyle, what's the deal, man?"

"What do you mean?"

"The girlfriend, Kyle. You know I remember what you told me."

"Look, Travis. It's way more complicated than you think. Things just change sometimes. I think I was just confused or something."

"And what if you weren't?"

"Well, I'm dating a girl now, so it's not like it really matters."

"Kyle, it does matter. Of course it matters. Are you happy? With her, I mean?"

"Yeah. She's great. I want you to meet her. Maybe next week?"

"Wait. Stop. I'm not done. Maybe I've been gone for a while, but I *know* you. I knew you back then and I know you now. You're gay. And it's fine. So why not just be yourself?"

"Shut up, please." He looked around, off behind me, and into the street like someone was just waiting for his sexuality to be called out so they could tell everyone they knew.

"Is it your parents?"

"Travis. Stop. It's nobody. I thought I was *gay* when I was sixteen. A lot of people think things like that when they're young. I was wrong. Move on, dude. I know you're just trying to help me, but let it go."

It was the way he said "gay" that worried me the most. His jaws were clenched, his teeth still together, and his eyes were fixed in front of him.

"I'm young now, Kyle. And I don't think I'm gay. I don't think it because I'm not gay. But you are, Kyle. Maybe you don't want to be, for whatever reason, or maybe something happened that made you scared, but please stop pretending to be someone you aren't. I'm scared too, man. We can handle this together, right?"

"You know what, Travis? Fuck off."

And he drove away without another word. I knew I'd gone too far, that I'd taken at least two steps in the wrong direction. Maybe part of my brain was still thawing out or something. Or maybe pretending is the only way for some people to be happy.

"Isn't that what you're doing too?" Hatton asked me the next day at school.

"What do you mean?"

"Aren't you just pretending you're the old you again?"

CHAPTER THIRTEEN

YOU   AGAIN

Since I'd missed out on getting my driver's license the first time, my dad had been eager to restart the driving lessons we'd begun before I got sick. So I had to turn down Hatton's offer to hang out on the Friday before Thanksgiving break to go driving on the interstate with Ray Coates, Backseat Driver. I was nervous as hell because I wasn't all that great with my old body, and I still wasn't too sure that this new one wouldn't just shut down at any moment. I kept imagining my arms and legs going completely limp and the car cruising right off the side of a bridge or something. But Dad was way more relaxed than he used to be.

"Come on, Travis," he said. "You're driving like my grandpa. Just chill out, okay?"

"You're making me nervous," I said.

He let go of the safety handle above the passenger

window and took his foot off the invisible brake pedal he'd been tapping on the floor.

"Sorry. Now fix your hands. Ten and two."

I liked doing things with my dad. He never got mad about anything—always kept his cool even in stressful situations. And he was always telling me some weird tidbit about something you'd never think anyone would know. If he hadn't been so excited to share these things, I probably wouldn't have ever wanted to learn them either.

"Did you know there are about sixty-one thousand people airborne over the US at any given hour of the day?"

"No, Dad. I did not know that."

"I don't see why people are afraid of flying with a statistic like that floating around. Get it? *Floating* around?"

Oh yeah, and he was also a big fan of puns. And when he'd laugh at himself, he'd sort of crouch over a little, holding his stomach. He was always searching for a way to make someone laugh. When I had my first round of chemo, he sat in the room with me the whole time and read aloud from this huge book of jokes. It was awesome in that way that you realize immediately and want to cry because this other person cares about you so much that they'd do anything to make sure you're okay.

After our driving lesson Dad and I met up with Mom at the Triton, which was the little indie movie theater where I first told Cate I loved her. You know, the one in the painting. We got our popcorn and soda and took a seat right in the center, me in the middle. We were seeing a movie Mom had read some great reviews for, some coming-of-age teen angsty crap. I mostly came for the popcorn.

Then, just as the previews were about to start, I saw her walk in. The screen was glowing and flashing on her face, and she looked exactly how she was supposed to look, like time had happened to her more slowly than the others. They saw her at the same time I did, and Mom immediately reached for my hand.

"What should we do?" she asked.

"I don't think she can see us," Dad whispered.

She couldn't. She took a seat in the third row from the front and slumped down the way I knew she would, the way she always did. I needed her to see me the way I saw her. I loved her, and even if those years she'd lived had twisted her memory a bit, had helped her get over me, she loved me too because she said so. She said it wasn't fair. I heard her say it. She said it so many times. She just needed to see me now so we could fix it. She needed to see that after all this time we could wind up there together in the place where it all started.

"I'm going up there," I said, standing.

"Travis, are you sure?" Dad asked, looking over at my mother.

"I have to."

So I made my way over toward the aisle, tripping over strangers' legs. That settled it, I thought. She'd see me in this theater, after all this time, and she'd know what to do, she'd know that the right choice, the *only* choice, was to be with me. And we would set the Earth back on its axis with a dramatic kiss in the glow of the movie screen.

Then he walked in holding two sodas and a popcorn, and I stopped right in the middle of the aisle. Turner, the fiancé. Shit, this guy was good-looking. Even in the dark I could tell that much, and I could see from the way he walked that he knew it too. Then he sat down beside her and handed her a soda.

"Excuse me. Are you going to stand there all night?" a woman said from a seat beside me.

"Yes. I mean, no. What?"

"Oh my God, it's the head kid," someone beside her said.

"Please shut up." I barely looked over at them.

"From the news? Holy shit. Can we get a picture?"

"No, you can't get a picture. I'm busy, okay? Just please leave me alone."

"Asshole," one of them whispered loudly.

"Travis." Mom had walked up behind me and tapped my shoulder.

"What?"

"We can go. Should we go?" Mom whispered.

"No," I said.

"I don't think this is right. Just not the right time and place for this, okay?"

"She wants to see me, Mom."

I walked away from her and instead of going over to Cate, I went to the back, through the purple double doors, and sat down on a bench next to the entrance. I was breathing so heavy, and I felt like my face was on fire. It couldn't be this hard. She was there. I was there. There was no reason we shouldn't be there together, and there was nothing to stop me from walking right up to her and telling her that, setting everything straight again.

I went back inside after a couple of minutes with the full intention of marching over to her, grabbing her hand, giving Turner the finger, and walking out of there to start my life the way I should've been able to weeks before. The way we always promised it would be. But then when I got close enough to get a clear view of them, I saw him leaning his face toward hers. And she was doing the same. With one little kiss that wasn't on my lips, I froze again, lowered my head, and returned to my seat, where both Mom and Dad stared at me until I said something.

"I'm fine."

But you and I both know I wasn't fine at all. I don't remember a thing about the movie because the only film I was watching was the one playing in the two seats they occupied, the one where they casually passed a bucket of popcorn back and forth and glanced at each other any time something funny happened on the screen. That was supposed to be me down there laughing with her. She was supposed to be whispering things into *my* ear and leaning her head on *my* shoulder. This guy stole my life and he didn't even know it.

When the movie was over, we waited a few minutes before walking out. I watched as they held hands and made their way toward the front exit. From the way they left so quickly, I thought maybe she'd seen us. But that wasn't something she'd do. She'd never hide from me.

Part of me wanted to stand up in the seat and scream out so she wouldn't leave. I wanted to get it over with already, just tell her and everybody else the real reason I thought I was back. It wasn't for my parents and it obviously wasn't for Kyle. It damn sure wasn't so I could go back and be miserable at Springside High, either. It was for her. I was back there in that theater in Kansas City five years after all reason and all logic and all history collided together to say I was gone forever because this girl needed me just as much as I needed her. The universe made a decision the second Jeremy Pratt's lungs started breathing my air and his heart started pumping blood up and into my brain. It decided that Travis Coates wasn't done with what he started. It decided that sometimes you love someone so much that going and doing something crazy like having your head frozen and convincing everyone you're coming back isn't as ridiculous as it sounds. So why was it so absurd to think she'd be glad to have me back? Why couldn't I just show up at her door and take her hand and say thank you? Thank you for still being here.

CHAPTER FOURTEEN

THANK YOU

I spent most of Thanksgiving break moping around the house and watching old movies on cable. Hatton was visiting his grandmother in Kentucky for the week, and it looked like Kyle wasn't talking to me. I couldn't blame him. Even I wasn't sure what I was trying to get out of confronting him about his sexuality. Ugh. "Sexuality." That makes it sound like the opposite of what it is, I think. "Lifestyle" is even worse. No wonder he wants to keep it to himself—nobody seems to understand things they aren't a part of—I guess that's why I keep getting called a freak on national television.

I just wanted him to be okay. I *needed* him to be okay because, well, I don't think I was anywhere close to that, and I needed at least one of us to have things figured out. Yeah, maybe I was dying when he told me before and it didn't matter, but you didn't see his face after he'd said it. I wasn't so naive to think it would be all that easy for him this time. I'm not stupid. But I wanted him to realize that he didn't have to keep hiding who he was, at least not from me.

And then there was Cate. Seeing her with Turner was like seeing your parents having sex—it's something you never want to see and after it happens, you're forever haunted by it, no matter what you do. It's like someone shaped a branding iron of the two of them kissing in that theater and scorched it right into my skull. The Triton might as well have burned to the ground because it was possessed by the spirits of that night. And I was bound to see her with him again. I knew I'd eventually come face-to-face with the biggest obstacle that stood between us. He'd have to go—that's all there was to it. Turner who works with computers would have to be a victim of fate. It was inevitable.

Something else inevitable was seeing my entire family for Thanksgiving. This wasn't necessarily a bad thing. I liked my family okay . . . I just wasn't sure how they'd react to the dead guy in the room. I'd already seen my grandmother and aunt several weeks before, and that went okay. But this would be different. This would be little cousins who weren't little anymore and aunts and uncles who'd visited me in the hospital, who'd helped my parents move on with their lives after I'd gone.

Everyone in the family volunteered to drive to Kansas City for our big holiday dinner, instead of the usual trek to Grandma's in Arkansas. I was anxious to see what had become of all these people who'd already seemed to age and change so much between our annual visits back before I was gone. Every year there'd be some new growth spurt to marvel at or a cousin with an accompanying girl-friend or boyfriend to whisper about in the kitchen or after they'd gone to bed.

The morning our first guests, my aunt Cindy and her gang, were to arrive, my mom walked into my room and handed me a stuffed elephant.

"Why?" I asked.

"It's for Ethan. That's Chloe's son."

"How old is he?"

"He's two. Cutest thing you've ever seen. Didn't I show you any photos yet?"

"No. Wait, how old is Chloe now?"

"Twenty. Don't ask. It's been a wild couple of years for Cindy and Jim."

The last time I'd seen my cousin Chloe, she had dyed, jet-black hair and was wearing fingernail polish to match it. She had an eyebrow ring, too, and I distinctly remem-ber walking up to her as she was staring at a candle that was sitting on the windowsill in my grandmother's den and asking if she wanted any dessert.

"Did you know that if you stare at a flame long enough, you can see its soul?"

"No, Chloe. I did not know that."

That was also the Thanksgiving she kept bringing

up some "Veronica," who Mom was certain was her girl-friend. Aunt Cindy would get this look on her face any time Chloe said her name, and I saw Uncle Jim gently set his hand on her shoulder during dinner, almost like he was preparing to hold her down in case she decided to jump up and rip the ring out of Chloe's eyebrow.

"I thought Chloe liked girls." I inspected the elephant, rubbed its plush against one cheek.

"That was either a phase or a ploy to get attention and drive Cindy crazy."

"Did it work?"

"Yes. That girl is the most spoiled human being I've ever met. Cindy practically raises Ethan while Chloe goes and hangs out with her friends. Beats all I've ever seen."

"Classy. Is her husband coming?"

"Her boyfriend, you mean. And no, your grandmother won't allow it. She thinks he stole a spoon from her house last Christmas."

"Did he?"

"Probably. You know, they use spoons to smoke those drugs."

"What drugs?"

"I don't know. Whatever kind they're smoking these days."

"Don't ask me."

I'll admit that when they all arrived and were standing in the driveway, I was completely speechless seeing Chloe as an adult holding a two-year-old on her hip. I was even more shocked to see her younger brother, Toby, who was no longer a Dr. Seuss—quoting and adorable eight-year-old but a full-fledged skinny teenager with shaggy hair and big headphones around his neck.

"Toby?" I walked up to him, and he looked over at his mom before doing anything.

"Toby, don't be rude. You remember Travis," Cindy barked.

"Hey, man," I said. "I can't believe you're so *old*. You're almost my age now. Trippy."

He still didn't say anything, but he smiled and exhaled a subtle laugh, holding out a closed fist. I bumped it and walked over to give Chloe a hug.

"Ignore him—he pretty much hates everything," Chloe said into my ear.

"This is for Ethan," I said to her, holding up the stuffed elephant.

"Elwapunt?" he said. I laughed and let his outstretched arms grab it.

"Yeah, elephant," I said. "He's cute."

"Quality genes, you know," she joked.

I liked her immediately. I mean, I'd always liked Chloe and we'd never had any problems or anything, but she was one of the cousins who stayed pretty distant during my whole illness, and I guess I just thought it would be weirder than it was. But we were laughing and joking already.

"You look great, kid." Uncle Jim shook my hand just as

firm as ever, and I could be mistaken here, but I'm pretty sure he had tears in his eyes.

"We certainly have a lot to be thankful for this year, don't we?" Aunt Cindy said, moving in to hug me.

The next group to arrive was Uncle Pete, Aunt Mary, and their twins (the aforementioned Chase and Chad), along with my grandmother, who they'd picked up on the way. Pete was my mom and Aunt Cindy's only brother, but you'd never have guessed that from the way Mary so easily fit in with her sisters-in-law. When I say fit in, I mean that she talked nonstop and a little loudly, just like my mom and Aunt Cindy. And I loved it. The chaos of their combined voices seemed to make me forget all about my situation for once, if only for a few minutes. It was like if I closed my eyes and didn't look at any of them, didn't see how they'd aged and changed, then I could pretend away the dying and the surgery and the waking up to a new world. If every moment could just have this effortless familiarity, then I could be okay.

Chase and Chad were now fourteen, still identical in every way, and even though they both gave me a hug when they walked in, I could tell they weren't quite sure what to say to me or even if they believed that I really was me. They sat next to Toby on the couch and were discussing movies by the time I walked in and took a seat across from them in my dad's recliner.

"Dude, the CGI was so epic," Chase or Chad said.

"I know, right? What about that last battle scene? The

Troll King? So cool." Toby sat up and grabbed a chip from a bowl on the coffee table.

"What movie you guys talking about?" I asked.

"*Troll Wars*. Dude, tell me you've seen it," Toby said.

"Haven't even heard of it."

"Holy shit. Holy shit," one of the twins said. "We have to go. We have to leave this house and go right now."

"I don't think they'll let us," I said.

"Tomorrow, then. Tomorrow you're taking us to see *Troll Wars*. Settled."

"I don't have a license," I said.

"What? You're sixteen, right? Like, almost seventeen?" Toby asked.

"Lame," one of the twins added.

"So lame," the other agreed.

"I have to wait ninety days before they'll let me take the test. It's a medical thing."

"You didn't have one before?"

"Ran out of time," I said.

This made the three of them get quiet, that weird quiet where everyone thinks the same thing and waits for a brave soul to creatively change the subject. So I knew I had to just go for it if this day was going to work out at all.

"Here," I said, standing up and lowering the collar of my shirt. "This is where they did it. This part is me and this part is him. No, it doesn't hurt and yes, it feels exactly like it felt when I had my first body."

They all stood up and stepped closer. Chase and Chad,

as if they'd discussed this beforehand, each stuck out a finger and slowly went in to touch the scar. As they did this, Toby held up his phone and snapped a photo.

"This is the single coolest thing I've ever experienced," Toby said.

"Get in here, then." I pulled him over beside me and smiled as he held his phone out above us and snapped another shot.

"You guys are so weird," Chloe said as she walked into the room.

"He is one of *two* people in history to come back from the dead," Toby said to her. "I think we have the right to freak out a little."

"He was never actually dead, dumbass," Chloe said to him.

"You know what I mean. And watch your mouth. You're a mother now, you b-word."

By the time they were done pretend fighting, Chloe had Toby in a headlock and was asking me if I thought he'd make a good candidate for head transplant surgery. You have no idea how amazing that felt either. To joke about this thing that everyone took so seriously was such a relief. I was so afraid that everyone would get there and we'd all be sad and moping around and talking all about when they lost me and everything.

When dinner was ready and the scent of the turkey was wafting its way through the house and causing us all to turn ravenous, my cousin Thomas finally arrived.

Thomas was Chloe and Toby's older brother and had been twenty when I last saw him. He was dressed in his fatigues, hat and all, and gave my uncle Pete, a former Marine, a salute after he'd given everyone else a hug.

"Travis," he said, hugging my neck. "So good to see you, cousin."

"Alive and well, huh?" I tried to joke.

"Absolutely," he said. "Damn, you look exactly the same."

"Look at his neck," Toby said.

"I'll kick his ass for you later, Travis. Food ready?"

I sat at the flimsy card table with the other kids, where I belonged, and watched Chloe and Thomas at the grown-up table. I'd been outranked. They did not mention this in the cryogenics brochure. Chad, Chase, Toby, and I waited for our moms to fix our plates, and even though it all happened the way I'd always remembered it, it still felt strange to be a part of this new generation of cousins and not sitting across the room with the ones I'd grown up with.

"So you mean to tell me," Toby began, quite loudly, "that if someone in this family gets frozen for a bunch of years, they still have to sit at the kiddy table until their new body is old enough to graduate?"

"Yes, Toby. Eat your food," Aunt Cindy said to him.

"If Travis wants to sit over here, we can make room," my grandmother said.

"I'm fine," I said. "Really. This is nice."

"Come on, Travis. Thomas, move over. Travis, you belong over here." Chloe stood up and held her plate, making her way to our table.

"No. Really, this is silly. I'm sixteen. You're twenty. Stay put."

"You sure?" she said, her head tilted a little, a half frown on her face.

"I'm sure. Everyone, eat. Please."

"Well, I do want to make a toast," Grandma said, standing up. "To Travis."

"Oh man," I said. I still hadn't eaten a bite. My stomach was about to attack my spleen for nutrients.

"No, now you only get to come back to life once, so we're going to toast you all we want tonight," she said.

"Here, here." Uncle Jim raised his glass of iced tea into the air, and everyone followed suit.

"Sharon," my grandmother said. "Would you say grace?"

"Everyone please bow your heads," Mom began. "We thank you, God, for all the miracles in this room tonight. For little Ethan, for Chloe. For Toby, Chase, Chad, and Thomas. And, Lord, we especially thank you for bringing us our Travis back. We missed him so much."

When I opened my eyes, which were fairly wet, I saw that everyone in the room had the same expression, one of those sad-but-happy ones that you see when there's a good memory or joke shared in a eulogy or when your grandparents talk about their childhoods. This look they all shared, some with tears and others with shaky lips, it made me realize something that I hadn't quite thought about up until that moment. It made me realize that no matter how often you see or talk to someone, no matter how much you know them or don't know them, you always fill up some space in their lives that can't ever be replaced the right way again once you leave it.

"Travis," my sweet grandma said. "I always knew you'd come back."

CHAPTER FIFTEEN

COME   BACK

It's always weird going back to school after a holiday. There's this strange sort of feeling in the air and this distant look in everyone's eyes—like no one really knows how to catch back up with their routines, from walking down the hallway to turning locker combinations. You see people stopping to remember what books they need for which classes, and sometimes you even see a kid or two wander into the wrong room at the wrong time. As I sat in my desk in geometry that morning, I wished I could raise my hand and explain to the teacher and to everyone that this feeling they all had, this out-of-time-and-place feeling, was exactly what I felt every second of every day. I wanted them to know, just for a second, what it might feel like to be this way, to be unable to catch back up, to make sense of the littlest things going on around you.

Hatton showed back up at school with a black eye,

courtesy of Skylar and a dictionary that he'd thrown at him from across a room. He was smiling, though, even took his thin wire-rimmed glasses off to give me a closer look. It was like he was proud of the thing.

"I *am* proud of it!" he said. "I look like a total badass now."

"You look like someone who lost a fight."

"Even so. I look like I was *in* a fight. That's all that matters."

"Yeah, with a dictionary."

Though I was relatively famous at school, and everywhere else for that matter, Hatton Sharpe was pretty much the only person I ever talked to, voluntarily at least. If high school couldn't be the same—with Kyle and Cate, I mean—then at least Hatton was there to make it bearable.

"What do you think the likelihood of a guy like me hooking up with a girl like Audrey Hagler is? Be honest," he asked at lunch one day that week.

"I dunno, Hatton. Do you really want a girl like that?"

"Every single second of every day since I was twelve."

"Doesn't she date Matt Braynard?"

"Yeah. That guy's a tool."

"Seems nice to me."

"You haven't spent that much time around him yet. He uses that whole president of the Christian Youth Club thing as a way to cover up what he really is."

"Which is what?"

"A sadist."

"That makes sense."

"You never answered the question. What are my chances?" Hatton was biting his thumbnail.

"Okay. Seeing as she currently dates a sadist pretending to be the biggest Christian in school, and, adding to that, she's about a year older than you are and doesn't know your name, I'm thinking maybe one in about three million?"

"Well, that's not very promising."

"No. But you know what, Hatton?"

"What?"

"One day when we're older and we've got jobs and families and all that, you're gonna run into Audrey Hagler somewhere and you're probably gonna forget her name too. It'll take you a minute to figure out where you know her from, and when you realize who she is, you'll laugh to yourself."

"And she'll still be bangin' hot and we'll, like, start an affair or something. That could be cool too."

"You're hopeless."

"I know. But thanks anyway."

"Sure. Has anyone asked you about the black eye?"

"Couple of people. I told 'em I got in a fight with some private-school kid in my neighborhood. I kicked his fake ass."

"Nice."

"You still haven't talked to Cate?"

"Nope. It sucks."

"Maybe it's like you said, though. Maybe she just needs to see you once and she'll realize you're the same guy."

"That's what I'm hoping. I just don't want to scare her away before I get the chance to prove that."

"You think your new body's gonna freak her out? Travis, not to be weird or anything, but your old one couldn't have been any better than this. Aside from your scar, which makes you look badass anyway, there's nothing wrong with you. I think if I'd been there when you were sick, then getting to see you like this now would be completely incredible."

"I know. It's just . . . it's not going to be the same. When we touch, it'll be different, you know?"

"When you touch? Wait, I'm confused. She's engaged, right?"

"Right."

"Oh." Hatton sort of stared down at the ground for a few seconds.

"What? Say it."

"Travis, I just think it's a bad idea to expect her to see you and automatically be your girlfriend again. I know that's what you want, but have you considered how unlikely that is?"

"No," I said. "And I don't really care if she's engaged. She'll see me and it'll all be okay again. So do you wanna help me or not?"

"Help you do what?"

"Help me get her back."

"You're not going to give up on this, are you?"

"Not a chance. Can you be at my house at six?"

"Sure, man. As long as it's okay for me to run away when her fiancé comes to kick your ass."

"Fine. But I thought fights made you look badass?" I asked.

"Yeah, but I've reached my weekly quota already."

Even though I knew Hatton was wrong about her, that she *would* be my girlfriend again, even if it took a little work and a little time, I knew that sitting around waiting on her to come to me was not the right strategy. She wasn't going to hunt me down and tell me she still loved me and that it didn't matter what the world thought about any of it. She was waiting on me to do those things. I had to find her and tell her, show her, that Travis Coates might be mostly ash in some mystery container hidden in his parents' house, but that the part of him that found its way back would always be incomplete without her. I wasn't dead anymore, so we could be together. It was so simple and I just needed to tell her. So I'd either make it happen, or I'd die again trying.

CHAPTER SIXTEEN

DYING AGAIN
T R Y I N G

The night I told Cate I was sick, she was driving us to a concert downtown. We were on the interstate when I decided I couldn't keep it from her any longer. So I just came out with it and closed my eyes and held on to the handle on her passenger-side door and wished for the moment to pass as quickly and painlessly as possible.

"I wanna die," she said a few minutes later.

"Cate, don't say that."

"No. I wanna die!" She got louder this time, both of her hands gripping the steering wheel tightly, her arms stretched into straight, powerful rods jutting out from her chest.

"Just pull over and let's talk for a second. It's okay."

"I wanna die! I wanna drive this car right off the road and die!"

She was sort of flailing now, her hands still on the

steering wheel, but the rest of her was shaking back and forth against her seat. Her hair was flying around her face. She kept repeating it over and over. "I wanna die. I wanna have a wreck and die!" Then she paused for one quick second, her crying stopped and her body motionless, and she reached over and set one hand on my left arm and said, "But not with you in here," in the most normal, emotionless voice I'd ever heard.

She never had a chance to start freaking out again because we were both laughing too hard. The tears, this time, were running down my face and neck, and I was pretending that they were all from the laughing, but I'm pretty sure some of them were from something else. No one else ever would've reacted that way. No other girl in the world would've gone so quickly from wanting to wreck her car and die to laughing as loudly as she laughed that night. And hers was a loud, contagious laugh that surprised you at first, caught you right off guard and made it impossible for you to even consider not joining in.

I wanted to hear it. I wanted to make her laugh again, and I didn't really care if it meant I'd have to see her cry a little too. I felt like seeing her cry would only prove to me what I thought was the absolute truth. Then I'd know she'd been waiting for me. Maybe not before, maybe not exactly the way I'd have hoped, but she'd cry and laugh and I'd know my death wasn't the end of us after all.

Before Hatton got to my house that night, I walked into the living room and caught my mom watching a news show on mute and crying. I did *not* want to see *her* cry. No one ever wants to see their mother crying. I'd seen it plenty—back when I was dying, of course, and now again that I was back. It still never got easier, though. My mom was always very in control. Not cold, just *together*, I guess. She was always the one to keep her cool in an emergency when everyone else would be coming unglued. So to see her not in control was pretty terrifying. I sat down beside her and didn't say anything, just looked over at the TV screen and saw my face.

It was the same photo they'd been using for a month—a school picture from before I got sick. I had on this blue shirt, and it really bothered me that they kept using this photo because it reminded me of how great my hair used to be. Well, maybe not great but the way I liked it. It was sort of shaggy, I guess. Not curly but wavy enough to flip up in the front, right above my eyes, and jut out a little over each ear. And that smile I had. I looked so dumb. With no teeth showing, just this smirk like I didn't have a care in the world, like I didn't know it was all about to change.

"They just won't let up, will they?" I said to Mom.

"I thought I'd get used to it by now," she said, never averting her eyes from the screen.

"Yeah. Well, they'll eventually run out of things to talk about, I guess. What's going on today?"

"There's this group of people in Florida saying you and Lawrence could be the second coming."

"The second coming? Of Jesus? Like we're *both* Jesus? That doesn't even make sense."

"They've been holding up pictures of you two and having prayer meetings, and they claim all these people have been healed since you came back."

"I haven't healed *one* person, Mom. Promise." I held my hands up in surrender, and this made her laugh.

She paused for a minute and turned to look at me. She reached over, smiled a little, and tugged at a clump of hair from the side of my head.

"It's growing out pretty fast, yeah?" she asked.

"I guess so. I'm never cutting it. Ever."

"Hippie," she said.

"Yep. That's me."

"Travis? Can I ask you something?"

"Sure, Mom."

"Are you afraid?"

"Of what?"

"Are you afraid it's all a dream? Sometimes I wake up in the middle of the night and I have to go make sure you're still in your room."

"Creepy," I said. I was about to cry, so humor was my only defense.

"And when you were gone . . ." She paused. She was about to lose it. I thought about bailing, but Jeremy Pratt's heart wouldn't let me. "No. It's too embarrassing."

"Please," I said. "Tell me."

"When you were gone, we used to keep your door closed

and any time I walked by it, I'd knock and I'd wait for you to open it. It sounds so stupid now. I know it does. But once I started doing it, I couldn't stop. I'd just give it a little knock, wait a few seconds, and then go about my day."

"That's pretty sweet, Mom."

It wasn't sweet. It was the saddest thing I'd ever heard. I wanted to go up and shut myself in my room so she could knock on the door and see me open it a million times. It was so easy to forget how many days they'd all spent without me. I can't imagine going that long without seeing her or Dad. I can't imagine not hearing their voices. I wonder if they ever forgot what my face looked like, if maybe they had to get photos out any time they felt like they were starting to forget me.

"Yeah, well. You're back, and I'm not about to waste your whole life whining about almost losing you."

"Let me lay hands on you, child," I said in a deep voice. "I'll heal the pain away."

She took a throw pillow from the couch and hit my arms with it as I frantically waved them toward her.

"Would you please quit watching the news now?" I asked, standing up.

"Yes. Good idea. Want to watch reality shows with me?"

"Over my dead bodies, Mom."

Hatton showed up a few minutes later, and we went up to my room. Dad was working late again, something he'd been doing pretty regularly since I'd gotten back. He was more important now, in charge of a lot of people at the company. All I knew is he always had some long story to tell me about someone I didn't know screwing something up at work.

"So what's the plan?" Hatton asked, meddling around with stuff on my dresser.

"We've got to go find her."

"This sounds kind of dangerous."

"We aren't gonna kidnap her. I just want to find her and talk to her."

"Where's all your stuff? This looks like a hotel room."

"They got rid of it."

"Like, everything?"

"As far as I can tell."

"Weird."

"Very. We had to go buy me new clothes, and they keep asking me if I need other stuff, but I'm not sure where to start."

"What was your old room like?" he asked.

"It was a mess. I had movie posters all over the walls and stacks of books and magazines in that corner over there. I'm not sure I could re-create it if I tried."

"I think there's a dead hamster somewhere in my room. So yours sounds nice."

"You *think*, Hatton?"

"All I know is we had a hamster, and then we didn't have a hamster, and there's a pretty big pile of clothes and shit by my closet."

"Isn't your dad a vet?"

"Yeah. Don't tell him. He thinks we buried it in the backyard."

I shook my head in disbelief, hoping Hatton didn't have any other pets.

"So . . . Cate," he said. "How do we find her? Do you know where she lives now?"

"I know she's in Springside. And I know she lives with Turner. But that's about it."

"We need your computer."

"Over there." I pointed toward the desk by the window.

"You got a Facebook page?" he asked.

"No. Deleted it before I left. Didn't really think I'd need it again."

"What? How do you stalk people? I mean, how do you keep up with people?"

"Kyle gave me his password a few weeks ago."

"Okay. Well, we don't have to do it now, but you need to get a new page soon or I can't be your friend anymore."

"Deal."

I forgot to tell you about getting my computer back. Dad said he couldn't bring himself to get rid of it, said he thought he'd be brave enough one day to open it up and see if I'd left anything interesting behind. Thank God that didn't happen because between you, me, and every other teenage boy in the world, you do *not* want your mom or dad going through your computer. Anyway, the night I first got back home from Denver, Dad walked into my room holding the gray Dell laptop and set it down on my desk. When he left the room, I opened it up, ready to find out everything I could about all the things that had happened while I was gone.

Only I'd deleted my account just before I died. Aside from getting tired of "Get well soon, Travis" posts, I didn't want to risk leaving behind one of those creepy-dead-guy pages that people turn into virtual little memorials that never end. So then there I was with no account and no access to Kyle's or Cate's page. I did a Google search on their names, but nothing came up but a bunch of useless information about other Kyle Haglers and Cate Conroys from the past and present. It was torture.

"This your computer from before?" Hatton asked.

"Yeah."

"It's a dinosaur," he said.

"When I first turned it on, it took three days for the Windows Updates to install. I think it almost exploded."

"Okay, so first we get you a new computer and then a Facebook page. Priorities, you know," he said, typing in Kyle's password.

"What would I do without you—"

"Found her," he interrupted. "She's at Carrie's OK Bar. It's downtown."

"What the hell is Carrie's OK Bar?"

"It's a karaoke bar. Travis, come on."

"Wait, how do you know she's there?"

"She checked in there about twenty minutes ago."

"What does that mean?"

"Oh. Right. Since you left, it's become very important that we all constantly know each other's thoughts, locations, and birthdays."

"That's really stupid. Except for in this one very specific situation. I can't go if her fiancé's there, though. That would be too weird."

"He's not."

"How do you know?"

"Because she put 'Girls' Night' with about five exclamation points after it."

"Are people just asking to be murdered?"

"Pretty much. So are we going?"

"I don't have a license or a car, Hatton. Remember?"

"I've got a license."

"You have a *license?*"

"Yeah. I've been sixteen since August. Mom's just weird about her car. She'd rather cart me around everywhere than let me borrow the damn thing."

"Wait here. I'm gonna go do some groveling."

Mom was still on the couch doing what she always did on Friday nights—watching TV and eating a cup of reduced-sugar ice cream. Everything my mom bought, in my old and new lives, was somehow fat-free or sugar-free or some other something free or reduced enough for it not to taste completely terrible, but just right at that level under good or satisfying. And we were "off cow's milk" because it "has no nutritional value anymore." Whatever that means.

"What's up?" she said.

"Nothing. Kind of bummed, I guess."

"Did Hatton leave?"

"Nah. He's upstairs on the computer."

"Then what's the matter?"

"It's just that we have some friends who are hanging out downtown, and we don't have a way to get there."

"He didn't drive over?"

"Nah. His mom's weird about her car. I don't know why—he's a stellar driver."

"Stellar?"

"Stellar. I've seen it. It's like he's been driving for decades."

"So you want the car, then?" She set her bowl down and straightened up a little, muting the TV.

"Nah, it's fine. I know that would make you uncomfortable."

"Do you want me to drive you downtown?"

"I can't be the kid whose mom drops him off," I said.

"Fine. Then just ask me for the car, Travis."

"Can we borrow the car?"

"No. Are you crazy?"

"Well, that wasn't nice."

"I'm not sure I'm ready for this."

"Mom, please. I've been sitting in this house for weeks. I know you're scared. I know you don't want anything to happen to me, but you have to see this from my perspective a little bit."

"And what's your perspective?" She crossed her arms.

"That I am *sixteen* years old, and I want things to be the same way they were when I was sixteen the first time. I went out with my friends. You let me go out with Kyle and Cate all the time."

"I was scared then, too, you know?"

"Yeah, well, what's the good in being back if I'm just going to be stuck in one place all over again?"

"That's not fair, Travis."

"No, Mom, it's not fair that every single time I wake up, I have to remind myself that you're all different and that nothing will ever be the way it's supposed to be again. You're scared? I'm *so* scared. I'm scared that if something, at some point, doesn't feel a little normal to me again, then I'm going to lose my damn mind."

"Travis, I—"

"One night, Mom. One night to feel normal, like I wasn't sick and I didn't go away and I'm just a kid riding around and hanging out with his friends. Please."

"I want to see Hatton drive," she said, standing up.

"What?"

"Go get him. I want to see him drive. Then maybe I'll let you take the car."

Five minutes later we were in her car, in the driveway, with a visibly nervous Hatton behind the wheel. As Mom buckled her seatbelt in the passenger seat, Hatton looked back at me with his eyes opened really wide, like this was the scariest and most important moment of his life. I really hoped that wasn't true. But I was scared too. I had to get downtown and we were running out of time. How long does someone stay in a karaoke bar anyway? Maybe she was already gone.

"So, umm, where to?" Hatton asked. I loved this guy.

"Hatton," Mom began. "I want you to drive us to the Walgreens on Center Street, turn around in the parking lot, and drive back here. I'm not going to tell you how to drive, I'm just going to make sure you can."

"Yes, ma'am," he said, cranking the car.

We weren't even down our road yet when she started asking him about his glasses.

"When's the last time you updated your prescription?"

"I think it was, like, three or four months ago," he said.

"And your mom can confirm this if I give her a call?"

"Yes, ma'am."

This was ridiculous, but I kept my mouth shut and I let her keep interrogating. I wasn't about to ruin our chances after getting this far. He eventually turned into the Walgreens, and Mom told him to pull into a parking spot and then back out of it. I think at that point she was just messing with us. But I didn't laugh because she never once even cracked a half of a smile for the whole ride.

When we got home and Hatton pulled all the way into the driveway, Mom turned back toward me and sighed. Her eyes were watered over and, without looking at him, she said, "Very good job, Hatton."

"Thank you," he said.

"Travis," she said. "If there is one single hiccup, if one tiny thing happens to you or Hatton tonight, I will live the rest of my life in complete and miserable regret. Do you hear me? You will ruin my life if you screw up. Hatton, do you hear me?"

"Yes, ma'am. Loud and clear."

"Be back by eleven. Text every thirty minutes, both of you, and you'll be subject to a Breathalyzer and a drug test when you get home. I have access to these things, you know that, Travis."

She exchanged numbers with Hatton and hugged me a little too long in the driveway before letting us leave. Then she stood there watching us as we backed out, and I thought that maybe she'd still be there in that same spot when we got home. She'd have that same worried expression on her face, and she'd breathe this heavy sigh of relief when she saw me. That's how it must have been when I was gone, I guess. Like she was holding her breath for five years.

"I like her," Hatton said as we made our way down my street. "She's scary in that sort of sexy-older-woman way."

"I will kill you. You pervert."

Since it was already after eight o'clock and there was plenty of Friday-night traffic, I was getting really worried that we'd missed our chance of seeing Cate. Add to that the thirty minutes it took to find parking downtown, and we ended up not walking up to Carrie's OK until about nine o'clock. I was so worried that this had all been for nothing. But Hatton kept promising me otherwise, saying that no one in their twenties would leave a bar that early on a weekend. And, you know, it was just nice to be out of the house.

"I've never been in a bar before," I said as we got out of the car and started walking down the street.

"Me neither. Do you think we look old enough to get in?"

"No. Shit," I said.

"I have a plan. Stop worrying so much. Worry about what you're gonna say to Cate instead."

There was a girl at the door with tattoos covering her arms all the way up to her shoulders. She had a lip ring and purple highlights, and I could tell without even asking him that Hatton had just fallen madly in love with her.

"You got IDs?" she asked as we approached.

"Boom," Hatton said, handing her his driver's license and my learner's permit.

"Yeah, okay," she said, taking a quick look at each of them. "Have a nice night."

"No, look. We really need to go inside. Please?" Hatton clasped his hands together. "This is a matter of life and death."

"Are you being chased?" She was trying not to laugh.

"Time, my dear. Time is chasing us. Well, it's chasing my friend here. He's running out of time. The woman he loves is in your fine establishment, and if he can't see her tonight, then it may all be over. Forever."

"Did you really think this would get you in?"

"No. But there's something else."

"Sorry. Twenty-one and up."

"Look a little closer." He pointed to the birth date on my ID.

"Bullshit," she said. "No way this is real."

Then Hatton leaned in and started whispering into her ear, and she looked over his shoulder and right at me. I knew what he'd done.

"Hey, come here, kid," she said.

I stepped closer to her, and she lowered the collar of my shirt a bit. She stared down at the scar and nodded her head with this sinister, fascinated grin on her face.

"Wicked," she said finally. "Go in and don't you dare make a scene."

"Oh my God, I love you. Do you wanna make out? I know you won't believe this, but I'm very available." Hatton leaned in and kissed her on the cheek before throwing himself back far enough not to be punched.

"Thanks," I said.

"Good luck," she said, winking. "Don't lose your head in there."

I wasn't afraid of losing my head. I was afraid my entire body would shut down before getting to see Cate. I was shaking all over, like I was lying on one of those creepy coin-operated vibrating beds you see in old motels.

Seriously, I had to stop for a second when we walked inside and lean against the wall. Hatton walked ahead of me, and it was so crowded and smoky that I lost him in seconds. I stumbled my way through the noisy crowd and eventually saw him standing by a little stage in the back. He was waving me over with this big smile on his face. I wished I could be more like Hatton sometimes. He always seemed completely unfazed by everything around him. Me? I felt like I'd just walked into hell—only it had worse music and a lot more cigarette smoke than I'd ever imagined.

I didn't see her anywhere either. She'd probably gone home. This didn't seem like her kind of thing anyway. I could just see us making fun of a dumb place like that, of all the people drunkenly singing songs with a beer in one hand. I was still wondering about "Girls' Night," too. My Cate would never say something like that. Is that what growing older had done to her? Had it made her completely cheesy and ordinary like the rest of these people? If I saw her smoking, I'd probably fall to the ground and start weeping. My girlfriend was better than a place like Carrie's OK Bar. None of this felt right.

"You see her anywhere?" Hatton asked when I got over to him.

"No," I said loudly. "This place is so gross."

"It's awesome!" Hatton yelled. "I feel like shotgunning a Budweiser and punching someone."

"Maybe she left already, man. God, this sucks."

"Travis," he said into my ear. "If it were up to me, we wouldn't have even come here tonight. You want your girlfriend back, right? You want her to see you? Well, make her see you." He pointed up to the stage.

"What do you want me to do, Hatton? Just go up there and start singing her a love song?"

CHAPTER SEVENTEEN

SINGING HER A LOVE SONG

"Yes!" Hatton yelled into my ear.

"What?"

"You have to go up there! There's a microphone and everything. Just go for it! Tell her how you feel!"

"I can't do that! I'll just find her and maybe we can talk outside!"

"No! Dude, this is zero hour!"

"I don't even see her! Let's just go!"

"Weak! You're weak! Get your ass on that stage and go for it! You are Travis Coates! You kick death in the ass like it happens every Tuesday!"

He was right. I could do this. I could get up there and tell her exactly what I'd wanted to tell her every second since I'd opened my eyes in that hospital in Denver. What was there to lose? It would either work or not work. It would change everything for the better or change nothing at all. That's not quite a win/win, but it was at least a win/give in to reality and move on with my stupid life. Before I had much more time to think about it, Hatton grabbed my arm and led me to the stairs on the side of the stage. I still hadn't spotted her in the crowd. Between the smoke and the noise it was pretty impossible. So I gave Hatton a look that told him I was going for it, and I climbed the stairs.

I stood in front of the microphone and looked out over the crowd. No Cate. I scanned the entire room, hoping I'd see her and that she'd either run out of there as fast as she could and spare me the humiliation I was about to endure, or head over toward me. There were tall, round tables with barstools scattered throughout the place. And people stood around them, mostly drinking and shouting at one another over music being played through the speakers hanging to the left and right of the stage. No one seemed to be anxiously waiting a turn to sing karaoke. But as Hatton had said, the night was relatively young. Maybe people needed a few more drinks in them before they started making asses of themselves in front of a hundred or more strangers. Not me, though.

I looked over to Hatton, and he was mouthing "Do it" and pointing toward the microphone. I was sweating profusely, and I suddenly became super paranoid that everyone could see my scar, that they were all about to stop what they were doing and focus right in on it. But I'd worn a button-down, collared shirt that I knew was doing its job of mostly covering the thing. It didn't matter—I felt like an exposed nerve up in front of them like that. I was frozen in one spot when Hatton jumped up onto the stage beside me and whispered into my ear.

"Do you trust me?"

"Not really," I whispered back.

"Please. This will work. I know it."

Then he ran back across the stage, hopped down onto the floor, and started flipping through a black binder sitting next to the lyrics monitor. His face lit up and he looked up at me, raising his eyebrows and nodding his head. He made it seem like he was almost asking me if I were ready, but he wasn't. He'd already typed in the code for the song, and a blue spotlight burst onto the stage and found me where I stood.

"Zero hour!" he shouted.

"I hate you!" I shouted back.

Then the music started—loud piano keys with an electric guitar riffing right behind it and an abrupt thump of drums. And then I started singing because that's what you do when you've got nothing to lose. You start singing with your eyes closed because you know the song and you know why your friend just forced you into singing it.

I managed to get the first few lines out with a sort of half-sing-half-whisper, my mouth touching the cold metal of the microphone.

I wanted to be with you alone. And talk about the weather.

Then I sort of mumbled for a while, a nervous, indistinguishable jumble of words to the general beat of the song. But when I looked up, there were people singing along. And a few were raising their drinks into the air and moving their heads back and forth. And then I saw her. She was sitting at one of the tables and looking right at me with her mouth slightly open, this look in her eyes that was both amazed and terrified.

So I grabbed the microphone, yanked it off the stand, and yelled the chorus out while looking right at her.

> *Something happens and I'm head over heels*
> *I never find out till I'm head over heels*
> *Something happens and I'm head over heels*
> *Ah, don't take my heart*
> *Don't break my heart*
> *Don't . . . don't . . . don't throw it away!*

I didn't finish the song because I saw her turn around and head for the door. I dropped the mic (not in the cool way, believe me) and jumped down from the stage, running through the crowd after her. When I got outside, I looked all around in both directions and didn't see her. I backed up to the brick wall behind me and slid down it, covering my face with my hands. Seeing her had done something I hadn't quite expected. It had nearly killed me all over again.

"Hey." Someone poked my arm.

"What?" I looked up. It was the tattooed girl from the door.

"She went into that diner," she said, pointing to the dive joint across the street.

"She did?" I stood up.

"Yeah. If she doesn't come around, I'm all yours, Tears for Fears." She smiled.

I ran across the street, didn't even watch for traffic, and looked into the window. There she was, sitting in a booth in the back corner. She looked right at me. She'd been crying. Of course she'd been crying—her dead boyfriend was stalking her. I gestured, pointing to my chest and then to her, asking if I could come in. She nodded her head, and I could actually see her breathing as I walked across the room toward her.

CHAPTER EIGHTEEN

TOWARD HER

"Hi."

"You look exactly the same," she said quietly.

"So do you." I sat down across from her.

"I'm sorry."

She buried her head in her arms on the table, almost the same position a school kid uses to take a nap in class. I wanted to just get up and squeeze in beside her, put my arm around her and tell her it was okay, that I wasn't mad. But I couldn't. I wasn't me anymore. Well, I wasn't to her yet, anyway. To her, I was only part me, and as much as that hurt, as unnatural as it felt not to touch her, I knew I couldn't go wrapping some other guy's arms around her and thinking that would make things better. I was Travis, sure, but I was Jeremy Pratt, too. It was an easy thing for me to forget, but I wasn't so sure it would be that easy for her.

"The song was a bit much. My friend made me do it."

I reached across the table, almost took her hand, then stopped myself.

"It was perfect," she said, her voice muffled by her arms.

She raised her head up, and she had half of her top lip between her teeth. She did this, my Cate. When she was sad, she would chew on her lips so much they'd be chapped for days. She was still beautiful like before, maybe even more so. Her hair was shorter than I'd ever seen it, cut just above her shoulders, and she was definitely wearing less makeup than she used to, maybe none at all. But she'd never needed it anyway. Her cheeks were flushed a bit, maybe from the crying or from her quick exit from the bar, maybe still from embarrassment or the cold. She had on a dark green sweater and light gray jeans. There was a necklace, a tiny gold sailboat, dancing up and down on her chest, never quite resting there because of the way she sat, slumped over a little with her shoulders jutted forward.

"Hi," I said again.

"When they told me you were coming back, I couldn't stop crying."

"We don't have to talk about it," I said. "Really. It's okay."

"No. I want to. They told me, your mom and dad, and both of them sounded so . . . shocked. I just couldn't believe it. I mean, I remember thinking that this was the absolute last thing I expected to hear when I picked up the phone. And then they had to go. They told me you were coming back, that it worked, and then they had more calls to make. Simple as that."

"It was weird. Waking up, I mean. And you not being there." I looked into her eyes, couldn't stop looking into them.

"I just . . . I wasn't sure what to do or where to start, really. I wanted someone to tell me what I was supposed to do. Was I supposed to go to Denver? What if I got there and you didn't wake up? What if it didn't work? And then I thought . . ."

She paused for a little more crying. This time I reached over and took a napkin out of the red plastic dispenser at the end of the table and handed it to her. It was a quick, almost instinctive gesture, but she looked up at me like I'd just handed her the Hope Diamond and then she started crying again.

"Cate, if you need me to go . . . if this is too much, I can go and we can—"

"No, stop. We have to. So I waited to hear news about the surgery, to make sure you were okay, and when I did, when I knew it had worked, I just sort of felt flooded by everything all over again. I couldn't stop thinking about that last time I saw you, in the hospital."

"You never turned around," I said.

"I wanted to. I wanted to so badly. I almost did. I almost ran back in, but I knew you were right. It couldn't feel like a real good-bye."

"You knew I was lying," I said.

"I knew you wanted me to think you'd come back."

"It seemed so impossible."

"Then I heard you made it home okay, and I got in my car, drove across town, and sat at the end of your street for a while thinking about what I'd say to you. I didn't have a clue. I'm not sixteen anymore and you are, and I have no idea how to deal with that."

"Me neither. I blinked and the world got older."

"It's so messed up," she said, sighing. "But amazing, too, you know?"

"I know. I can't believe I'm sitting here, let alone anywhere."

"You saw Kyle?" she asked.

"Yeah. A couple times. He's sort of not talking to me right now."

"Oh. Why?"

"'Cause I'm a jerk. Your parents tell you I went to see them?" I tried to change the subject as quickly as possible.

"Yeah. They were thrilled. Mom's been begging me to at least call you."

"I understand, Cate."

"It's not right, though. I just . . . I still wasn't sure what to say. 'Welcome back' seemed too simple."

"I just need you to say we're still the same. Everything else can be different, but I need this to be the same."

"Travis." She flashed her sad eyes.

"I know the body thing is weird. I know. But it's actually better. This one is better. Embarrassingly better, actually."

She smiled, looking down at my shoulders and chest, and my arms, too.

"You look incredible," she said. "Healthy. I've seen you on TV, but it's different like this. You're not hunched over or pale. It's nice seeing you like this."

"Seeing me not dying? It feels pretty damn good too. On a scale from one to ten, I give dying a solid screw-that."

"Can I see it?"

She reached her hand over and peeled down the collar of my shirt. Then she touched just above the scar first, then just under it. It was a soft touch. She whispered something, but I couldn't make it out.

"What?"

"Impossible," she repeated.

Then I grabbed her hand with both of mine, sort of enveloped it safely between them, and I was breathing really heavy and could hear her breathing too, like we'd both suddenly forgotten how to take in air properly.

"I love you. You know that. And I know maybe love doesn't stay there after someone dies and this many years pass, but I don't care. I needed to see you and I knew you needed to see me. So here I am."

"Travis, I'm engaged."

"I know. And if you can forgive me for leaving, then I can forgive you for that."

"I have to go," she said. "Thank you, though. Thank you for finding me like this. If I ever stop crying, I promise I'll call you."

She stood up and leaned down, kissed my cheek as she

slid her hand from my grasp, and walked out. I knew it wasn't fair to go after her, to make her talk anymore or feel any worse for not talking. I watched her cross the street, her arms folded over her chest, protecting her from the cold air, and soon enough she was back inside the bar. I called Hatton and told him where I was.

"You hungry?" he said, sitting down a few minutes later.

"Starving."

"Anything you want, dude. On me." He waved over to a waiter across the room.

"This was a disaster," I said. "But I'm glad we did it."

"I'm assuming she isn't coming home with you, then?"

"No, but at least I got to see her," I said. "And now she's seen me. In person, I mean."

"Still think you can get her back?"

"Of course I can."

"And you're sure about this? You don't want to give it a little more thought maybe?"

"I'm sure, Hatton. Never been so sure about anything in my life."

I've got to say, serious Hatton wasn't my favorite, but it was hard not to appreciate how he could go from being completely ridiculous and carefree to being this support-ive, logical friend. It's just that he didn't understand my logic. My girlfriend was engaged to another guy. That had to be stopped. He had to go, and it was only a matter of time before Cate saw it my way too. There was no doubt in my mind.

CHAPTER NINETEEN

DOUBT IN MY MIND

We made it home just under curfew, and I was surprised to see that Dad still wasn't there. Because it was so late, Mom insisted that Hatton stay the night, and after we dragged the inflatable air mattress up the stairs, he and I took turns airing it up with a flimsy manual pump.

"This is ridiculous," I said. "There has to be a better way."

"You're kind of lazy, huh?" Hatton asked, grinning.

"I'm not lazy. I'm just . . . disappointed, I guess. The future's kind of a letdown."

"Wow, thanks," he said.

"You know what I mean. It's not this," I said, gesturing toward the half-inflated mattress. "It's everything else. I thought if this weird shit ever actually worked, then things would be—"

"Easier?" he asked. "Yeah. You're lazy, man."

"Maybe so."

"But hey, you're not a terrible singer, you know?" Hatton pressed his hand against the air mattress to test it out.

"Middle school choir."

"For real?"

"Yep. I used to fake it, though. Most of the time I just moved my mouth and never really sang."

"Was it convincing, you think?"

"I think so. I never got caught."

"I once threw up auditioning for a play in middle school. Stage fright, I guess. Puked right on my script."

"Cate has stage fright," I said. "Or she used to anyway."

"You really miss her, huh?"

"It's weird. I know I should miss my body, but that's not all that important to me. But Cate . . . *that's* what I miss. Her. Us. Like the surgery didn't have anything to do with my body or my head. It feels like they cut her off, and now she's dangling there and I can't have her anymore."

"That's maybe the saddest thing I've ever heard." He stared up at the ceiling.

"Yeah, well. It's been a long night. I'm gonna try to sleep."

School was harder that next Monday. Everything, actually, was harder after I'd finally seen her up close. And she'd seen me, right? So she was supposed to be back. That was the plan. She was supposed to be just like the old Cate— calling me all day and showing up at my locker to say hello in between classes. She was supposed to be waiting for me by her car when school was out, her book bag slung over one shoulder and her foot propped up against the door.

But she wasn't there, just like I hadn't been there all those times when I was supposed to be. If a few months felt this bad, then I can't imagine what five years was like for her. Every time I passed her old locker at school and tried not to look at it, I'd close my eyes and see her doing the same with mine. You have to forget about people when you can't have them anymore. That's the only way to be okay, I think—to forget how they looked and sounded and left Post-it notes on your desk and told you they'd come back from the dead someday. She had to get over me because there was no alternative. But I couldn't do that with her. I couldn't forget that she was still here and I was still here and we weren't together.

"Stacey Lowell wants to go out with me, I think," Hatton said, sitting down at lunch.

"So go out with her."

"She's too smart for me."

"You're smart enough."

"Not that smart. She's always talking about Sigmund Freud and psychoanalysis."

"She wants to be a therapist, I think. Maybe she just wants you for your problems."

"Nah. I don't have any problems. It's my hair. Girls love my hair."

"You do have great hair. It's so . . . big."

"It grows out instead of down. I think it gives me a one-up on all the buzz cuts around here."

"Watch it."

"No, no. Yours has grown out a lot. You look almost like a real live boy again."

"You never saw me before, dude."

"Yeah, I have. Yearbook in the library. I wanted to compare. And the news, of course. That old photo of you."

"Creepy."

"Are you thinking about her right now?"

"You don't have to ask. I'm always thinking about her."

"Would it help if I told you that I'm fairly sure it's illegal?"

"What?"

"You guys being together. It's illegal. Statutory."

"I turn seventeen in March. Then it's legal."

"Oh. Never mind, then."

"It wouldn't matter, though."

"It might. Do you want to visit your girlfriend in the pen?"

"Are you done?"

"Quite."

When I got home from school, Mom was asleep on the couch, still wearing her pink scrubs. She'd worked the graveyard shift, something she only had to do once a month or so. Dad had driven me that morning on his way to work, which was awesome because when he drove me, we always pulled through McDonald's for breakfast.

Here's what you should know about my parents: they had very opposing ideas of what was good for me. My mom, for instance, would've forced me to eat a bowl of oatmeal with a half a grapefruit or a banana before driving me to school. But my dad, he figured life was too short for stuff like that. So on mornings like that one, we ate our sausage biscuits and hash browns in secret, together, and we had a silent pact that my mother would never find out.

"Gonna be late again tonight, pal," he said when I got out of the car.

"Bummer. See you tomorrow, then."

I hadn't really thought about it too much at first, but these late work nights of his were starting to feel a bit strange. I'll admit that it was hard not to immediately jump to the worst conclusion—to see all the thousands of movie and TV show scenarios where the father starts working late and neglecting the mother, and the marriage ends after a big affair with a secretary or coworker is revealed. But I knew that couldn't be the case here. Not my dad. Not Ray Coates. His only secrets involved fast food.

After school I fell asleep doing homework, and when the phone rang, I nearly tumbled off the bed trying to reach it on the nightstand. I cleared my throat and tried to wipe the sleep out of my eyes before answering. I didn't recognize the number.

"Hello."

"Travis?"

"Speaking."

"It's Cate."

"Cate." It took a second to register. "Cate! Oh, hey."

"What you did Friday night wasn't fair."

"I know. I'm sorry. I just—"

"Let me talk. It wasn't fair. It was immature and it scared me. I don't like being scared. You know that."

"Yes. I know that."

"And I guess you thought that if you just threw yourself back into my life like that, then . . . well . . . then I wouldn't be able to keep ignoring you."

"In so many words, yeah."

"Travis, I'm an adult now. And I make decisions like one. That's probably hard for you to understand. Or maybe it isn't, but it's still hard for me to understand sometimes. We can't have what we had before. I could tell you the millions of reasons why that's true, but instead I want you to just trust me."

"I trust you, Cate."

"Trust me when I say that it's better this way. But it doesn't mean I don't want to see you. It doesn't mean we can't be a part of each other's lives again."

"Just not a big part."

"Just . . . different, okay? Friends. We were friends once. You remember that. We were best friends. All these years later and I still haven't found another friend like you, Travis. That has to mean something, right?"

"When can I see you, then?"

"I can't say when. I wish I could. Things are so crazy right now. Turner found out about that night at the karaoke place, and he's been really worried and acting weird about things. He really cares about me, Travis."

"And you love him? Like you loved me?"

"I do. I wouldn't be marrying him if I didn't."

"Oh. Right."

They say the heart is just a muscle. They say it plays absolutely no role in our emotions and that its use as a symbol for love is based on archaic theories of it being the seat of the soul or something ridiculous like that. But as I quietly listened to every word she was saying to me, as each syllable shot a sharp arrow through the phone and into my ear, I swear I felt like my entire chest would collapse in on itself. I knew this feeling. They say a heart can't really break because there's nothing to be broken. But see, I once had to leave everyone I loved, and it felt this same way. Maybe Jeremy Pratt's did too. Before he died, I mean. Maybe his heart was torn to shreds and maybe that's why it hurt so bad now, like it hadn't had enough time to heal before receiving its next blow.

"I know this is harder than I can ever imagine, Travis. But I do love you. That can mean a lot of different things. I care about you and I'm glad you're back. It's nothing short of a miracle, and I only hope you see it that way too."

"I'm trying, Cate."

"Can I ask you something?" she said.

"Of course."

"When they did it . . . after you'd said good-bye to us and they were putting you under, were you scared?"

"Not really. I was tired. I just needed it to be over."

"I was so angry," she said.

"You were?"

"It's so selfish, but I just wanted you to stay as long as you could. They said seeing you go peacefully or whatever would make it better. Everyone said it would be so much easier. But it wasn't, Travis. It was the worst thing that ever happened to me."

"I'm so sorry."

"You came back, Travis Coates."

"God, can you believe it?"

"I guess maybe some part of me wanted to think it might happen someday. Like maybe when I was an old lady or something. Like we joked about. But this is just—"

"Bizarre?"

"Different, yeah?" she said. "Just different and incredible and kind of sad, too, I think."

There it was. That's all I needed her to say. I knew why it was sad and so did she. I was gone just long enough for her to move on, and now she was starting to wish she hadn't. Turner? Turner who? Maybe she loved him. I didn't expect her to go and destroy the guy. That wasn't Cate. But I *was* back. And she knew, just like I did, that this was going to change everything. There was no hiding from it.

CHAPTER TWENTY

HIDING FROM IT

One night, just a couple of days before a chemo treatment that was sure to kick my ass, Cate showed up at the front door holding two blankets and a big red thermos, the kind where the lid doubles as a miniature little mug. She was determined and her face showed it. Anyone who knew her less than I did, which was everyone, would have taken it for anger, both of her sharp eyebrows pointing inward toward her nose a bit, her lips pursed, her gaze dead-on and purposeful. This just meant she had a plan, though. And I knew not to stray from her plans.

"What gives?" I asked, still standing in the doorway. I liked pretending to go against her wishes, like we were opposing forces and not completely entangled.

"Leonids."

"Say what?"

"It's a meteor shower. Peaks tonight. Does your dad have a ladder?"

"Oh. Yeah, I think so."

"Get out of the way, stupid. We've got to set up shop."

She never changed her expression, even when she leaned over to kiss me on her way inside. I followed after her, taking the blankets and thermos out of her hand and watching as she walked nonchalantly through the kitchen and over to the door that led into the garage.

"Ladder?" She pointed before opening it.

"Yeah. Let me get it."

"No, no. Stop. I got it."

"You know, I can lift a ladder, Cate," I said, frustrated.

"And I can kick your ass, Travis," she said, smiling.

No one let me do anything anymore, which was nice but also made me feel even worse about being sick, like I was just there to be a constant inconvenience to everyone. I knew that wasn't the case, but still. Dying's hard enough without everyone reminding you all the time.

I couldn't believe Cate let me climb the ladder, actually. But I got up just fine, and she was situating both blankets on the flat, slanted side of the roof, the side that perfectly faced the sky.

"Our own private planetarium," she said.

We'd sat up there once before, with Kyle, on Halloween night so we could scare the trick-or-treaters at the front door. That night ended after Kyle fell from the roof when a kid threw a handful of mini Butterfingers at his face. He lived.

"What's in the thermos?"

"Mexican hot chocolate." She handed it to me with the lid off, and I smelled it, the spices tickling my nose, warming me up instantly. I took a sip straight from the thermos.

"Here, at least use the cup," she said, handing it to me.

"It's too good." I took another sip, swallowed loudly. "Must drink it all."

"Save some for me, you maniac."

"Did you see that?" I handed her the thermos and sat up.

I'd seen one, a meteor. It was yellow—maybe gold, even—and it streaked right across the sky. Younger kids would have called it a shooting star. But we'd reached that age where the science behind it mattered, where the wonders of the universe needed to be further explained to mesmerize us. But still, it was beautiful and, even though this sounds weird, it made me feel really tiny and insignificant. And I liked that. Maybe I wasn't supposed to, but I did.

"I missed it. Stop distracting me."

She took a sip of the hot chocolate and leaned back onto the blankets. I watched her for a minute, just watched her look up at the sky, a blue-purplish glow shining down on her face. Her foggy November breaths hung a little in the air in front of her. She eventually caught me and started smiling.

"You're missing quite a show, Travis."

"No, I'm not," I said.

She rolled her eyes, but she was smiling. "You're a cheesy bastard sometimes, you know that?"

"You love it." I slid closer to her, set my chin right on the curve of her shoulder.

"I do," she said, looking back up at the sky. "You know, about four billion meteoroids fall to Earth every day. Most of them are just too small to notice."

"Maybe someone sees them," I said. "Kind of sad to think they disappear just like that."

"Oh boy, you're on a roll, cheeseball." She shook her head with a little half smile on her lips. But she didn't look at me, and I knew we were thinking the exact same thing.

Two weeks went by, and I hadn't heard a thing out of Cate. *Two weeks*. And she wouldn't answer any of my calls or texts. Just like that, I thought, Travis and Cate were doomed to be a thing of the past. A perfect little blip on the airwaves of time. I could tell you I got angry and threw things across my room and kicked at the walls and punched a hole in the back of my bedroom door. But I didn't. One night, after I'd tried to call her, I walked quietly down the hall to the bathroom. I closed and locked the door, turned on the bathtub faucet, and then held on to the cold porcelain as I lowered myself onto the floor and wedged my legs between the toilet and the tub.

And I cried. It was the kind where it's hard to catch your breath, where every muscle in your body aches and you aren't sure it will ever end. And my parents never heard a thing.

The next day at school Hatton was still trying his best to make light of it all. And I couldn't blame him for it, really. I would've tried cheering me up too, even if I thought it was impossible.

"Travis, man, you're a good-lookin' guy. You can pretty much pick any girl in this school, and she'd probably be more than happy to help make you feel better."

"Thanks, Hatton."

"No, I mean, for real. I think you're really missing out on a rare opportunity here, man. I see the way they look at you. Hell, if I got looks like that, I could tell my parents to cancel our Internet."

"I think they're just interested in the freak head thing, Hatton."

"Oh, they're interested in the *head*, all right."

"Gross."

"You bet it is," he said, grinning.

It was little conversations like this that reminded me so much of how it had been with Kyle. It was strange how sometimes I'd be talking to Hatton and, if I didn't look right at him or pay that much attention to his voice, it was almost like Kyle Hagler had walked into the school, sat down, and picked right back up where we'd left off. I'd been so stupid about Kyle, and now he wasn't there. I guess I had to stop thinking there'd be a day when everything I wanted, everything I had, would be set back perfectly into place. Truth is, I *was* the past and I had to find some way to exist in the future. It wasn't going to be easy, that much I knew, but I had to try. That's what people do in these situations, right? They try even when they know it's impossible.

CHAPTER TWENTY-ONE

THE   IMPOSSIBLE

My first priority was getting Kyle to talk to me again and, of course, apologizing for being such an ass. It wasn't any of my business if he was gay or straight or both or neither. That didn't matter. What mattered was that we were friends. Since I couldn't get Cate back as easily as I'd thought, and maybe never, I at least had to salvage what I had with Kyle. So I called him up one afternoon, and I honestly still can't believe he answered.

"Hello."

"Kyle. Don't hang up. Please don't hang up."

"I'm not hanging up. Chill out."

"Oh. Good. Umm . . . how's it going?"

"Pretty good, I guess. Class is kicking my ass right now. Never go to college. It isn't worth it."

"Noted. Look, I'm really sorry about everything."

"Travis, you know . . . if we could just not talk about it, that would work for me."

"Okay, but just know that I'm sorry."

"Deal. I mean, sure. That's fine. Listen, I talked to Cate yesterday."

"Shit. Cate. What'd she say?"

"Well, she told me about the karaoke place. *That* was bold."

"I was . . . desperate, I guess."

"She liked it. It's sort of hilarious, too. But she's just really worried about you, I think. She feels bad about how everything's . . . turned out."

"We've only talked once since then. It's weird, Kyle. It's so hard to explain how this feels to me. You guys haven't seen me in so long, and I've just seen you a few weeks ago."

"That's got to be really hard."

"I feel like I was reborn into a never-ending episode of *The Twilight Zone*."

"Pig faces. The horror."

"You wished all the other kids away into the cornfield, Anthony."

And just like that, we were making TV references like we used to. Maybe he was so quick to forgive me because of what Cate had said to him, that she was worried about me. Or maybe he needed me too, couldn't stand the idea that I was back and that we weren't at least trying to make it work. Either way, talking to Kyle, joking around with him like this, made me feel like everything that had happened was all just a daydream. I decided right then and there that I'd try to have as many of these moments as possible until the day I really did die.

Before we got off the phone, Kyle invited me to a concert at his college that next weekend. An '80s cover band
called Judd Nelson's Fist was playing, and he promised I'd
know at least three or four songs, that we'd ditch the thing
if it turned out to be lame, and that college girls would
think I was the most adorable thing that ever happened. I
was ready to say yes at "'80s cover band," but the last bit
of his argument was awfully intriguing too. I was single,
after all, right? Fine, fine. I had no intention of even flirting with a college girl. And I definitely wasn't going to go
flashing my scar around like some cryogenic gigolo.

"I'm in. What should I wear?"

"Clothes, preferably." Kyle started laughing.

"No, I mean, what do people wear to, like, college concerts?"

"Oh, you're being serious?"

"I am."

"Jeans and a shirt. It'll probably be cold, so maybe a
jacket. I feel like you should know these things, Travis."

"I just don't want to look stupid or out of place, you
know?"

"Travis, it's a concert, not prom. You've got to lighten
up."

"Fine. You can pick me up, then? Friday?"

"Yeah. Let's say six o'clock. Oh, and don't forget your
glow sticks."

"What?"

"Kidding."

• • •

Friday at six, Kyle pulled into my driveway in his truck and waited as I hopped inside. He had the radio on and was listening to some slow-paced indie crooner, and I immediately noticed how the truck smelled exactly like his old bedroom, like a combination of patchouli and Old Spice.

"You might get to meet Valerie tonight, cool?" he asked.

"Sure. She gonna be at the concert?"

"We may meet her afterward, if that's okay. Do you have, like, a curfew or anything?"

"Mom said eleven, but I can get around it."

"Awesome."

I'd expected us to be going to some auditorium or food hall on Kyle's campus, but instead we parked down the block from this old three-story house that had people hanging around on the porch and out in the yard. Several of them were holding beer bottles.

"My permit says I'm technically twenty-one. Do I need to get it out?"

"First off, weird. And second, they aren't checking. Don't worry about it."

"But people are drinking." I nodded over toward a group yelling and hanging all over one another at the end of the porch.

"Oh no. They've just been pregaming. They can't serve alcohol at school-sponsored events like this."

"Pregaming?" I asked, embarrassed.

"Yeah, like, getting a little buzzed before something. You missed that part of high school, huh? Some people need it, I guess."

I was surprised how many people were inside. The whole bottom level of the house had been hollowed out to make a huge room with a small stage and a dance floor. People were standing all around, laughing, flirting, and taking photos with their cell phones. It was louder than I'd expected and with way more polo shirts. I don't really understand polo shirts.

I guess we made it just in time because as we sifted through the crowd and found a spot to stand in, a guy (wearing a polo shirt) got up onstage and everybody started cheering.

"Ladies and gentlemen of KC State, how are you feeling tonight?!"

The crowd started yelling all around me, and I felt sort of intimidated by it. The only real thing I could compare it to was the karaoke bar that night, except I wouldn't be the one onstage. Thank God. What Kyle had said before, about the part of high school I missed, was right. I never made it to the wild parties and concerts and pregaming. I got sick before any of that could happen.

"Tonight we are pleased to bring you not one but *two* amazing acts!"

"Oh no," Kyle said into my ear. "I knew they'd have some lame opening act. We should've come later."

"Before we present to you the amazing Judd Nelson's Fist, we have, as a special guest, KC State's very own Floorboard Johnson!"

The crowd cheered some more, only not as loud, and a few people started laughing. Then this guy—he couldn't have been any older than Kyle—walked out onto the stage wearing a fedora and holding an acoustic guitar. He grabbed a stool from the back corner, set it up right in front of the microphone stand, and started playing.

"Every song this guy sings is about flowers or stars. Bet." Kyle extended his hand to shake mine.

Five songs and twenty minutes later, I handed Kyle a crinkled-up dollar bill, and he laughed much louder than I'd expected. A girl standing behind us started laughing with him before leaning over and asking my name.

"Travis," I said. But she didn't hear me.

"What?"

"Travis!"

"Nice. I'm Lindy."

"Hey."

"You're that kid! The one with the . . ." She pointed to her neck.

"No. Different Travis. But I get that a lot."

"But I recognize you!" She was getting louder.

I leaned forward and whispered into her ear, "Please?"

She nodded her head and winked at me, her silent agreement to keep my secret to herself. I was happy I'd zipped my jacket all the way up and even happier that

Floorboard Johnson was done. I think everyone was happy, judging from the applause. He put his stool back and sauntered offstage. I imagined he lived out back in a teepee with a dream catcher hanging over the entrance and slept on a pile of Hacky Sacks.

"And now . . . the band you've all been waiting for. . . . Give it up for JUDD NELSON'S FIST!!!!"

As soon as the five-person band ran out onto the stage, they started playing "Video Killed the Radio Star" by The Buggles, and everyone was dancing and singing along. It was amazing, not only how good they sounded but how much fun everyone was having. It was the kind of fun that creeps into your skin and spreads all over your body, and even if you want to be cynical about something, you just can't manage it. Hell, I was so relieved that people still loved '80s music that nothing could bring me down.

After songs by Madonna, Cyndi Lauper, Dexy's Midnight Runners, Men at Work, Queen, and Talking Heads, Kyle asked if I was ready to go.

"Is it almost over?"

"Nah, man, but they'll keep going until they've covered the entire decade. Trust me. We've seen the best."

So we made our way back through the crowd, which was much more difficult with people dancing and singing and jumping up and down. When we got to the front door, I saw that Lindy girl pointing at me and saying something to a friend of hers. I guess the enthusiasm in the room had gotten to me a little, because without even thinking,

I waved at her and pulled down the collar of my jacket really quickly before we walked out. Why not, right?

Out on the porch Kyle stopped for a second to say hello to a friend, and I checked out the crowd. The music was almost as loud as it had been inside, so I was bobbing my head a little with my hands in my pockets. Then I saw her. Cate. She was sitting right on the rail of the porch at the opposite end from us. I'm not sure why I was so surprised, really. I knew she went to KC State too—part-time, at least. I guess it would work out that the *one* night I hadn't spent hours obsessing over her would be the same night we'd run into each other.

She spotted me as I approached, and hopped down from the rail.

"Travis, what are you doing here?"

"I'm with Kyle." I pointed over toward him. "You look great."

"You think they'll sing 'Head Over Heels'?" She laughed.

"They've got nothing on me."

"You . . . you okay?" She kept looking over my shoulder like maybe she was waiting for someone. Hopefully not Turner.

"I'm okay. Getting out of the house has helped."

"So you guys are good now?"

"Yeah."

"Travis?"

"Yeah?"

"It's really nice to see you."

She reached out her hand and sort of tapped the side of my arm before letting hers swing back to its place. She was sincere. It *was* nice to see me. And I'd have sat through ten more hours of Floorboard Johnson's songs to see her.

"Cate! Oh my God, wow!" Kyle walked up and hugged her.

"She's following me," I joked.

"No, no," Cate said. "He's following me."

Kyle laughed and for a second, just a second while I watched him and heard her chuckle a bit, I thought maybe I'd slipped into a time machine. I could've stood there listening to them talk for five more years, never getting tired of how familiar and comfortable it sounded.

"You here alone?" Kyle asked her.

"Nah, my friend Sara's inside. I think she ditched me, actually. She does that sometimes."

"Come with us," I blurted out. I couldn't stop myself.

"Where you going?" She looked at me in a way I hadn't quite expected.

"Umm . . . maybe get something to eat?" Kyle suggested.

"Uh, yeah . . . you know what? Yes. For sure. Let me go find Sara and let her know."

She walked into the house, and Kyle looked at me with his eyebrows way up high on his forehead.

"What?"

"Nothing. Just . . . crazy night."

"Crazy night, yes."

"Don't overthink this."

"No. No overthinking. Just a chance encounter with my soul mate. No overthinking here."

"Travis. I'm serious."

"Kyle, I'm kidding. I don't care what's going on—I just need to be around you guys. In some capacity."

She came back out a few seconds later and we all walked down the street to Kyle's truck. I crawled into the backseat, and as soon as Cate shut the door, she turned around and gave me this look, this look I don't think I'll ever forget. She was so happy to be there with us.

"Burgers?" Kyle asked, cranking the truck.

"God yes, burgers. Burgers all around! Burgers for days." Cate held her hands up dramatically as she answered.

"It's nice to see you haven't lost your ladylike appetite," I said, smiling.

"Never!" she said, returning my smile.

Steak 'n Shake wasn't too different from the way it had always been. I wasn't sure if either of them could remember it, but my last time there had been with them, and I'd puked most of my food out in the bathroom after we'd eaten. Needless to say, I was pretty excited to try it without the chemo.

We ordered at the counter and found a booth near the back. We each got a burger, fries, and a chocolate shake. The burgers there were good, but the shakes were a religious experience. I wouldn't tell them, but I was half expecting to wake up from a dream with every second we spent together.

"So, boys, what's been going on?" Cate asked.

"Ah, you know," Kyle said. "School and . . . lemme think, oh yeah . . . school."

"Yeah, me too. I mean, work *and* school. It's a bitch."

"So you're at the law firm still?" I asked.

"Yeah. Umm, I work there three days a week, just mostly clerical stuff while I'm getting my degree."

"Awesome," Kyle said.

"No art school?" I asked.

"Nah, that sort of faded away years ago."

"That sucks," I said. "You were so good."

"That's sweet. But no, I wasn't. Everything looked too, I dunno, cartoonish."

"Probably hard to find work with an art degree nowadays too, huh?" Kyle said.

"Yeah. And I have no interest in teaching it, so I had to let that go."

"Do you still paint at all?" I couldn't let it go as easily as she could, obviously.

"Not really. Hey, you think we could talk about something more interesting? Like how you died and we're all sitting in a burger joint five years later?"

We laughed. Especially Kyle. His laugh, I noticed, was something that hadn't changed at all. It was still this aggressive and quick inhalation of breaths with a few snorts mixed in. I loved it. I would've liked to record it and play it any time the world started freaking me out. I almost asked him if I could.

Our food arrived soon enough, and for a minute or two we were all too busy eating to say anything. We just sort of looked at one another, nodding and smiling with our mouths full. I'd say, it was on par with all of our late-night dinners at Steak 'n Shake—only better because it had been too long. And because it was unexpected. All the best moments are, I guess.

"I need to tell you guys something." Kyle got this serious look on his face. I was sure this was it, this was what I'd been waiting for since confronting him in my driveway that day. He was going to tell us the truth.

"Go on," I said.

"I'm going to ask Valerie to move in with me. It just feels right."

"Why would you do that?" I nearly yelled it.

"Travis, geez," Cate said.

"You know, I love her. And she loves me, and I'm tired of visiting her creepy dorm room all the time. I'm really excited about this, Travis."

"Yeah," I said. "I mean, yeah. That's cool. I need to meet her. I thought we were gonna see her tonight." I was trying desperately to save face. I'm not sure it was working.

"We were, but she said she didn't want to intrude on our impromptu reunion."

"She is *so* sweet, Kyle," Cate said. "I think it's a great idea."

"I was thinking about asking my parents to move in with me, but it turns out they're already there," I said. "Because I'm trapped in teenageland."

"Not forever," Cate said.

"Yeah, man. You don't get to cheat your way around that one. We all had to be stuck there."

"Come back," I said. "It was so much easier with you two."

I'd meant the whole thing as a joke, but of course it hadn't gone as I intended, and we all got quiet for a while. As much as I didn't like to be reminded about not having my own body, it seemed like other people didn't like being reminded of all the things that were also out of their control.

"Sorry, guys. I was just kidding around."

"Travis Coates," Cate said. "You weren't funny in your first life, so why think you can be funny in your second?"

When we finished eating and got up to leave, Cate told us to wait up while she went to the restroom. We stood around outside the door, and I could tell Kyle was pissed at me all over again. I was consistently being an ass to him. I'm not sure why he would even keep trying at that point.

"Weird night, huh?" He broke our silence and kicked at a rock on the sidewalk.

"Yeah. Nice, though."

"Yeah. Travis, I need you to promise me you won't bother her anymore."

"What?"

"Cate. She's being really nice and cool about every-thing. Especially considering the way you've been acting."

"The way I've been acting? What the hell does that mean?"

"Your little karaoke stalker shit. And even tonight. You knew she wanted space and needed more time, and you just walk right up to her like that."

"Gimme a break, man. You have no idea."

"See, Travis. That's the thing. You come back and you expect everyone to be just the way they were when you left. But it's not that easy, okay? You can't just force us all to be how you liked us."

I didn't have time to respond because Cate walked outside. I think she could tell things were getting pretty tense because she made a big display out of talking about how full she was to lighten things up. I loved her so much for it. Well, for everything, really.

After we dropped her off at her car, Kyle and I didn't say a word to each other. I wasn't just thinking about our conversation, though. I was also bummed that I hadn't gotten any alone time with Cate. Maybe that was for the best, but it sure isn't what I wanted. We pulled up to my house, and before I went to get out, I looked over at him and I promise you I tried to stop myself, but I just couldn't. Sometimes you have to say what's on your mind or the whole thing will implode in on itself.

"Kyle, it's not that I want you to be the way I liked you. I just want you to remember *why* I liked you is all."

"And why's that?"

"Because you were never full of shit about anything."

"Good night, Travis."

I shut the door and leaned into the open window of his truck. He had both hands on the steering wheel and stared straight ahead, refusing to look my way.

"What?" he said.

"Sorry. Just, listen. If I can be the head kid, then you can be his best friend who happens to be gay. None of it matters, Kyle. Screw what people think. Just let it go. It's that easy."

CHAPTER TWENTY-TWO

IT'S THAT EASY

Over the next week Cate and I talked on the phone about four times. And she was actually the first one to call. It was the day after the concert, and she wanted to thank me for "being so cool" and not "acting weird or anything" with her around Kyle. I told her I wanted to be friends just as much as she did and that I'd do whatever it takes to make sure she wasn't uncomfortable or scared to be around me.

I called her the next afternoon, and we caught up a bit more. She mentioned Turner a couple times, and I somehow managed not to throw up into the phone. I guess she was testing the waters a bit, making sure I still didn't have the wrong idea or anything. But both times she said his name, it felt like she'd walked into the room and samurai-style ripped my gut open. It was brutal, but not so brutal that I couldn't get over it just to hear her voice.

The third phone call was a bit weird at first. She was upset about something, I could tell. I asked her what was wrong, but all she would tell me is that she'd just had a bad day. That made me happy, which is sort of sick, I know, but still. It made me happy to think that after a bad day she'd want to talk to me and not anyone else, especially Turner. Maybe old feelings were coming back to her again. Maybe I was growing on her more quickly than she'd predicted. I was just me, after all. I was just Travis 2.0—all the same files in a brand-new, fully functioning operating system.

It was our fourth phone call, though, that confirmed for sure that I shouldn't give up on us so easy. At first she just griped about something that happened at work. Someone had been rude to her—one of the lawyers— and she was thinking about trying to find a job some-place else. Then she started talking about her art. It surprised me, for sure, since she'd seemed so determined to avoid that topic after the concert. But now she was asking me if I remembered these different paintings she'd done in high school and that mural she'd designed for the English hall.

"Of course I remember the mural," I said. "*The Canterbury Tales.*"

"Yeah. You helped."

"I painted about five square inches of the blue back-ground before Mrs. Campbell refused to ever let me touch a work of art again."

"You weren't that bad," she said.

"Cate. For real. She told me she'd give me an A if I'd run errands for her, keep everyone supplied with clean brushes, and never make her grade a piece of my art again."

"Hilarious."

"I thought it was pretty fair. I was only there to watch you anyway."

"Travis, come on."

"It's true. You were so good at everything. You remember that stained-glass window you made for the library? It's still there."

"Really? Wow. I haven't thought about that in so long."

"I go in there sometimes just to see it, you know. I like seeing something you left behind."

"That's sweet."

"Do you still have it?"

"What?"

"The painting you made me. The theater?"

"Yeah. It's here. I told you I'd keep it."

"Thanks. I just missed you so much, Cate."

"I know, Travis. I missed you more than I can even begin to explain."

"So can I see you soon? I know that's not what we talked about, but we were okay the other night. It was okay, wasn't it?"

"Yeah. It was okay. I think Kyle helped a lot."

"He did. Sure he did. But I just want to see you. We can get coffee or something. It doesn't have to be anything serious. Just coffee. Two old friends having coffee and catching up."

"I want to say yes, Travis. This is so weird. All of it."

"Look, tell Turner about it. I know you don't like secrets, and I know how you are. You probably beat yourself up inside every time we talk. But he needs to know I'm not going away, right? I think that's only fair for both of us, if he knows that."

"Okay. Yes. You're right. I'll talk to him and then maybe we can meet up sometime next week."

"Yes. Okay. Good. This is progress, Cate."

"Progress," she said. "*Friendly* progress."

The next day I was sitting in my room watching a rerun of *The Bob Newhart Show* when I heard a car pull up in the driveway. Then I saw Kyle through my window, so I ran downstairs to beat him to the door. I opened it, taking a deep breath and not entirely sure he hadn't come over to give me the punch in the face I probably deserved. Then he sort of just fell onto me, his arms wrapping around my entire body, squeezing tight. He was crying. I couldn't have moved if I wanted to, even with Jeremy Pratt's strength.

"I'm so sorry," he said, finally letting me go.

"Here, come in. Sit down. It's . . . it's fine."

I followed and watched him take a seat on the couch. I sat on the big puffy arm of my dad's recliner and let him gain his composure. He was leaning forward with his elbows on each knee.

"I'm an asshole, Kyle. And *I'm* sorry. I don't blame you for a second."

"You should. It's my fault. You come back and you try to help me, try to be my friend, and I just treat you like shit. It's not right. It's not."

"I overdid it. I should've minded my business."

"You were right, though. That's why I got so damn mad at you."

I was right? Wow. I'd been so worried about him showing up and crying that I hadn't considered this being the reason. It took me a few seconds to register what he'd said.

"Oh. Okay. Does Valerie know this yet?"

"Yeah."

With that he started crying again but silently, just letting tears fall freely, not even wiping them away.

"It just . . . it bummed me out to think that you weren't happy, you know?" I sat down in the chair and leaned forward.

"Ten years," he said. "Ten years of praying every night for something to go away, knowing it doesn't work like that. Ten stupid years."

"God, Kyle. I had no idea."

"It's like . . . maybe *everyone* thinks about it sometimes. Maybe we all think we're gay at one point or another? That's how I rationalized it for so long. I convinced myself that I was just thinking the same way every guy thinks . . .

just choosing to wash away thoughts that I shouldn't be having."

"Look, if I ever made you feel bad about—"

"No. That's just it. No one ever made me feel bad about anything. And my folks, they're the best people I know. It's just . . . it's like I wanted so badly for it to be a phase and I convinced myself that if I made it one, then it was one. It was just something to linger there forever and never get its way."

"I guess I thought if you were ready to tell me back then, you know, that maybe you were getting ready to tell everyone."

"That's the worst part," he said. "After I told you . . . after you went away, I just sort of got more and more paranoid about it. I mean, you're the only one who ever knew, so I had this weird chance to just keep it a secret forever. But once I'd said it to you, once I'd said it out loud, I was so scared that people would be able to tell. Like, they'd see it in the way I talked or in my hand gestures or whatever. It's ridiculous. It's like this—I felt like if I could be as different from all the stereotypes about gay guys as possible, then it would just go away. I couldn't be gay . . . I like sports. I hate shopping. I think Broadway musicals are bullshit."

We both laughed, and I could see that with each new thing he said, with each little confession, Kyle sat up straighter and began to look less sad and defeated. It was like watching an actor slowly separating himself from his most famous character, like he was shedding an artificial skin.

"Can I tell you something?" he said.

"Of course."

"You remember Jake Brassett?"

"Yeah. Soccer guy."

"He liked sports too."

"Okay . . ."

"And making out with me in his grandma's basement senior year."

"Wow."

"Sorry. Too much?"

"Hell no. I'm fascinated. Anyone else?"

"Not really. A couple of guys you wouldn't know, from college. I got really tired of the secrets, so I just kept it from myself, too. I started dating girls when I was a sophomore."

"Yeah . . . how does that work exactly? Do you just picture a dude when you're with them?"

"Not really. It's more like I just shut off my brain and go for it. That, and pretend that I want to wait for marriage."

"You're kidding, right? No sex at all, Kyle?"

"Nope."

"This is so much worse than I thought."

He told me he'd dated three girls in college, all fairly pretty and sweet, all patient or religious enough to wait for sex. He said that was the worst part—when he would be with one of them long enough to realize they were seeing him as this great, respectful guy who cared more about love and companionship than anything else. He said it was the most painful thing in the world to repeatedly break these girls' hearts just because he was too scared to stop trying, to stop hoping that one of them would change the way he felt.

"And I loved them, I think. At least a little. But that's why I had to end it, I guess. I couldn't keep lying to them and knowing that if we stayed together, then they'd be missing out on their chance to be with a guy who really could love them all the way."

He said he was done. He said Valerie would be the last girl he dated, the last person he'd lie to about being gay, or anything at all. Secrets, he said, will boil under your skin until it feels like every time you speak, every time you look in the mirror, every time you hug someone or kiss someone or tell someone you love them, it feels like you're going to die.

"One last thing, Travis," he said to me before he had to leave.

"What's that, buddy?"

"It's you, man. I'm in love with you."

"Oh . . . I . . ."

"I'm just screwing with you. Don't be an egomaniac."

"Shit. That's not funny."

Kyle told me he was planning on coming clean to his parents that weekend. He said his mom would probably cry a little but would eventually realize the perks of having a gay son. He said she always hated his girlfriends anyway. And his dad would give him a hug and awkwardly tell him to "be safe" or something like that. Kyle said he felt guilty for how easy he knew it would be to tell them and for how hard he knew it was for so many others.

I didn't mention Cate. I wanted him to say everything he needed to say, and I wasn't quite sure how he'd react to the situation. I sure didn't want him to know what my real plan was, that I had no intention of being her friend and every intention of making her fall in love with me all over again. He'd say I was ridiculous and immature and selfish. Maybe he was right, but I was also in love. So logic and maturity weren't all that important to me.

I dreamed that night that Cate and I were lying on my roof, and we kissed and held hands and her head was resting on my shoulder. Mostly it felt just like before, like we could pretend the years away. Or she could. When I woke up, all I could think about was how the familiarity of it all made me wonder what would happen if I stayed there in that one spot and closed my eyes again, if I refused to acknowledge everything and everyone in the world around me. Maybe time, as they say, is just a human invention. Maybe I never really left because leaving wasn't possible. Maybe we're all on a string, and maybe our past selves are on that string and our future selves are too and maybe Jeremy Pratt's there. Maybe he's there lying awake at night and wondering if his family will be okay after he dies. Maybe we all just exist, all versions of us exist at all times, and we have to figure out a way to get to each of them, to find each one and tell that version that it's okay, that it's all just the way it works, a concept too powerful to ignore but too complicated to explain.

CHAPTER TWENTY-THREE

TOO COMPLICATED TO EXPLAIN

It was the first week of December when I saw Cate again. We met at this new little coffee shop downtown called the Grindhouse, which I guess was supposed to be funny, but sort of grossed me out. I kept picturing people drinking coffee and dry humping. But as I'm sure you might have guessed, this is not what happened when I met up with Cate.

Even though it was pretty cold, she was waiting for me outside when I walked up. I'd told my mom to drop me off around the corner because I was a little embarrassed about not being able to drive yet. Before, when I was sick, it hadn't mattered. But now with Cate being a little older and all, I didn't want anything extra to remind her of our age difference. She stood up to hug me, and I counted to three and then let go of her, being careful not to touch the small of her back or press myself too close against her. She wanted to be friends, so we'd be friends until she wanted something more than that. Damn, it was hard, though. I wanted to be like this couple I saw in a horror movie when I was a kid and be Super Glued to her forever. Only without the murder by the demented serial killer that followed.

"Should we go inside?" she asked, shivering.

"Hell yes," I said.

I stepped just past her and opened the door. Then I stood back and waited for her to walk in ahead of me, and I swear it was like nothing was different. For a few seconds there, nothing had changed at all. Not her, not me, not the world around us. I'd call it déjà vu or whatever, but that's sort of what my whole life was right after I came back. Just one big moment of "Hasn't this happened before?" that no one else could understand.

"This okay?" she asked, stopping at a table by one of the front windows.

"Works for me." I took my jacket off and hung it on my chair before sitting down. She did the same.

"This place is pretty good," she said. "They've got the best chai I've ever tasted."

"You and your chai," I said. "Still no coffee? I thought maybe you'd grown into it or something."

"Oh no. No, thanks. I've tried. I really have. It's still like . . ."

"Drinking dirt?" I said, finishing her thought.

"Yeah." She smiled. "Plus, Turner says tea's much better for you anyway."

Turner says tea's better for you? What is he, a doctor? Last I heard, he worked with computers. So he knows how to use Google, then? Good for him. I bet if I Googled "people who are destined to lose their fiancées to miracle cryogenics patients," his name would pop right up. So suck it, Dr. Computer.

"Well, I'm still getting a coffee. I'll be right back. You want medium or large?" I stood up with my wallet in one hand.

"No, Travis. Here, let me get mine." She handed me a five from her pocket.

I took it from her and then set it back down on the table.

"No way. You crazy?"

Then I walked away before she could argue. I ordered our drinks at the counter and looked over to see her texting someone. I bet it was Turner—probably checking in to make sure I hadn't kidnapped her and tried to take her back in time with me or something.

"Here you go." I handed her the tea and sat down.

"Thanks," she said. "Sometimes they have music and stuff here. Over on that stage. We saw this guy doing an acoustic set here one night, and it was surprisingly good."

"Oh yeah? We?"

"Me and Turner. He doesn't drink or anything, so we usually end up coming to places like this whenever we need to get out of the house."

Oh, Turner doesn't drink? Well, isn't he just Mr.

Awesome? I swear this guy was getting on my last nerve and I'd never even met him. Why couldn't he be some jerk who made her miserable? I mean, I didn't want her to be miserable, but I also didn't want her to be in love with some guy who sounded perfect, either. Even her parents said they liked him, and I never thought they'd like anyone as much as they liked me. This was going to be harder than I thought.

"He's a recovering alcoholic?" I asked, sort of whispering.

"No, Travis. Jesus." She laughed.

"You're sure?" I kept a straight face.

"He says he doesn't like it. His mom was a pretty big drinker when he was a kid, and I think it just left a sour taste in his mouth, you know?"

"Yeah," I said. "That sounds like a good reason."

"Travis?"

"Yeah?"

"You okay?"

"I'm fine, yeah. Still getting used to you having a boyfriend who isn't me, I guess."

"I'm sure it's weird," she said. "And I appreciate you trying so hard."

"Did you date much? After I left?"

"Not really. I was completely shut off to even the idea of it for a long time. Then senior year Jake Brassett asked me to the Homecoming dance."

"Jake Brassett? The gay football player?" Shit. I probably wasn't supposed to say that.

"Yeah. That one. But he wasn't gay at the time. Or he wasn't all the way gay or whatever."

"How long did you date him?"

"Not long. Maybe two or three weeks. Then I saw Ryan Fielder for a while after that. He was nice."

"Ryan Fielder? Wow. Did you guys play Magic: The Gathering, like, every night?"

"No." She laughed. "He'd grown out of that by then. Mostly we just drove around town and stuff."

As hard as it was to hear her talk about dating other guys, it also made me proud of her. She hadn't let my "death" ruin her, you know? She hadn't let it keep her from trying to just be a normal kid who did normal-kid things. That being said, I made sure to add Jake Brassett and Ryan Fielder to my list of Assholes Who I Will Find a Way to Destroy. I mean, let a guy actually die before you go taking away his girlfriend.

"Let me ask you this," I said.

"Oh boy. Okay. I'm scared."

"Were either of them as good a kisser as I am?"

"I'm not answering that," she said with surprise.

"Okay. Fine, fine. But at least tell me you never took either of them to the park. Please just tell me that."

"Nope. Never once. Some things are sacred, Travis."

"I haven't been back since," I said. "Feels too weird."

"You're kidding. Okay. Let's go." She stood up and started putting her jacket on.

"What?"

"We're going to the park. We have to. It's weird if we *don't* now."

I followed her out and to her car, which was parked on the street just about a block away. She was still driving the same thing she'd always driven, this black '90s Jetta her stepdad had rebuilt an engine for and given to her on her sixteenth birthday. It felt so familiar that I didn't think twice about kicking my right foot up to rest on the edge of the dashboard above the glove compartment, like I'd always done.

"Weird," she said.

"What?"

"I just got the strongest déjà vu when you put your foot up there."

Soon enough we were turning into a small parking lot beside the Colonnade at Kessler Park. We used to drive up here all the time, just the two of us. It seemed otherworldly, this massive collection of stone columns that stretched along the road and looked down onto the park. She liked the way it opened out to the nature all around, how nothing was confined to any small space. It was like a long corridor that only pretended to lead somewhere, but instead could've taken you in any direction you chose. Concrete benches lined the section we liked most, the one with no real roof, just rectangular beams lying across and connecting the two long rows of columns. If you sat there at the right time of day, just late enough in the afternoon for the sun to still be blazing bright, but on its downward path toward the west, the shadows from the beams and columns would intersect and slice dark lines through your face and chest and arms. Maybe even your neck.

And so we got out and sat on one of our benches, and I immediately noticed how different this place felt without the sound of kids in the distance or tourists walking around snapping photos or cars driving past. Winter had driven these things away. And it *was* cold out, but it was a good cold, the kind that reminds you you're alive, that every inch of your body is still able to feel. Even painful, uncomfortable things are good for a guy who never thought he'd feel them again.

"I love it here," I said.

"I couldn't let you go any longer without seeing it again."

"Thanks. Coming up here alone would've been too weird."

There was that feeling in my chest—the one where it feels like something is drilling into your ribs on each side and the vibrations are sort of meeting in the middle. And then it starts radiating down your arms and you're not sure if you can steady them enough to reach out for her, to touch the sides of her face as she leans closer. Your voice even starts to shake, matching the nervousness of your body, of Jeremy Pratt's body, as she finally gets close enough to hear you, and you say to her that this is the most perfect moment of either of your lives.

"You okay?" She snapped me out of my daydream.

"I'm fine. Just thinking about something."

"What?"

"Okay. So I was wondering—how do you refer to me? Like, when I'm not around."

"By your name. It is still Travis, right?"

"No, you know what I mean. Do you call me your ex-boyfriend? Or maybe former boyfriend? Dead boyfriend?"

"Well, in high school I tried not to talk too much about you. It was hard for me, I guess. I didn't like saying things about you in past tense. It never felt right."

"And after that?"

"After that, especially around the time I started dating again, I just decided that not talking about you was worse. That it actually made me feel more like shit. So I just called you Travis, my first boyfriend."

"That's not so bad, I guess."

"I don't think I ever called you my ex-boyfriend even once. So at least there's that."

"We should do this again," I blurted out.

"Yeah," she said. "We should. I'm super busy with school and work, but we'll make it happen, okay?"

"Okay."

And just like that, we were friends. It wasn't exactly what I wanted, but it would do. Anything that got me nearer to her would definitely work until I found a way to get even closer.

A few days later she called looking for a good excuse to skip her night class the next day and offered to pick me up from school. I immediately thought that maybe this was it—maybe this would finally be the day she came clean about how she *really* felt about us and how she couldn't keep pretending with Turner anymore.

"Are you sure it's okay to skip these classes?" I asked when she picked me up.

"Yeah. It's fine. I told them my grandmother was dying."

"Oh. Is . . . well, never mind."

"What is it?"

"Is she? I mean, is she still alive?" I whispered *alive* like I wasn't supposed to say it.

"Yes, Travis. My God. You weren't gone for twenty years."

"So where are we going?" I asked.

"Not telling. Just wait and see."

We eventually drove up to the Nelson-Atkins Museum of Art, which I hadn't been to since a school field trip back when I was a freshman. We parked in the underground garage and went inside.

"Close your eyes," she said as we walked past the gift store.

"If I close my eyes, I won't be able to see the art," I said.

"No. You've seen all this. I want to show you something else."

Then she grabbed my hand. I'll tell you this much—if

I'd never gotten to open my eyes again but could still feel her semi-sweaty grasp and the rough scratch of the tips of her fingernails, I would've been okay. She could've taken me anywhere as long as she kept pulling at me that way, tugging Jeremy Pratt's arm and making my shoes squeak against the slick linoleum floor with every step.

"Okay," she said, letting go of my hand and positioning me by the shoulders. "You ready?"

"If someone isn't naked, I'm going to be unimpressed."

"Shut up, pervert. Okay. On the count of three."

"Do I open my eyes *on* three or right *after* three?" I took every opportunity I could to prolong this moment. Talking to her with my eyes closed felt more like it was supposed to feel than anything else had.

"On three. Okay. One . . . two . . . three!"

I thought I might cry. To be completely honest with you, I think I had at least one tear rolling down my cheek as soon as I saw it. I never thought it would happen, so it hadn't even occurred to me that I'd open my eyes to see the one thing I'd always wanted to see before I died. But there it was, right in front of me. Katsushika Hokusai's *The Great Wave off Kanagawa*. You've probably seen it on television or in someone's dorm room or something. And maybe it was lame to be so infatuated with a piece of artwork that was so popular, but I didn't care. I used to have this huge print of it hanging across from my bed, and I'd stare at it for hours, especially when I was sick. They'd even moved it down to the guest bedroom for me when I couldn't make it up the stairs anymore. Standing beside Cate, I looked at that thing like I was seeing the entire world for the first time. She'd remembered, of course, because I used to have this whole scheme about taking a trip to New York to see it in person before I died. But we ran out of time.

"It's on loan from the Met," she said quietly.

"Cate, I—"

"I need to be honest," she said. "I never really understood what all the fuss was about until I saw it up close. It's really beautiful."

"I used to imagine I was in one of those boats," I said, pointing toward it. "And you know I don't really like water or anything. The ocean, I mean. But it never scared me. The idea of this huge wave crashing down on me was sort of peaceful in a weird way."

"Do you still have your poster?" she asked.

"They got rid of it," I said. "They got rid of everything."

"We'll get you a new one, okay? They'll have some in the gift shop," she said, just barely gripping my arm.

"Thank you, Cate. This is . . . just, thank you."

"Sure," she said.

After standing in the same spot for a while, and completely ignoring the several other patrons who wanted to get the dead-on view that I had, I broke my stare and looked over at her with a big smile. And as we started to walk toward the exit, I held up my finger and turned back around to get one last look.

Before we left, Cate insisted on buying another poster for my room, and even though I argued with her a bit, I was excited to have this one familiar thing to hang up on my wall.

On the drive home I must've had a dumb grin on my face because Cate, with one hand on the steering wheel, used the other to take her phone out of her purse and snap a photo of me.

"There he is," she said. "Travis Coates in his natural habitat."

When she picked me up later that week and we drove out to the park, we started talking about movies. I was quite a movie addict in my previous life, and I'd spent a lot of my time with Cate trying to teach her the difference between a movie and a film. I was never one of those film snobs, though; don't get me wrong. I loved a good silly movie as much as the next guy. But I had a hard time when people at school would say their favorite was something like *Dumb and Dumber* when they had literally thousands of better options. It wasn't entirely their fault, though. They didn't have someone like my dad to provide them with factoids about every movie playing on cable, or my mom to paraphrase entire life biographies of Hollywood's most awarded and acclaimed actors. And, well, they didn't have me to regurgitate that information and force them to sit in indie movie theaters or have director-themed marathons on the weekends. But Cate did. And because she was Cate and we were perfect together, she loved every minute of it.

Except this one night a few months before my procedure. I'd been begging her for weeks to watch *The Shining* with me. She'd only seen bits and pieces of it, but she always remembered the little-girl ghosts and the blood rushing down the hallway and, though Cate usually wasn't all that squeamish, these images had terrified her as a young child innocently flipping through the channels. It was in those days when the various therapies and medications I was receiving were kicking my ass so hard that going out wasn't really an option anymore. She'd drive over after school every day and on weekends, and we'd watch just about every movie that had ever been made.

One of those weekends I finally convinced her to watch my favorite Stanley Kubrick film. And it was a terrible idea that led to maybe the best night of my life.

But first I should tell you about my theater seats. When I was thirteen, a group of investors decided to reopen this old theater in downtown KC called the Triton. You'll remember this as the same theater where I professed my love for Cate and much later, after I'd thawed out, saw her with her fiancé. It was during the renovations of the Triton that my dad happened to see, right there in the *Kansas City Star*, that they were giving away all of the original theater seats to anyone who could show up with a way to transport them. The next day I had two red-cushioned theater seats that dated back to the 1950s sitting right there in the back corner of my room. It took me a little over an hour to scrape off the decades-old wads of gum stuck to the underside of each seat using a butter knife, which I threw away and never told my mom about. I had to screw each rusty metal leg base to a small two-by-four just so the seats would stand upright, and every time you sat in them, they wobbled a bit from side to side and may or may not have sounded like a car being ripped open by the jaws of life. I loved them so much. In fact, I'd say I probably missed my theater seats more than just about anything else from my room. But I knew they couldn't be replaced, so I didn't even bother asking about them.

"If we're going to watch this movie, I need a lot of candy and you have to promise not to make fun of me." Cate was visibly nervous, her top lip between her front teeth, her nostrils flared a little bit.

"I make no promises."

Here's the thing about *The Shining*: it's terrifying. No matter how many times you watch it, no matter if it's pitch-dark in the room or every light in the house is on, it is the scariest shit you've ever seen, and you are doomed to replay its most horrific scenes over and over in your mind for days to follow. But nevertheless, it's a master-work of cinematography, and I couldn't let Cate avoid it any longer.

We waited until nighttime, took our seats, and used

my roller desk chair to prop our feet up in front of us. We never held hands much, but that night she didn't let go of mine for the entire movie.

When it was over, she didn't really say anything for a while. It was pretty late and she needed to head home, but she also wasn't moving from her spot in the theater seat.

"So . . . good, huh?" I tried to stand up, even though my body really didn't want me to.

"I don't think I've ever been so freaked out in my entire life," she said in a shaky, low voice.

"Cate, come on. It's just a movie."

"I don't think I'll be able to sleep."

"I'm . . . sorry?" It was becoming really difficult not to smile.

"No, don't be. I think I loved it. But yeah . . . I'm totally scared shitless too."

"That's exactly how you're supposed to feel. It worked!" I managed to finally get myself standing upright, and I held one hand up for her to high-five. She did, very slowly, still staring toward the TV screen.

"I guess I better get home."

"Are you okay?" I wanted to laugh. I'd never seen her like this.

"Yeah. Sorry, I'm fine. Okay. I love you." She leaned in and hugged me, and kissed me on the cheek. "You need help with anything before I go?"

"Nah. I'm good. Let me walk you out."

"Travis. You can barely stand. Get in bed and I'll talk to you tomorrow, okay?"

"Okay. Love you. Night."

I made it to my bed and was lying with my eyes closed by the time I heard her car pulling out of the driveway. Then my phone rang.

"Hello."

"Travis?"

"Cate Conroy? It's been *ages*."

"Stay on the phone with me until I get home. But, like, not just home. Maybe until I'm in my room with the door locked."

"Are you serious?" I was laughing.

"Yes, I'm serious. I told you I didn't want to watch that scary-ass movie, and now I can't even drive home without looking out the window and into the backseat, like, a hundred times and—"

"This is the best moment of my life."

"Stop it!" She tried to be mad, but I could tell she was smiling. When you talk to someone as much as I'd talked to Cate, you know how their voice changes when they smile.

"Hey, Cate?"

"What?"

"Heeeeeeeeeeeere's Johnny!" I couldn't resist. I mean, come on.

"I hate you. Oh man, I hate you so much."

"You'll miss it."

I talked to her that night for about an hour after she'd gotten to her room, locked the door, and checked under her bed and in her closet.

I replayed the whole thing to Cate in the park that afternoon, remembering every single word that we'd said. She seemed amazed at how much of it she'd forgotten. She looked at me with these bewildered eyes and held her hand up to her mouth, her fingertips touching her lips. It was weird that she hadn't remembered it the way I had. And I could tell it bothered her. But in that moment I understood what they say about nostalgia, that no matter if you're thinking of something good or bad, it always leaves you a little emptier afterward. I didn't like it. It reminded me of everything I was trying to ignore. Was this going to happen every time we talked about the past? I wasn't sure I could do that to her and, well, I wasn't sure she'd let me.

The next day I was walking from chemistry to lunch, and I ran into Audrey Hagler. She walked up to me and didn't say a word, just hugged me, and I could feel the warmth of her cheek on my own.

"Everything okay?" I asked.

"You're a good friend, Travis."

"Okay . . ."

"To Kyle, I mean. Thank you."

"Sure," I said, feeling a little embarrassed.

She smiled really big and squeezed one of my arms. And then she walked away and I was left standing right in the middle of the hallway, my cheeks flushed, my palms sweaty, my arm feeling as if her hand was still there gripping it. There are moments in your life when you imagine things happening in slow motion, when your movie-addled mind won't let you experience things the way they're actually going down, but instead replaces it with fictional special effects. And it was in this moment that I came to realize something very important, something that I hadn't quite given much thought since my return. I considered the idea that maybe my death had slowed everyone down a bit. If I'd still been there, Kyle wouldn't have felt compelled to live a lie for so long. It seemed to me that I'd screwed up years of his life. I wondered what things I'd screwed up for the rest of them. I'd wanted them all to move on and stop centering their lives on a kid who stood no chance of survival. I'd volunteered for all this craziness because I thought it was the least selfish thing I could do, the *only* thing I could still do for them. But in that hallway with all those people moving by me in a half blur and a cloud of noise swarming around my head, all I could think about was how badly I'd let them all down. Dying, as it turns out, may not have been the best decision I ever made.

CHAPTER TWENTY-FOUR

THE BEST DECISION I EVER MADE

Now that Kyle and Cate were both back in my life, in some form or another, I was feeling almost . . . peaceful. It wasn't exactly like before, but it would certainly do for the time being. And Cate and I were on the right track to becoming something even better than before, I'd say. And having Hatton was just an added bonus to it all.

But it was inevitable that these two worlds—the one where I was just another teenager and the one where I was pretending not to be—would collide. And I needed it to happen without one destroying the other. I'd planned on eventually getting Kyle and Hatton together to show them how one was pretty much the past or future version of the other. And Cate? Well, I wanted to tell them both at the same time that I'd been hanging out with her, figuring maybe they'd try to one-up the other as my most supportive friend and I'd be left unscathed in the process.

But see, things don't always go according to plan in my life. So the day after I got out of school for Christmas break, Kyle called me and I could immediately tell he had something to say that I didn't want to hear.

"Travis?"

"Yeah?"

"Why didn't you tell me you've been seeing Cate?"

"How'd you know that?"

"Because she told me. I saw her last night at school."

"Oh well. I haven't really had the chance to tell you."

"Bullshit. She says you guys have been hanging out for, like, two weeks."

"Yeah. What's the big deal? We're just friends, Kyle."

"Then why didn't you tell me?"

"I was going to," I said.

"You forget I know you just as well as you know me. You can't ruin things for her."

"You know this is right. We're supposed to be us again. I'm not doing anything wrong. I'm being her friend, and it seems like she's been pretty desperate to have someone to talk to."

"I just . . . I just hope it's not the wrong decision. For either of you, okay?"

"Why would it be? She didn't stop loving me because I died, Kyle. I don't blame her for trying to move on. But now she'll see that it can go back to how it was, okay?"

"I don't think you get where I'm coming from here, Travis."

"The future?" I tried to joke.

"Stop. I'm being serious."

"Sorry."

"Look, I'm just afraid you're going to find out that no matter how perfect you guys were before, that maybe that doesn't last forever. Plus, she has a fiancé. She is getting *married*."

"That *is* quite a complication," I said. "But still. Let me figure this out. You know I have to."

"I'm not kidding around. Be careful, okay? I've seen her with him. She seems happy. Happy like she was with you."

"Don't say that."

"I'm just looking out for you. Like you did for me. *And* Cate. You're not the only one who loves her, Travis. She's my friend too."

"I know. Look, can we just talk about this later? When's Christmas break for you?"

"Started today. I'm so damn happy I could puke."

"Me too. Don't have to go back till the second of January. You got plans tomorrow?"

"I'm going to sleep for as long as humanly possible. Then I've got no plans."

"What say we go to Arnie's? Like old times?" I asked.

"Perfect. Should we invite your new friend from school?"

"Huh? Oh, Hatton?"

"Yeah, I guess. Audrey says you guys are inseparable."

"Sure. I mean, if it's cool with you."

"Travis . . . I'm not mad that you have a friend. That would be a little bit messed up."

"I know. It's weird, though. You guys not being there, I mean. It feels like cheating or something sometimes."

"Well, at least you made a friend. I'm really glad."

"Cool. So pick me up at noon? We can get Hatton on the way to the arcade."

"Sure. And Travis?"

"Yeah?"

"I finally told my folks."

"And?"

"I can't say it was the best moment of my life, but I survived."

"They were pretty surprised?" I asked.

"I think so," he said. "Mom cried. She just doesn't want my life to be harder because of it. But I told her I'm pretty sure gay people rule the world, and she started laughing. She'll be fine."

"And your dad? What'd he say?"

"He was the most surprised. He thought I was just really picky. We still haven't really talked about it that much since I told them, but I know they're okay."

"You tell Audrey, too?"

"Yeah. She says she knew already, but I don't know if she's just trying to be nice or what."

He paused for a few seconds, and I wasn't really sure what to say. All I could see was that gawky sixteen-year-old version of him sitting beside my deathbed in the middle of the night, his whole body shaking as he told me the truth. I wanted to ask him if he felt the relief he'd been looking for or if it was something different. I wanted to know how it felt to tell the truth even when you think it could change the way everyone looks at you.

When Kyle picked me up for our afternoon at Arnie's Arcade, he looked different from before—he wasn't dancing and singing or anything, but I thought I noticed some change in his demeanor, like letting go of his secret had lightened him up a bit.

"That's his house. The red one," I said.

We pulled into Hatton's driveway, and he was already standing on the front steps waiting for us. He wore his usual hoodie, zipped halfway up over a T-shirt that said "Are you kitten me?" and had a crude drawing of a cat on it. His favorite T-shirt.

"Gosh, he's small," Kyle said as Hatton walked over to the truck.

"You're just old," I said.

After Hatton had climbed into the backseat and he and Kyle had awkwardly shaken hands, we were all quiet for a few minutes.

"So, Kyle." Hatton finally broke the silence, leaning up a little.

"Yeah?"

"Just curious here . . . on a scale of one to ten, how attractive am I to the average gay male?"

"Hatton, Jesus!" I turned around and thought seriously about throwing him out the window.

"Travis, chill out," Kyle said, laughing.

"Like, what . . . like a one? Tell me it's not a one." Hatton never acknowledged my reaction.

"Hmm . . ." Kyle looked into the rearview mirror at Hatton. "I'm gonna say a solid three."

"Three. *Hell* yes. I'll take it. Thank you."

"It's the glasses. They work on you."

"Hear that, Travis? These babies work on me."

"Why do you care?" I asked.

"Travis, *anyone* finding me attractive is a score for me."

"Fair enough."

"Travis is a seven, closer to an eight," Kyle said.

"That's not fair. He cheated when he got his body."

"Don't worry," I said. "I'll ruin it before too long."

I guess Hatton's bravery had done the trick with the two of them, had broken all the ice that needed to be broken, because they spent that afternoon at Arnie's like they'd been friends forever. They moved from game to game, raced each other on clunky fake motorcycles, and placed bets on who could earn the most tickets. I didn't join in because as soon as we'd walked into the arcade, I had a mission.

Arnie's wasn't all that different overall—the carpet was still a deep, dark red, dim track lights still hung in diagonals across the ceiling, and the prize counter was still full of cheap plastic toys and erasers and Chinese finger traps. But the game floor had been changed. New games had been added, replacing the classic pinball machines and Pac-Man and Asteroids. And the most harrowing thing I noticed was that my favorite game of all time— Space Invaders—had been replaced by quite possibly the most frightening thing I'd ever seen. It was called Dance Till You Die and there were two middle schoolers, one boy and one girl, doing just that. They were dancing so hard, jumping up and down and twisting, that sweat was pouring from their foreheads. You could see it dripping from the boy's hair onto the shiny, illuminated platform below him. It was horrifying.

I walked over to the counter and asked this kid who was probably no older than I was where they'd moved my game.

"Oh, that's in the Retro Room. Back corner."

Retro Room? Why would Arnie's Arcade have a section marked "retro" when, five years before, the whole damn place existed and thrived for the sole reason that it was *entirely* retro? I walked over to Hatton and Kyle, who were playing some futuristic shooter game that I couldn't care less about.

"What's wrong with you, Travis?" Kyle asked.

"This place is freaking me out a little. I thought it would be more . . . the same."

"It's fun, dude. You wanna play?" Hatton asked.

"I need to go check something out. You guys keep having fun."

The Retro Room was not a room at all. It was a dark corner, sectioned off by wavy purple curtains. The past, just covered up enough to give everyone the option to forget it ever happened. I was looking at the neon letters above the entrance and wondering if entering would somehow set everything back on its proper course, if the past would become the present and I'd finally feel like I was standing in the right place.

Just so you know, nothing spectacular like that happened when I stepped inside. It was still just me, part Travis, part Jeremy Pratt, and all disappointment. Pac-Man, Asteroids, Ms. Pac-Man, three pinball machines, Frogger, Centipede, Lunar Lander, and Space Invaders. If these games were the children of the arcade, then the Retro Room was their time-out, punishment for never changing the way they were, for not growing up like everyone else. And I belonged there with them.

When Space Invaders was still in its proper place near the main entrance of the arcade, I used to stand there and spend hours every weekend defeating the never-ending alien hordes as the electronic music got faster and faster. Sometimes Kyle would be there to lean against the machine and cheer me on. Sometimes more people would gather behind us and watch as I fought to beat my record from the previous week. My top score was the highest they'd ever seen at the Springside

Arnie's: 29,601. That's a hell of a lot of aliens and bonus ships.

So I slowly approached the machine again, looking down at the buttons, amazed at how the red shooter one looked just the same but how the four white buttons had faded and worn to a dull yellow. The token slots, too, were damaged and aged, their faces unreadable. But I knew how many tokens it took to play a game, and soon enough I had my hands on the buttons, and I could hear the music that had been the sound track to so many of the afternoons before I got sick—the ominous *dun dun dun dun*'s that I used to hear in my sleep like echoes from an era that I hadn't even lived through, an early '80s electronic metronome.

I started shooting, tapping the buttons with as much speed as Jeremy Pratt's hands would allow, but it felt weird. Of all the things to feel different, of all the moments that I could have so quickly remembered my unique situation, this one pissed me off the most. I'd been able to do everything I'd done before I got sick—even more than that, I'd been able to do things that I'd never been able to do before—skateboard, run without getting winded, do fifty push-ups in a row without crashing to the floor and crying. And now? Now I was struggling to match my eyes to my hands and shoot the same little digital aliens that I'd annihilated so many hundreds of times before. This was total bullshit. This, the Retro Room, the whole damn thing.

It was Game Over before I could even clear out one level, my score a measly 850. An 850? I hung my head down low in shame and frustration. I was about to walk away, defeated, when I glanced back up at the screen. And then I saw it, flashing there, taunting me with its accompanying music. HI SCORE: 29,601. That's when I knew I couldn't stop. I knew what I had to do.

CHAPTER TWENTY-FIVE

WHAT I HAD TO DO

In 1978, when coin-operated Space Invaders machines first appeared in restaurants and arcades all around Japan, the game became so instantly popular that there was a brief national shortage of hundred-yen coins. Can you imagine? So many people were putting these coins into Space Invaders machines that they actually ran out of them. This is just one of many things my dad made sure I was aware of when my obsession with the game began. I think he was proud of me, in some small way, for choosing this game that had trail-blazed a path for so many others. He once said to me, his tone surprisingly sincere, that he was glad I wasn't "one of those Pac-Man people."

I played and lost three more games even quicker than the first two. My heart was racing—I could feel it in my throat and in my thumbs and even in my feet.

Okay, Travis. Last token. Then you're all done.

I let the token slide into the slot and listened as the game started back up, my eyes closed for just a second before I started shooting. I cleared one whole screen and then, of course, the game got faster and faster, harder to shoot and dodge lasers to the frantic beat of the music and the white flashing lights on the screen. I was sweating and rocking from side to side on my feet. It was during this game that Hatton and Kyle found me and watched as I furiously pushed the buttons and cursed the machine.

"Ah. Game over," Hatton said. "Good try, though."

"Just a few more times."

"Travis, yeah . . . you're covered in sweat and your face is pretty red. I don't want to be *that* guy right now, but I think maybe we should take you home. You're not looking so great." Kyle had his hand on one of my shoulders the entire time he spoke.

"I'm fine. What're you talking about? It's just hot in here. I'm having a blast."

Hatton looked at Kyle like he was silently asking him what to do, like he trusted this guy he just met over me. I didn't say anything about it, but to be honest, it sort of ticked me off. I walked off to get more tokens and when I came back, they were both just standing there like they'd been talking about me or something.

"What?" I asked. "Everything okay?"

"Yeah," Hatton said. "Let's see you beat that score."

Seventeen games later Kyle leaned in and started talking to me in this calm sort of low voice that reminded me of being sick, of being treated like something less than a free-thinking, fully functioning being.

"Dude, I get it. The score still being here, that's really crazy, but you don't have to prove anything today, okay?"

"I know I can beat it," I said, never looking up at him. "Or at least match my score. Damn thing isn't gonna win."

"Travis, I know this has all got to be really hard for you. I can't imagine. And you've been doing so well with everything. I don't think anyone else could've handled it all the way you have."

"Shit!" I slammed my hands down on the machine. "You just made me lose, man. Damn it!"

He backed away a little bit, gave me this look of mixed horror and disappointment, and then walked off. I started to yell an apology after him, but he'd walked out of the room so quickly that it didn't quite work. I was soaked. Even my hands were wet, leaving smudges of moisture all over the buttons. I wiped my palms on my jeans and looked over to Hatton, who was staring down at his phone.

"Hey, we've been here, like, two and a half hours, so my mom needs me to come home. She's gonna pick me up in a few. Cool?"

"Oh. Okay," I said, turning around to face the game again.

"Okay . . . so I'm just gonna go wait for her outside. I'll see you later, Travis."

I just kept playing. I could deal with Hatton the next

day. He didn't understand. I guess Kyle didn't either, even if he said he did. No one can understand something that hasn't happened to them. Meaning, of course, that no one could ever understand anything that was happening to me. Well, except for Lawrence Ramsey. Maybe he liked Space Invaders too.

A few minutes later I heard Kyle walk up behind me, and without even turning to face him, I asked if he'd mind letting me borrow some money. I wasn't even getting close. All those games later and I hadn't even scored a third of what I needed to beat my record. I blamed Jeremy Pratt and his stupid hands.

"Travis," a familiar voice said from behind me. I let go of the buttons and turned around. It was Cate.

"Hey! What're you . . . what're you doin' here?" I went in for a hug.

"You're soaking wet. You feel okay?" She barely hugged me back, an expression of worry on her face.

"Yeah. I'm fine. Did Kyle call you?" I looked around, expecting him to be standing nearby.

"He's outside. He was worried, Travis."

"Worried? Geez. They don't understand. See, I have to beat this score. You remember my high score, right? It's still here, Cate. Isn't that incredible?"

"Yeah, Kyle told me everything. It's pretty awesome."

She was humoring me and, for the first time since I'd been back, I felt like she was seeing me as some dumb kid. Her voice and the way she was looking into my eyes and that worried expression on her face made me let go of the controls and step back a little.

"It's time to go. You've been here all day."

"All day? I don't think we've been here *all* day."

"Travis, it's dark out. Kyle says you've been playing for three hours."

"I just need to try a few more times. I feel like I have to. I'm broke, though. You got, like, ten bucks? I'll pay you back, I swear."

"Travis Coates," she said sternly, leaning in to look me right in the eyes, her nose almost touching mine. "You are done. You are being silly and childish, and I am going to take you home now. Okay?"

"But I—"

"No. Stop. Let's go."

She pulled at my sleeve and I followed her out, looking back at the machine like once I looked away, it would disappear forever. We got outside and Kyle was standing by his truck. He walked over to us and put his hand on my shoulder.

"You okay, man?" He looked at me like he used to look at me before, like I was dying again. I hated it.

"I'm fine. Sorry."

He gave me one of those half-body guy hugs and then hugged Cate and said he'd call me the next day. I waved at him as he drove off. Cate was looking over at me and she was still very worried; I could see that. I was embarrassed. I felt like I'd just thrown a three-year-old's temper tantrum in front of her. Probably not the best way for a teenage guy to win back his grown-up girlfriend.

"Okay. Let's get you home, champ."

"Champ?" I asked.

"Champ," she said more clearly. "Champion. Champione!"

I laughed a little as we pulled onto the street. Then I started breathing really fast. I noticed it first in my chest, like it wouldn't rise all the way, like my lungs were blocked or something. I sat up and put both hands on the dashboard. I was hyperventilating. My heart was trying to force its way out of my chest, and I could feel my legs shaking.

"Travis! Travis, are you okay?"

"I can't breathe."

"Okay . . . okay . . . just close your eyes, okay? Close your eyes and lean back."

"I can't . . . my heart's beating so fast . . . I feel like I might pass out."

"You won't pass out, Travis. Just close your eyes and breathe really deep. Deep, deep breaths. Just trust me."

I kept my eyes closed, breathing really deeply and steadily like she said, until we were at my house and she had the passenger door open and was kneeling down and holding my hand, asking if I was okay. I'd calmed down a bit, my breathing was better, and it didn't feel as much like I was having a heart attack. So we walked inside and sat down on the couch.

"Thanks," I said. "I'm not sure why that happened."

"Has that happened before?"

"No. Not really."

"Before I got there, you were really hot, right?"

"Yeah. You saw, I was sweating like crazy."

"And were you . . . irritable? Like, did you want to punch someone in the face every time they spoke to you?"

"Kind of, yeah."

"Yep. Okay, so you definitely had a panic attack."

"How do you know for sure?"

"Because I had about one of those a day for six months."

"Damn, Cate."

"It was a while ago. It's fine now. I've got it under control."

"A while . . . like . . . five years ago?"

"Yeah."

"Six months?"

"First they tried meds . . . but they gave me headaches. You know I don't like taking medicine. I don't even take aspirin. Then I saw someone for a while, and I got to where I could stop them before they got too bad. Like what I told you in the car . . . you just have to close your eyes and breathe. As long as you know it's gonna pass, you just have to stay calm and wait it out."

"Can you stay for a little while? I guess Mom and Dad are working or something. I can't keep up with them anymore."

"Yeah. I guess I can stay. But look, Travis. I don't want you getting the wrong idea either."

My girlfriend who used to dare me to make out in public places and play footsie with me at the dinner table and park down the road to sneak into my house in the middle of the night didn't want me getting the wrong idea. My girlfriend who hadn't seen me in half a decade, who had come to save me from my breakdown at Arnie's, *that* girlfriend needed a little more convincing. I wasn't sure I could keep this up for much longer. Being her friend was fine, but I needed things to go back. I needed them to be the same as before, and the longer I waited, the less possible that seemed. Maybe that's why I freaked out in the car. Maybe, like some transplanted organ in an unfamiliar body, I was being rejected by the world around me. I had to fix things before I ran out of time.

CHAPTER TWENTY-SIX

OUT OF TIME

I should probably tell you about my last Christmas. I mean, the one I thought would be my last Christmas. And, well, to tell you about it means that I also have to tell you about my last New Year's, Valentine's Day, Easter, and Halloween. Because they were all on the same day.

You'll remember that Kyle and Cate came with us to Denver so they could say good-bye to me. But what I haven't told you is that we arrived there about six days before my actual surgery. For fear that I wouldn't make it much longer, Dr. Saranson flew us all out and put my parents, Kyle, and Cate in a couple of suites they had at the hospital. I call it a hospital, but this place, the Saranson Center for Life Preservation, was more like the starship *Enterprise*. The walls were all shiny metallic or foggy white, and all the doors were glass and moved silently out of the way whenever someone approached them. My room was designed to make sure my (very probable) last days of life were more comfortable than all the ones before them. The mattress had all these settings that I could control with a touch screen, and I could use that same screen to completely shut out the light from outside and make the ceiling glow with a million little digital stars. It was beautiful. I usually made fun of things like that, but they got it right, I think. It was peaceful without being creepy like those weird clown murals you see in some children's hospitals.

I'd already said my final good-byes to the few family members we'd told about my procedure because you don't need an audience to die and, plus, we knew how uncomfortable it made them feel. My grandmother especially had a hard time understanding why I'd want to take such a big risk and lose even one extra second of the life I was living. She kissed my cheek for the first time I ever remembered, and she told me that if it came to it, I should probably tell my grandfather hello for her. I thought that was sweet, the way she said it like I was just going to visit a foreign city or something.

We got to Denver and I settled into my room. Cate helped me while my parents and Kyle went to put their things in the guest suites across the building. She and I played around with the touch screen that the nurse had shown us, opening and closing the curtains, making fake stars twinkle one second and then turning the room into a bright, almost blinding white the next.

"So if you see a bright light, it's not you dying. It's me playing around in this room," Cate said, both of us squinting at each other.

Soon enough it was the early evening, and I noticed that this was the time when everyone always got the saddest. I think there's something about the sun going down that maybe pushes you just over the edge if you're standing too close to it. Mom was crying because she was always crying, and my dad was holding her hand and trying to make casual conversation with everyone. But I think it had hit us all at once that we were suddenly there. We had reached our final stop on the Travis Coates Is Dying Express, and now no one knew what to say.

"It's a shame," I said. "What is it, like, September?"

"Yeah. School starts next week," Kyle answered.

"I thought I could at least squeeze in one last holiday before I had to go."

"There's always Labor Day," Dad suggested.

"I think that only requires resting. I've got that down to an art," I said. "It's a real shame. I like how people act on holidays. Everyone just seems . . . I don't know— lighter, maybe. Like they're allowed to have fun all day long and eat anything they want and do silly things, and no one cares because, hey, it's a holiday, so why not?"

"When you were little," my mom started up, her tears still flowing, "you had that calendar. Remember that? Remember your big calendar?"

"Yeah. With the marker."

"That's the one. He had this big calendar on his wall. Thing must've been, oh, probably about the size of a movie poster, and he used to use this green marker to fill in some made-up holiday for every single day of every month. Every *single* day. So I knew when the first rolled around, Travis would be tearing off one sheet and starting on the other."

"What were the holidays?" Kyle asked.

"Oh, things like Squirrel Day or Dad's Ties Day," I said.

"What about Talk While Breathing In Day?" Dad said. "That was my favorite."

"And you'd celebrate them all?" Cate asked.

"*He* would. He'd try to get us involved in any way possible, but it wasn't always very successful. How does one celebrate The Way Porcelain Figurines Make a Popping Sound When You Move Them on a Shelf Day?"

"That was a good one," I said. "Probably my favorite."

"Do they really do that?" Cate asked.

"They do at my grandma's house," I said.

"So it was basically just everything you liked, right?" Kyle asked.

"I guess so, yeah. I was a weird kid."

"The best weird kid," Mom said.

Then she walked out of the room because I think she wanted to spare us some pretty ugly crying. Dad followed after her, and we all watched some TV until I felt like I couldn't keep my eyes open any longer. Eventually Kyle headed back to his room and left Cate and me alone for a few minutes.

"What would you call today? I mean, if it had to be a holiday?"

"Hmm . . . maybe Travis Gets Lucky in Denver Day?" I laughed.

"Okay, rock star." She rolled her eyes.

"Oh. Denied. That's pretty harsh, considering."

But she didn't laugh. She just bent down and quietly kissed me on the forehead and then paused for a second with her eyes really close to mine, looking right into them. You ever feel like you know someone so much that they can breathe for you? Like when their chest and your chest rise and fall, they do it together because they have to? That's how it felt. That's how it always felt.

The next morning I was feeling pretty good for a guy who couldn't sit up by himself and had to pee into a bag. Mom and Dad brought in a huge thing of doughnuts, and the three of us watched some TV while we smothered our emotions with sugar and lard. I asked where Cate and Kyle were, and my parents acted like they had no idea. Dad said maybe they'd slept in.

"You'd think they could wait a few days, huh? I said, a little miffed.

About an hour after we'd eaten, the door opened and in walked ten nurses, all dressed in homemade costumes. Dracula, a princess, the Hulk, Batman, Superman, a zombie—I think one of them may have been a hooker, but

I was afraid to ask. These were maybe the worst costumes I'd ever seen. They were made mostly of paper and hospital gowns that someone had used Magic Markers on. But it didn't matter because they were laughing and holding out their hands, fists closed. Kyle and Cate walked in behind them, both wearing surgical masks and scrubs.

"TRICK OR TREAT!" they yelled in unison, followed by some laughter. A couple of them looked very visibly uncomfortable with all of this.

They took turns coming up to the bed and putting handfuls of candy in my lap. Each one smiled at me, and the young guy dressed as Batman gave me a high five and shouted "YES!" afterward. The last two trick-or-treaters were my girlfriend and best friend, and they lifted their masks to reveal sneaky grins. Then they all yelled, "HAPPY HALLOWEEN, TRAVIS!" and walked back out.

"That was awesome," I said, sad it was over.

"Just be patient," Dad said.

Sooner than I could unwrap a piece of the candy, the lights in the room dimmed to almost pitch-black, and I couldn't really see anything until the first nurse walked in, holding a lit candle. Several more filed in behind her and there were some doctors, too. Then, of course, Kyle and Cate. My parents stood up, took candles out of their pockets, and lit them on Kyle's flame.

"Guys . . . I don't know what to—"

"Travis Coates," a middle-aged male nurse said. "Merry Christmas."

Then he counted, "A one … two … three …," and they all started singing. And it was "O Holy Night," and my mom and dad were crying, but they were still singing. Cate and Kyle, too. And the yellowish glow on all their faces was maybe the most beautiful thing I'd ever seen.

When it was done and they'd all walked slowly out, my parents followed behind them. But not before I felt something being put on my head. I sat in the darkness for a little while until I felt someone walk up to me.

Then the room lit up with stars, and all the nurses were dancing around to music that started piping out of a black boom box in one of their hands. And they were cheering and blowing on party horns and wearing hats, just like the one on my head. Kyle ran into the room wheeling an IV cart and said, "Who's ready for the countdown?"

He knelt down and disappeared for a second in the dark. Then a faint glow suddenly illuminated the room— he'd haphazardly wrapped an empty IV bag with little twinkling lights, like the ones you see on miniature Christmas trees—and now we all started to count down from ten as he used plastic tubing to raise the bag up from the floor. When we got to one, everyone cheered even louder and started singing "Auld Lang Syne." I joined in because how could I not, and we all laughed when my dad started dancing in the middle of the room with a nurse who was still very much dressed up like Dracula.

They kept dancing and the music kept playing until the room was clear of everyone. But the stars were still covering the ceiling, and I laid my head back on my pillow and watched them, waiting to see what would happen next, hoping it wasn't over. Kyle walked in a few seconds later and handed me a bouquet of flowers.

"Why, thanks, Kyle," I said.

"No, no. These are not for you."

He walked out quickly and pushed play on the little boom box that the nurse had set by the door. It was some beautiful violin music, something romantic. And Cate walked in smiling at me. She was still wearing her jeans and a hoodie, but her hair wasn't in its usual ponytail. It was flowing wild around both sides of her face. She was beautiful. Of course she was.

"Happy Valentine's Day," she said, leaning in and kissing me.

I handed her the flowers and she acted surprised, throwing her head back and being really funny in her dramatic way. "You shouldn't have, darling. Why, I must be the luckiest girl in the world." We laughed and kissed a little more, and I think maybe we were both crying when she finally said it wasn't quite over yet.

Suddenly the lights were back on, and before I could protest or even think about protesting, she and Kyle were helping me down from the bed and into a wheelchair. My parents were smiling in the hallway as we wheeled past them, and every time we approached a nurse or doctor, I got a head nod or a high five or a little cheer. It was the craziest thing I've ever seen.

We took an elevator down to the ground floor, and Cate told me to close my eyes, which I did because, at that point, there was no telling what was about to happen and I couldn't stand the thought of ruining the surprise.

"Okay, open up!" Kyle shouted.

We were in the center of a beautiful green courtyard. There were flowers all around the edges, reaching up to the windows of the first floor. I looked up and even though it was cool out, the sky looked like a bright blue triangle, shaped by the sides of the buildings around us.

"You'll notice, Travis, that there are Easter eggs all around you," Kyle said.

I did notice. There were bright plastic eggs scattered all around the yard, the grass just short enough not to cover them completely. I couldn't keep quiet anymore. I had to ask how they'd done all this.

"We had all night. You go to sleep at, like, six p.m., dude," Kyle said.

"Yeah, but the costumes and the eggs and the Christmas candles. I just—"

"We're not done, Travis," Cate interrupted. "In each of these eggs you'll find something special. Not candy, though. These eggs are magic."

"I don't think I can really get to them." I felt a little defeated, like I was screwing this all up.

"Hey!" some guy in a suit shouted from the sidewalk. "You guys can't be on that grass. What're you doing?"

"We have permission," Cate said.

"From whom?" he asked.

"From God," I said.

"What?" He wasn't amused at all.

"I'm dying."

"Oh." He looked down at the wheelchair and then up at our faces. "Okay."

"Happy Easter," Kyle said, waving as the man walked away.

"I think I want down," I said. "Can you help me?"

They did and I lay there in the grass, looking up at the blue triangle and then over at each of them. Kyle walked over and grabbed a purple egg, opened it, and unfolded a tiny slip of paper that was inside.

"What's it say?" I asked, not even able to lean up to see him all the way.

"It says: *Travis, do you remember that time we beat the final level of Zelda and we both teared up?*"

"It was *you*. I didn't cry. I never cry. Read me some more."

Cate opened a pink egg and began reading.

"*Do you remember that Halloween when I locked you out of the car in that grocery store parking lot when those kids were throwing eggs at you?*"

I did remember that. And even though I was laughing with her and Kyle, I need you to know that those hooligans could've put one of my eyes out.

Kyle started reading another note before I could say anything.

"Do you remember that time Seth Martin heard you talking about how dumb he was?"

They kept on like that for a while, and we laughed and told jokes and made fun of one another. But that's why they were there, I guess. Even though I was almost gone, they were still there to remind me that I wasn't quite dead yet. And to be honest, I wouldn't have minded just closing my eyes right then and letting go. Wouldn't that be perfect? Just dying right there with your two best friends helping you remember everything you loved about being alive?

And that's how, five days before having my head sawed off my body and carefully placed in a cryogenic freezer in the basement of the Saranson Center for Life Preservation, I got to have the best day of my life. Isn't that something? Isn't that the greatest thing you've ever heard? I bet most people don't even get one person who cares about them that much. And me, I got four of them. Yeah, maybe I got a bad deal the first time around. Sure, it wasn't fair to be dead at sixteen. But you know what? At least I got to live every single second before they finally turned off the lights.

CHAPTER TWENTY-SEVEN

THE LIGHTS

I woke up with Cate's elbow stabbing me in the ribs at about three a.m., the house dark and cold. There was a blanket on us—evidence that someone else had come home and quietly left us to sleep side by side on the couch.

"Cate," I whispered, gently pushing her away from me.

"Hey. What time is it?"

"Three in the morning," I said.

"Oh shit," she said. "Your folks home?"

"Blanket came from somewhere." I sat up and stretched a little, and wiped the sleep out of my eyes.

"You feeling better?" she asked.

"I am. Cate, I—"

"You'll walk me out?" She got up, walked over to the window by the front door, and peeked outside.

"Sure."

"I don't see your dad's car. It's the same one, right?"

"Yeah. Weird."

"Travis?"

"Yeah?"

"Why isn't your dad home at three a.m. on a Tuesday?"

"I don't know. He's been working really late since I've been back."

"Could he . . . never mind." She sat back down and yawned. I liked it when she looked sleepy.

"You think he's having an affair or something?"

"No. Forget I said anything. Your dad is not that kind of guy, Travis."

"I'm sure everyone who's ever had a cheating father has said the same exact thing."

We sat there in the dark for a few minutes. We could hear neighborhood dogs barking somewhere, and we looked at each other with surprise when we heard a car drive past. It wasn't my dad. When she got up to leave, Cate pointed at me with this funny look on her face, like she was trying to end this quiet moment in the dark before things got uncomfortable.

"I'll see you after Christmas."

She was going to spend the holidays at her grandparents' house in Dallas. She hated Dallas. She said the lack of cowboy hats and Wrangler jeans made it seem like it had misrepresented itself to the entire world. She didn't like things that weren't what she thought they'd be. But who does?

I walked her out to her car, and just before she opened

the door to climb inside, I leaned into her and kissed her cheek. No doubt, Jeremy Pratt's body was doing things that Travis Coates's body had done many times before in that very same spot, but she suddenly held up both of her arms and shouted, "Hey, whoa . . . what?" She was definitely caught off guard, but she was also laughing a little.

"I'm sorry," I said. "I'm really sorry."

"No. I am. Wow. That's happening, isn't it?" She looked down to my, you know, my . . . umm . . . *space invader*.

I quickly covered the front of my jeans with both hands. She started laughing and I joined in, knowing full well that even in the dim moonlight she could see how red my face had turned.

"It's my fault. I shouldn't have fallen asleep. Hell, I shouldn't have even stayed."

"I love you."

"I think Jeremy Pratt does too."

"I'm sorry, Cate. I really am. I just . . . this is so hard."

Then we both laughed, and she sat down in her car and let the door hang open. She peered up at me with those eyes she used to get just before she cried. I felt like shit. I deserved to feel that way too.

"I'll talk to you when I get back, okay? Can we just talk when I get back?"

"Yeah. Merry Christmas."

• • •

They say you can fall out of love with someone just as easily as you fall into it. But is that also the case when the person you love dies? Do you have to fall out of love with them so you can fall in love with someone else? If that's the way it works, then I could understand why Cate was taking her time, and I could at least respect her for not telling me something just because I wanted to hear it. You don't have to tell someone you love them if they already know it in every molecule of their body. I'd known it in two bodies, and no matter what anyone says, it isn't something that goes away.

Christmas Eve arrived quickly, and I still hadn't seen Hatton since that day at the arcade—only talked to him on the phone a few times. After my little freak-out I wasn't sure I could blame him for keeping his distance. I think maybe the Travis Coates Experience isn't all that entertaining when it gets too serious. I'd basically tweaked out like a junkie in front of him and, well, I'm sure it wasn't too fun to watch. Leave it up to me to suck the fun out of a building full of games and prizes.

And Kyle? Kyle had been busy with a mess of his own. After coming out to his parents and sister had been such a relief to him, he decided he'd just go ahead and tell a few college friends of his too. But his roommate, Evan, hadn't reacted the way he'd expected. He said it gave him the creeps and asked Kyle to move out. You always hear about these kinds of people—parents and friends who can't accept someone being gay and who treat them like they're less human because of it—but listening to Kyle talk about it made me feel so angry and defeated. Now he was staying with his parents until he could find a new place.

"You know what it's like, Travis?" Kyle said to me on the phone. "It's like being in the only group of people still left that it's okay to make fun of . . . that it's okay to call unnatural."

"Not the only group," I said.

"Oh. Right. I guess you *do* know what it's like."

"Well, technically mine was by choice. I chose to be a . . . whatever I am."

"Cryogenic American?" Kyle said.

"Exactly. Know what, man? Screw that Evan guy. People like him are few and far between, right? Maybe try to see it that way. At least he's in the minority."

"There's more of them than you think," he said. "Audrey's pissed because her boyfriend keeps telling her they should pray for me."

"Pray for you to do what?"

"I dunno. Change? Pray me straight. I tried that. It doesn't work."

"That Matt Braynard's a tool anyway. He's always walking around school like he owns the place."

"It really bothered Audrey. Said she might break up with him."

"Well, it sounds like Hatton's prayers were answered," I said.

• • •

My parents managed to make Christmas morning in my house feel the same as it always had. We had the fireplace on, and there were twinkling lights wrapped all around the tree and down the rails of the staircase. Mom even got up early to make pancakes shaped like Santa heads (yes, I see the irony). And Dad? He was on the back patio having his one recurring Christmas gift from my mom: a single smoke from a pipe he'd had since before they met. He'd promised to quit before they got married, and she'd promised that he'd get to smoke one pipe-full on every Christmas morning for the rest of their lives. Outside.

Mom would always tell me not to be tempted by my father's bad habits, and we'd always laugh and eventually eat our pancakes around the kitchen counter. I could smell the sweet smoke soaked into his clothes and, in a weird way, that's how I expected every Christmas for the rest of my life to smell. Not like holly or peppermint or ginger-bread. But like my dad's tobacco.

After breakfast we sat on the floor like always, and my mom passed out the gifts from under the tree. We had a long-standing rule that everyone in our small family would give only two gifts, big or small, expensive or cheap, to everyone else. Once our four were lying in front of us, we took turns, youngest to oldest, opening them one by one.

"Feels like socks," I said, unwrapping the soft package.

It wasn't socks. It was a green and black scarf. I'd actually asked for this after seeing it in a store one day. I wasn't even trying to hide my scar anymore—there was no use—but I'd grown accustomed to wearing all the ones Mom had bought me. I immediately and expertly tied it around my neck. Next it was Mom's turn. She started with one that I'd gotten her and she was tearing up before she'd even gotten all the paper off it. She paused.

"I don't even want this if it's a million dollars," she said. "If I can just have you here every Christmas till I'm dead, then I don't need anything else."

"That's nice, Mom. But I didn't keep the receipt," I joked.

"Travis! I love it! I absolutely love it!" She held the terry-cloth bathrobe to her chest and then out again, examining the embroidered initials on the front.

For Dad's turn he chose a gift from me as well. When he opened it to find a black T-shirt with a large green Space Invaders alien on the front, he started laughing.

"This'll show those cherry-chomping sons of bitches." Man, my dad really hated Pac-Man.

When I opened the first gift from my dad and saw that it was a skateboard, I was sort of stunned. I hadn't told them about that day at Hatton's.

"How'd you know?"

"I was clueless what to get you, so I stole Hatton's number out of your phone and asked him. It was the first thing he suggested. Will that one work okay?"

"Four wheels and a deck. It's perfect."

Mom opened a sweater from Dad, and then he did the same from her.

"We went shopping for these together," she said. "When you get old, it's just easier that way. Okay, Travis. Now open mine."

I'd guessed that it was a book, but I was wrong. It was actually a tablet loaded with games, movies, music, and TV shows. I was speechless. I hadn't even seen one in person, only on television a few times.

"Mom, this is . . . wow. So cool. How much was this?"

"Don't ruin this for me." She held up her phone to take a photo of me holding it.

After they each opened their other gifts from me—a gift certificate to a spa for Mom and a book about Bob Dylan for Dad—it was time to open my last present. It was from my dad, and it was money. I knew that much. One of his gifts was always an envelope with two hundred dollars inside. But this time he handed me a stack of five envelopes, each with my name written on the front in the exact same way.

"What's this?" I asked.

"Couldn't quite break the tradition after you left," he said. "I thought if you ever came back, you'd find a good use for it."

"So this is . . . a thousand bucks? Dad, come on. That's ridiculous. What am I going to do with all this? Here, take this back. I can't take this . . ."

"Hell, I haven't gotten to do this for a long time. Merry Christmas, Travis," he said, not even pretending to listen to me. "Promise to use it for something fun, okay?"

Christmas night ended in the most perfect way possible. Around the time my dad and I were beginning our third or fourth consecutive viewing of A Christmas Story, there was a loud knock at the door. I opened it up to find Kyle and Hatton standing there with huge smiles on their faces. They said I had two minutes to get my shoes and coat on and meet them in the driveway.

"Resistance is futile," Hatton added in a deep voice, slowly backing away into the darkness outside.

I was already shivering by the time I got from my front door to Kyle's truck, so when I was inside, I pressed my cheek right up against one of the dashboard heating vents. Hatton had crawled into the backseat, and instead of saying anything about the arcade, he simply reached up and patted me three times really hard on the back and said, "Travis Coates!"

"Where are you taking me?"

"Secret." Kyle never took his eyes off the road.

"Hatton, tell me," I said.

"He's in charge," he said.

It took us about twenty minutes down the interstate to get to wherever we were going. It ended up being a neighborhood, not unlike the ones we all lived in, but with a little less light on the streets and a little more junk in each front yard. I started getting anxious when we pulled into a driveway and Kyle turned off his ignition.

"I knew it," I said. "You guys are murdering me. Damn it."

"Why would we murder you in a stranger's house?" Hatton asked.

"It's the perfect crime, really," Kyle said. "Drive some-one to a random stranger's house, kill them, disappear. Confuse the hell out of everyone."

"Okay. No, but really. What's going on?" I was looking out every window, not knowing what to expect.

I followed Kyle and Hatton to the front door, and we waited after knocking three times. Eventually a little kid holding a toy gun opened the door. He was wearing Spider-Man underwear and nothing else.

"Mom!" he yelled, running away from us.

Kyle stepped inside first and we followed. The small living room was covered in red and green wrapping paper. It was a Christmas war zone. There were toys everywhere, some put together and some not even partially. There were other kids too, at least three of them. And one teen-ager with half-open eyes, sitting on the couch playing a video game. I wondered how many houses all over town looked exactly this way inside . . . one big simultaneous holiday hangover. The present-less Christmas tree made me sad. They always did.

Finally, a woman in a nightgown stepped out from a darkened hallway and gave us a silent stare. Then she put her hands up quickly and said in a high-pitched voice, "Oh! Yes. The listing!"

"Forget we were coming?" Kyle asked.

"I guess I did. You know how Christmas goes. It's been crazy here all day. Did you remember our deal?" She grinned.

"Yes, ma'am," Kyle said.

"Boys, get up and come over here for a picture," she said loudly toward the couch.

"Do we have to?" the one playing the video game asked.

"Yes, you have to! I'm framing this and putting it up on the wall. Hell, we might use it for our Christmas card next year."

She picked up the Spider-Man–underwear kid and held him on her hip while the other boys got up and stood in front of the Christmas tree. She walked over and stood beside them.

"Well, come on, then," she said, waving me over.

I looked at Kyle and Hatton, who both shrugged, and walked over to stand with the family. She pulled at her sons' arms to move them in closer and started combing the tallest boy's messy hair with her hand.

"Okay. Ready."

"Everybody smile," Kyle said, holding up his phone and trying not to laugh.

"Cheese," I said.

When we were all done, the kids took their places back on the couch, and the woman started walking toward the kitchen.

"Okay, let's go out back and I'll show you where they are."

"Where *what* are?" I whispered to Hatton. He ignored me. He was busy dodging things scattered all over the floor.

We followed her through the kitchen and out the back door. She flipped on a light and the entire backyard, which had even more junk in it than the front, lit up with a dull, dirty yellow. I looked up at the porch light to see hundreds of dead bugs collected in its glass. My mother would've insisted on cleaning it out for them. She wouldn't have taken no for an answer. I just cringed and kept walking.

We got to the back corner of the yard, and the woman opened up the heavy metal door of a rusted shed. Kyle helped her prop it open with a half-broken cinder block while Hatton looked at me with this really excited expression.

"There you go, boys. If you can haul 'em, you can have 'em."

She pulled a string that was dangling down from the ceiling, and the little metal shed lit up much brighter than I'd expected. And right there in the center was a set of two theater seats with red cushions standing perfectly on faded green metal legs that led up to dark wooden armrests. They looked nearly identical to the ones I'd had before, except there wasn't a single wad of gum on either one.

"Merry Christmas, buddy," Kyle said, walking over and sitting down in one of the seats.

"Boom! Surprised?" Hatton held up his hand and gave me a high five.

I knew it was possible that I might cry in front of them and in front of this woman who I'd never seen before in my life. But I didn't. I just watched as they both lifted the seats and started carrying them across the yard and then around to Kyle's truck. They loaded them into the back, and Kyle used a couple of ropes to tie them down so they wouldn't fall over or slide around on the way home. Inside the truck I was afraid to say much because I had that lumpy feeling in my throat, half due to amazement and half to trying not to blubber like a baby.

When we'd gotten them safely up to my bedroom and in their rightful place, in the corner by the window, facing my TV, I sat down in one of the seats and looked up at my two best friends. They wanted me to say something. Thank you, maybe. But that didn't seem like enough, I guess. Hatton threw himself onto the bed and grabbed the remote control off my nightstand. He tossed it over to me. Kyle sat down beside me and stared across the room at the black screen.

"Yeah," Kyle said. "This feels just about right."

"It's perfect," I said. "Better, even."

"Better than what?" Hatton asked.

"Than before."

I suddenly realized I hadn't gotten either of them anything. Here they'd obviously schemed in secret to do this amazing thing for me, to make me feel at least a little bit normal in my own room again, and I hadn't done a thing for them. I was suddenly overwhelmed with guilt, so I stood up quickly and said I had to pee. I didn't.

My mom and dad's door was shut, so I was careful to be extra quiet when I walked down the stairs and into the guest bedroom. I went into the closet and rustled around in a few boxes, but I didn't see what I was looking for. I wasn't all that sure what it even looked like anymore, but I knew it had to still be there, somewhere.

And then I saw it. Right in the back corner of the closet on the floor, covered by a couple of old throw pillows. I grabbed it and crept back up the stairs and into my bedroom. I held the green tin cookie jar in both hands and walked right up to Kyle and Hatton.

"Merry Christmas, guys. You wanna see something weird?"

CHAPTER TWENTY-EIGHT

SOMETHING WEIRD

They stared down into the cookie jar, both speechless and not moving. I thought they might even be holding their breath, afraid, perhaps, that one little stream of air could cause the ashes to explode all over the room. Hatton couldn't help himself and eventually started easing one finger into the jar. Kyle slapped his hand away.

"Why are these here, Travis? Oh my God."

"I think my parents are having a hard time figuring out what to do with them."

"This is the creepiest and coolest thing I've ever experienced in my entire life. Thank you, Travis." Hatton went to stick his finger in once more, and Kyle, once again, slapped it away without a word.

"What're you gonna do with them?" Kyle asked.

"Well, I was hoping maybe you guys could help me figure that out."

"I can't believe they didn't toss them out or something." Hatton leaned down, almost putting his face against the top of the jar as he spoke.

"Me neither. But they don't know I have these. So mum's the word."

"We should probably find something else to put them in, huh?" Kyle raised an eyebrow and looked around the room.

"I guess. But what'll we replace them with?"

"I have an idea," Hatton said. "But we can't do it today. Actually, I'll need a few days, maybe, but it'll work."

"What will work?" I put the lid back on the jar and set it on my desk.

"We can't leave it empty and we can't just fill it with dirt or something. That's real ash in there. I figure your folks are keeping it around for some reason. Say they look inside and find us out. You don't want to deal with that, right?"

"Right," I said.

"Right. So give me a couple of days and I'll get you some replacement ashes."

"You gonna have a bonfire somewhere?" Kyle asked him.

"My dad's a vet."

"Oh no," I said. "Hatton, I don't think—"

"It'll work. Trust me. They won't be able to tell the difference."

They both left well after midnight, and I quietly put the jar back in its hiding spot downstairs. If I'm being totally honest, I should tell you that the ashes really didn't mean anything to me. I wasn't looking at them as some haunting symbol of my former self. They weren't like the score at the arcade—they had nothing to do with my old life. I didn't feel the need to do something with them, to find them some special final resting place. That wouldn't change anything about my situation. But to Kyle and Hatton, it was different. It's like they instinctively needed to rid them from my life. That's the thing about having friends like the two of them—sometimes they know what you need way before you realize it yourself.

The next night Cate called me on her way over. She said we had to clear the air and get some things straight. I knew that couldn't be a good sign, but still, it was a chance to be alone in a car with her and I'd take it, no matter the consequences.

I met her in the driveway, and it felt a little like she was mad, like maybe she'd been rehearsing some long speech to deliver to me on her ride over.

"You okay?"

"I'm fine. I just . . . we have to talk about what happened the other day."

"Well, we don't *have* to. I mean, we could just chock it up to science if you want."

"That's not funny," she said, trying not to smile.

"Okay . . ."

"How was Christmas?" she asked, punching me lightly on the arm.

"It was good."

"Your mom and dad must've been over the moon, I'm sure."

"Over the moon? What're you, fifty?" I laughed.

"Shut up."

"They seemed happy, yeah," I said. "It's starting to feel normal again. Everything is sort of falling back into place, I guess."

"About that," she said. "I told Turner we've been hanging out. I had to. He thought it was just the one time, but I couldn't keep lying."

"What'd he say?"

"He was a little pissed at first. Of course he was. I would be too. Then he was glad I'd told him. He said if it was important to me that I see you, that we stay friends, then he was okay with it."

"Really?"

"Yeah, Travis. He's a really nice guy. I told you that. He just wants what's best for me."

"That's all I want too."

"I know. But the other night. You can't just do things like that. You can't just come at me like that and expect things not to be weird. You just came back *from the dead*, Travis, and as much as I'd like to put myself in your shoes and imagine what that feels like, I can't. I just know there are certain things you can't control that you just have to learn to deal with. The world isn't going to end if you don't get exactly what you want. Trust me, I know."

"How do you know?" I was stunned at this suddenly serious tone she was using with me. Maybe a few days away had given her time to figure out what I was up to.

"Because until I lost you, every little thing seemed so important to me. Then you were gone, and I was left wondering why I'd given a shit about any of it. For me, the world became something completely different, and I had to just deal with it and learn to get over it."

"How can you expect me to hear you say things like that and not feel the way I feel about you, Cate?"

"I don't know, Travis. That's what I'm trying to figure out. Turner wants to meet you before we can hang out again. That's cool with you, right? I don't ever want to be the kind of person who keeps secrets from my husband."

Husband? Wow. This was the first time I'd ever heard her say it. It took all I could do not to open the door and roll out onto the pavement.

She pulled down my street again, having just made a long loop around the block. As we got close to my house, I saw my dad walking out to his car and getting inside. It was eight in the evening.

"Hey, hang back a second, okay?" I said to her.

"Why?"

"Just . . . hang back, okay? Where can he be going this late?"

"Pick up dinner?"

"No. We already ate. Follow him."

"Travis, we are not following your dad."

"Please. You and I both know that his weird late nights are not okay. Something is up. I have to find out."

So we followed him. And maybe Cate's five years without me were a little more exciting than she'd let on, because I swear she was a pro at this. She even let him go through a stoplight or two and caught back up, so he wouldn't notice us. After we tailed him for about ten minutes, he turned into an apartment complex called the Villas at Red Oak. It was a fairly generic place, one of those two-level faux brick and aluminum siding buildings with exterior doors that all look identical except for their shiny gold numbers.

"Shit," Cate said, almost whispering.

"Pull in over there. I don't think he'll see us."

We parked on the other side of the wrought-iron fence that surrounded the swimming pool and separated it from the parking lot. The pool was covered by a large gray tarp that had a puddle of dirty water collected in its center, making it sag. We peered through the fence to where my dad had parked and saw him walking up the metal and concrete stairs to the second level. Neither of us said a word. I imagined it twenty times before it could happen, some strange young woman opening the door and greeting him with a kiss or a hug or both. Maybe, I thought, she'd take his hand and lead him inside, and I'd never be able to look at him again without wanting to cry.

He eventually stopped at one of the green doors. I made sure to remember it was the seventh one from the left. Then he took a key out of his pocket, turned the lock, walked inside, and shut the door behind him. He never saw us. But that didn't matter. We saw him. I saw him.

"I'm sorry, Travis," Cate said.

"What am I gonna do?" I asked.

What was there to do? My father, the best man I ever knew, the most honest one too, was doing something I'd never thought in a million years he would do to my mother. And all I could wonder was how long he'd been doing this and how long he'd keep it up if I didn't say anything. A big part of me wanted to call my mom right then. I thought it might be easier that way, if she just caught him in the act and then knew exactly why things had been so weird, why he'd been working late and on the weekends. But I couldn't. I couldn't let her see it, and I knew I had to calm down before I could try to see it for myself. So I told Cate to take me home, and I cried the whole way. And she never said a word. She only gripped my hand that wasn't really mine and listened to the sound of Jeremy Pratt's heart breaking.

CHAPTER TWENTY-NINE

HEART BREAKING

How I managed to go a whole week without saying anything about what I'd seen, what I knew, is something I'm
still not sure I can explain. They say when you're in a
state of shock, your brain has a way of detaching you from
the world and everything going on around you. They say
that once it's over, you feel like you can't remember huge
chunks of time from days and days of your life. That's
not unlike how I was feeling the day I had to go back to
school. It was January 2, a Wednesday. I remember that
because everyone was complaining all day long about
starting back in the middle of the week.

"They know we aren't gonna do anything today, right?"
Hatton whispered to me in class.

I didn't answer. I was tapping my pencil on my desk
and thinking about my dad turning that key and walking
into that apartment. I was replaying it in slow motion,

zoomed in. I could almost hear the sound of the key as it scraped against its matching metallic ridges.

"Travis? You okay?" he whispered again, poking at the back of my shoulder.

"I'm fine."

I hadn't whispered. I'd said it out loud as if the entire class were part of our conversation. Everyone turned around and looked at me, and Mrs. Lasetter stopped mid-sentence and glared right into my eyes.

"What was that, Travis?"

"He said he's fine," this guy named Adam Murphy said from the front of the room.

I didn't say anything. I just nodded my head and looked right at her. I wanted her to get angry. I wanted her to kick me out, to yell at me for interrupting the class. In the weirdest way possible, this is what I wanted more than anything right at that moment. I wanted to be separated from everyone just like my brain had been trying to do for days.

"Okay," she said before turning to the board and starting an endless scribble of equations and notes.

After class Hatton followed me all the way to my locker and then the cafeteria. We got our food and sat down without either of us speaking a word. For a few seconds we had this sort of stare-down. I speared a shriveled grape from my fruit cup and twirled my fork in front of me. He opened his carton of chocolate milk and took a sip. One of us would break first. It was only a matter of time.

"Dude, what the hell is up with you?" Hatton lost. I knew he would.

"Nothing."

"That's a lie. You've been acting weird all day."

"It's nothing. Really. Let's talk about something else, okay?"

"Okay. Here's something: I've got some ideas for your ashes."

"Oh yeah?"

"Yeah. I was reading all about these crazy things people do with them. There's some pretty bizarre shit."

"Like what?"

"Okay. For instance, you can pay to have your ashes sent into space. Which is pretty cool. But it's, like, a thousand bucks."

"Pass."

"Okay. Then there's some people who can do a fireworks display using your ashes."

"That's disgusting. What if it falls down on people?"

"True. I didn't think about that."

"Yeah. Or it falls down into a cow pasture and the cows eat it, and then people are having Travis Coates Ash steak the next week. No, thanks."

"What about having them pressed into a vinyl record? You can put whatever songs you want on it or even record a message. I thought that one was pretty cool."

"That's the dumbest thing I've ever heard."

"See, the problem here is that you're alive. So, really,

you don't need to be memorialized in any special way, I guess. But I think we should find something to do with them, right?"

"For sure. I can't have them in the house with me. It's like saving a severed limb or something."

"How willing would you be to get a tattoo?"

"Not very. Why?"

"They can grind up the ashes with tattoo ink and then . . . well, they'll be with you forever."

"Wow. No. You can get one, though. You have my permission to get a tattoo made out of my ashes. Go for it."

"Don't dare me, Travis."

"I'm not kidding. I'll pay for it."

"I'm scared of needles."

"Sure you are. Sure, sure."

"Okay. Last one. I think this may be the winner, too. There's a company that will use the carbon in your ashes to make two hundred and fifty pencils. They'll even put a message on the side. Imagine, we can give everyone we know a little bit of old Travis!"

"I don't hate it," I said. "But I also don't know why anyone would want a pencil made out of an incinerated disease-ridden body either."

"I'll keep looking. We'll find something appropriate."

"Maybe we should think more . . . globally. We could mail little Ziplock Baggies of ash to people all around the world and have them flush it down their toilets."

"Now you're just being crazy, Travis."

As we began discussing the difference between "crazy" and "creative," Matt Braynard approached our table and sat down beside Hatton. He even put one arm around Hatton's shoulders, which made him flinch.

"Fellas," he said.

"Matt," I mustered. Hatton was silent. He was so silent, in fact, that I was afraid of what he might do.

"Can you guys hang after school for a few minutes today?"

"For what?" Hatton asked defensively.

"Well, as you know, I'm the president of the Christian Youth Club, and we've been working on a little project that I think you guys—especially you, Travis—might be interested in seeing."

"What kind of project?" I didn't trust this guy for a second. His hair was too perfect, gelled up in the front and forming a little wave to one side.

"A secret one. You'll like it. Just come by, okay, guys? It won't take long."

He got up and walked away, but not before patting Hatton really hard on the shoulders. I thought Hatton might get up and tackle him, but he didn't. He was Hatton Sharpe. His rage would have to stew internally.

"Do we go?" I asked.

"Up to you. I'd just as soon never see that guy again."

"Me neither. I say no. In fact, I have an idea."

"What?"

"Let's leave right now. I don't want to be here. This is pointless."

"You want to skip class? We have no car, Travis."

"I think Kyle's still on break for the holiday. I bet he'd come get us."

"We'll get caught. We'll get caught and I'll have to repeat sophomore year, and my life will be over."

"Hatton. Geez. If we get caught, we might get detention. We never do anything wrong. And I'll take the fall for it. We'll lie and tell them I had an emergency or something. It'll be fine."

So we didn't go to chemistry but instead walked right out the front doors and stood at the corner of the parking lot to wait on Kyle. He'd answered on the first ring, said he'd go crazy if his mom asked him another question about his "lifestyle" or what kind of boys he was into, and that he'd be glad to assist two teenagers in breaking the law. Not one single person who walked by us in the parking lot asked us why we weren't in class. Kids like us, you know, we just looked like we wouldn't do anything we weren't supposed to do.

"Gentlemen," Kyle said once we were inside his truck. "Adventure awaits us."

"Where we going?" Hatton was still nervous, gazing back toward the school as we drove away.

"Well, I'd suggest the arcade, but . . ." Kyle rolled his eyes, smiling.

"Funny," I said. "I know a place."

I gave him the address for the Villas at Red Oak, but I wouldn't tell either of them why we were going. When we eventually pulled into the apartment complex, they both seemed really confused and pretty let down.

"This doesn't seem fun at all," Hatton said.

"Is this where Cate's living now?" Kyle asked.

"No. Look, guys. I've got something to tell you."

"Oh God," Kyle said, his tone one that I could remember well. I'd told him really bad news before, and I immediately felt terrible for misleading him.

"No, no. Nothing bad. I mean, it's bad but not for you, I guess."

"What is it? Why are we here?" Hatton was looking out all the windows like he'd still get caught skipping class across town.

"Last week Cate and I were driving up to my house, and we saw my dad leaving . . . and we followed him."

"You followed your dad?" Kyle asked.

"Cate? You're back with Cate?"

"No," Kyle and I said at the same time.

"Just let me finish, okay? We followed him and we ended up here. Now, I know I've talked to both of you about my dad's weirdness lately. Like, the late nights and the working on weekends and everything. Well, I think I figured out what's been going on."

"Is your dad a serial killer?" Hatton asked.

"Hatton!" we yelled.

"Cate and I sat here and watched him walk all the way up those stairs over there, take out a key, and walk into that apartment." I pointed toward the door.

"Shit," Kyle said.

"I'm confused," Hatton said. "Why's your dad have a key . . . oh."

"Yeah," I said. "And I need you guys to wait here for a few minutes while I go up there and settle this."

"What?"

"My dad's car is right there." I pointed to his maroon SUV, which was parked in the exact spot as one week earlier. "He's up there right now, in the middle of a work-day, probably doing something I do not want to see, but I can't let him keep this up."

"Are you sure, Travis?" Kyle said. "Maybe you should talk to your mom first."

"Nope. This is the only way. You guys just wait here."

So I walked up the metal and concrete stairs, my hand gripping the railing. I came to the seventh green door from the left and stopped in my tracks. I turned around to look down at Kyle and Hatton, who were watching through the front windshield of the black truck. I thought at least if I had to lose someone that day, then I still had these two people. Then I braced myself, planted my feet in front of the door, and knocked. And I knocked hard. It couldn't be ignored or missed. It meant business.

The door swung open, and Dad stood before me in a light blue T-shirt and khaki pants. His face was scruffy from a few days of not shaving, and his stance was weak, shoulders folded in a little with the realization of what was happening. His glossy eyes were fixed on mine, and his mouth was hanging half-open.

"Travis, what're you doing here?"

"You answer first." My voice was stern and cold.

"You should come inside." He stood back, opening the door wider.

"No. I don't want to come in *there*. Are you fucking crazy?" I was yelling now.

"Travis. I think you're confused. Come inside, okay? Come inside and we'll talk."

"Where is she? Is she here? Is she in there? I want to see her. What's her name?"

"There is no her, okay?"

"No her?"

"I'm the only one here. Now come inside."

Confused, frustrated, and freezing, I followed him into the warmth of the apartment and took a seat on a gray sofa. The place was sparsely furnished with bare walls and empty coffee and side tables. A large TV had muted football playing on it. My dad took a seat on the edge of a recliner that rocked back a little, making this tiny squeaking sound that would've made me laugh if this had happened at any other moment in time.

"Please explain what this is," I whispered, afraid of what would come next.

"We were going to tell you." He rested his elbows on the tops of his knees and leaned forward.

"Tell me what?"

"Everything, Travis. We were going to tell you everything when you woke up, but it didn't seem right just yet."

"If you don't tell me the thing you won't tell me, then I'm going to freak out." I got louder with every word.

"We're divorced, Travis. Your mom and I have been divorced for about three years."

Now he covered his face completely, like hiding from me would make this easier or make me disappear. I just looked down at the floor and tried to understand what he'd said, tried to figure out how it could even be a possibility.

"We were going to tell you."

"Seems like it." A cold tear rolled down my cheek.

"They told us not to," he said. "Dr. Saranson—he said to keep it a secret for a while, just until you'd adjusted to being back. Your mom almost told you, right when you woke up, but I stopped her. I was so scared to break your heart, Travis. She was too. She knew it would just make it worse to wait."

"Three years? *Three* years, Dad?"

"We tried, Travis. We tried so hard. Therapy, church, relationship books. We did it all. Nothing seemed to help."

"It's my fault, then? I die and you two can't stand each other anymore?"

"It's not your fault. That's not how it works."

"Then tell me this: Would you still be together if I hadn't died? Would you?"

"I can't answer that, Travis. You know I can't answer that, and what good would it do if I could?"

"How could you do this to me?" I stood up, started to pace. I couldn't look at him. "Damn it!"

"We did it *for* you, Travis. Please sit down. Please just calm down and take a seat, okay?"

"You know what? To hell with both of you!" I stormed toward the door.

"Don't leave like this. We can talk about this like adults."

"I'm *not* an adult! I'm a fucking kid! I *should* be an adult, but I'm not!"

"Listen to me!" he yelled right back. "Just let me show you something."

"Okay. Fine. What? Show me."

He led me down the hallway to a closed bedroom door and stopped for a second before opening it. He looked right at me, that kind of look you give someone when they're about to see something that will change them forever, and then he swung the door open

And inside was my entire bedroom. It was exactly the way I'd left it, plaid wallpaper and all, only across town and in this new apartment, in this place where my father secretly lived, where he'd made a new life for himself. I couldn't speak, couldn't form words with my lips or move my tongue. I wasn't certain I was still breathing. I was frozen in place, just looking in at all the stuff. Every poster, every stupid torn-out magazine page that I'd sticky-tacked to the wall. It was all there. The bed was the cherry-wood top bunk only with the bookshelf beneath it filled with the same hardcovers from my childhood— Hardy Boys first editions, *Treasure Island*, two copies of *Tuck Everlasting*. The theater seats were in their corner, and my print of *The Great Wave off Kanagawa* hung right by the windows. There were even the same exact curtains as in my old room, with the same hole torn in the bottom right corner where I once got them caught in the vacuum cleaner. Bedspread, pillowcases, the lamp on the nightstand—they were all mine and they had been placed here with strategy and care, replicating a time before I was sick, before my illness changed the way I lived, before it changed the way we all lived.

"This was part of the problem." He walked over and sat on the bed. "I've had a hard time letting things go."

"I don't understand, Dad. Why wouldn't you bring this stuff home? Why am I sleeping in a new bed in a roomful of stuff that isn't mine?"

"Because she doesn't know, Travis."

"Oh." I walked over to the closet, opened it to see all my clothes—my jeans, my shirts, my favorite jacket.

"I kept it all in storage for a while—when we were still trying to work things out."

"Who left who?" I asked quietly.

"I was a mess, Travis. I can't say I blame her."

"I'm not even sure what to say, Dad. I don't really know what's going on right now."

"I'm so sorry. I'm sorry it happened this way. Hell, I'm sorry it happened at all."

"Do you want her back? Is that why you didn't let her tell me? Why you waited?"

"No, Travis. I know that's not going to happen. Your mom and I love each other, we really do. And we're friends—we talk a few times a week, have for years. It's just one of those things that happens. I can't try to explain it because I'm not sure why it happens either."

"Like it is with Cate," I said. "Only I can't let go of it."

"You'll find a way, Travis. You'll have to."

"My head is going to explode." I took a seat on the floor. "This room, Dad. This is . . . weird."

"It's the only thing I knew to do. I never even come in here. I just open the door every now and then and look inside, imagine you sitting on the bed listening to music or inviting me in to watch an old movie."

"That's so sad." I was crying.

"Losing you was the worst thing I could ever imagine happening. I can't do that again, you know I can't go through that again. She can't either."

"Let's hope you don't have to."

"Can I tell you something else?"

"It can't get any worse," I said.

"I lost my job six months ago. Your mom doesn't know yet. Please let me tell her."

"What'd you do?"

"Nothing. Things change. The company grew faster

than I could keep up with, and they replaced me with some young asshole fresh out of college."

"Their arcades suck now anyway."

Dad held one hand down and helped me up. There was no emotional embrace or anything, but he let his grip linger for a few seconds and he nodded, looking into my eyes. I walked out of the room, amazed I hadn't started having another panic attack, and I didn't stop walking until I was opening the door to Kyle's truck and jumping back into the front seat. They didn't say anything. They were watching my dad up on the second floor looking down at us.

"I need to go home, please."

"Everything okay?" Hatton asked quietly.

"Everything is not okay."

CHAPTER THIRTY

E V E R Y T H I N G
IS   NOT   OKAY

By the time we pulled into my driveway, I'd told Kyle and Hatton everything. Kyle was astonished that he hadn't found out about the divorce somehow, and Hatton was too preoccupied by my dad's creepy bedroom museum of death to talk about anything else.

"You want us to come in with you?" Kyle asked in the driveway.

"I'm not going in there." Hatton was shaking his head. "Sorry. I mean, I think this is all you, man."

"He's right," I said. "I'll see you guys later. Thanks."

Mom was standing in the middle of the living room when I walked inside. Dad must've called her because she was pale, and her eyes were bloodshot. She looked at me like I was that doctor who first told us I was sick, with an expression so lifeless and haunting that no amount of good expressions or smiles or laughing could ever erase it from my memory.

"Travis, I—"

"You lied to me."

"Yes. I lied to you. Your father lied to you. We lied."

"And Grandma and Aunt Cindy? They all—"

"Yes. They lied for us. It wasn't okay to ask them to do that, but they did it anyway."

"Shit."

"Can you just sit down? Can we just talk for a little while?"

"What's there to say, Mom? Everything is so wrong."

"But it's not wrong, Travis. Look, you are *here*. Every science book on Earth says you should be dead and gone, and you are standing right here in our living room. This is complicated."

"Why'd you leave him?" I sat down because I was afraid I'd eventually collapse if I didn't.

"I want to tell you what happened after you went away, okay, Travis?" She sat down to face me.

"Okay."

"When you died or got frozen or whatever, we weren't sure exactly what to do. We talked to a therapist, we got rid of your things, we even thought about adopting a kid from Russia or China. But nothing worked because there was always, above all else, this silent and heavy shred of hope that you'd come back, that they'd find a way to bring you back and we'd be okay again. But a few months went by, then a year, and we heard nothing. I called to ask how far they were from saving you, and all I ever got were vague answers and impossible time estimates. The best they ever told me, after one year, was that maybe, if things worked out okay, then maybe we'd survive into our eighties or nineties and possibly be able to see you again before we died. And we knew it was crazy—the whole thing. Every part of me believed that when we said good-bye to you, that was it. But then after you really were gone, it was different. It wasn't so easy to just accept it, you know? And there was that small chance that it wasn't permanent, and that got so easy to cling to. So we ate healthy and we stopped drinking caffeine and alcohol. We exercised every day and took fistfuls of vitamins because we were determined that no matter what we did, no matter what our lives became, we would live to see you again, live to make sure that you would have a real life."

"Congratulations," I said.

"Let me finish, damn it. Sorry." She was crying. But she kept talking. "Then another year went by and we heard even less. We started talking to other families whose relatives had volunteered for this, and that just made it worse, made it seem even more hopeless. Eventually we saw a grief counselor because we could hardly talk to each other anymore. He told us that as long as we kept holding on to the idea that you'd come back, we'd never be able to move on or get over losing you. He told us we were sentencing ourselves to a life of perpetual mourning, a life where we'd feel like you were dying every single day over and over again."

"So you split up and everything was fine until I came back?" I wasn't playing fair. I knew that.

"We tried, but it was obvious that we were moving at very different paces. We just couldn't quite sync back up after you'd gone, Travis."

They say most marriages end after a couple loses a child. My parents were only doing their part to make sure the statistic held true. How could I blame them? How could I be angry at them when I wasn't there to see what it was like? Leaving had been so easy because I thought I was doing it for them. I thought letting go would give them their lives back. But it just messed things up even worse. As I looked at my mom and her sad eyes, I knew I'd been a selfish asshole. I never thought I'd come back, but I gave up anyway. What a coward. I was so scared and so tired that I let the idea of leaving for them overshadow the fact that I was really doing it all for me.

CHAPTER THIRTY-ONE

ALL   FOR   ME

After the talk with my mom I called Dad to apologize, and he asked if I wanted him to come home. I said he *was* home and that there was no reason to keep up their charade any longer just for my benefit. I told him I'd come over the next day and we'd talk about where to go from there.

I tried to sleep, but it wasn't working too well. I was worried about both of them, I guess. I was worried that they were doing the same thing I was—staring up at the ceiling in their lonely beds and thinking about everything we'd been through. They lied, sure, and I was still pissed about it and probably wouldn't get over it too quickly, but they hadn't given up. There was no reason in the world to think this crazy shit would ever work, but they tried anyway. These two people had waited on something impossible because they couldn't stand not to.

I'd tried to call Cate all afternoon, but she never answered or came over or anything. I wasn't sure what was going on, so I eventually gave up and went to bed. I lay there looking around at all the stuff in my room that wasn't mine. It couldn't be mine, because that was all sitting silent in a dark room across town, waiting for its ghost to come back and haunt it someday.

Mom drove me to school the next morning, and I don't have to tell you it was a bit uncomfortable for both of us. I wondered if Dad had told her about his job, if maybe the previous day's events had prompted him to come clean about all his secrets. I wouldn't dare tell her, though. The two of them had enough to deal with all on their own.

"Did Chloe and all the other cousins know too?" I asked in the car.

"No," she said quietly. "We only told a few people. Our friends know, but they're so few and far between that we knew it wasn't much of a risk."

"I can't believe I didn't figure it out."

"Your poor father's been sleeping on the floor of my bedroom for three months. I half think he wanted to get caught with all his late nights."

"I'd like to say I feel sorry for him."

"Travis, don't be too hard on your dad, okay? I know this seems bad, but he's much better than he's been in a long time."

"Yes, ma'am."

"You need a ride after school or you planning on skipping out early again?" she asked, suspicion on her face.

"Sorry. I had a mission."

In class that morning Matt Braynard passed me a note. It read: *Where were you yesterday, dude?* I crumpled it up and shoved it into my backpack and never looked his way for the entire hour. After class he blocked the door so I couldn't escape him.

"Look, Matt. I'm sure your project is nice and all, but I really have a lot going on right now."

"Five minutes, Travis. Give us five minutes. Come by Conference Room B in the library at lunchtime, okay? Bring Hatton if you want."

I'll admit that my curiosity, at that point, was pretty piqued. I told Hatton in geometry that we had to go check it out or we'd never hear the end of it from Matt. He agreed, with a pretty sour look on his face, and we headed that way when the bell rang. Audrey Hagler was standing at the door to Conference Room B in the far back corner of the library. She was smiling a huge smile and gave me a hug when I walked up. She said a polite hello to Hatton and pushed him off with one hand as he tried to wrap his arms around her.

"What's this about anyway?" I asked her.

"You'll see. Come inside."

She opened the door and there were ten or so members of the Christian Youth Club standing in a circle and holding hands.

"Okay, guys," Matt spoke loudly. "Thank you so much for coming. We have something to show you."

"I'm Jewish!" Hatton yelled. "I'm just putting that out there so it's clear. Okay? Okay. There."

"Okay," Matt said. "And I'm Lutheran!" he yelled with a fist in the air. The room filled with laughter.

"Travis," Matt continued. "And Hatton. We've been working on a little project for a few weeks now, and we decided over Christmas break that maybe it was time to show you."

"Well," Hatton began, "this is officially terrifying."

"Hatton, stop," Audrey said.

"Mr. Franklin said it would be okay," Matt continued.

"Said what would be okay?" I asked.

"Mr. Franklin? The counselor?" Hatton added.

"Yeah," Matt said. "It was his idea, mostly."

"What was his idea?" I asked.

"We should pray first," one girl said from the circle. "We start all of our meetings with prayer."

"Please bow your heads," Matt said.

I looked over at Hatton and he had his head lowered, his eyes closed, and one hand gripping Audrey's. He may have been Jewish, but I knew his true religion was girls, especially ones like Audrey.

"Dear Lord," Matt prayed, "thank you for this day. Thank you for bringing us together, and thank you for bringing our new friends here to join us. Amen."

They all said "Amen" in unison as they lifted their

heads and opened their eyes. I mouthed it with them, feeling as if I'd be breaking some cosmic rule if I didn't. And they were smiling at me in this way that was so welcoming but curious, too. It wasn't how all the others looked at me, though, not like they were seeing a science experiment or the famous kid from TV. These kids didn't expect anything from me. They were just glad I was there.

"Should we show him?" Audrey asked.

"For sure," Matt said. "Let's go next door."

I followed them out of the room and watched as they filed into Conference Room A one by one. I was the last to enter and wasn't too surprised to see that they'd all made a circle around the room. What was it with these people and their circles? I should go to church more, I guess.

In the center of the room there were two big tables covered in large plastic containers. Each one had words written on top in black marker ink. The first one that caught my eye read "Kentucky-Nebraska." I knew what was inside the boxes before they could tell me.

"Letters," I said.

"What letters?" Hatton asked.

"His letters," Matt said.

"Fan mail," I said. "Been coming since I got back."

"For real?" Hatton slapped my arm.

"I told Mr. Franklin I didn't want them."

"We haven't read them or anything," Matt said. "Just so you know. We just sorted them for you."

I walked over to one of the containers and took the lid off. Inside it had cardboard dividers to separate each state. I flipped through for a few seconds before putting the lid back on and looking around at the rest of the boxes.

"You've gotten something from every state," Audrey said.

"And overseas, too," Matt said. "Those two boxes are just from other countries."

"Shit," Hatton said. "I mean, *shoot*." He held his hands out and looked around the room.

"I told him I didn't want any of these," I said.

"I know," Matt said. "But we just wanted you to know where they are when you're ready. As long as they keep sending them, we'll keep sorting them like this."

"Thanks, Matt," I said.

Audrey stood beside him now, leaning against his shoulder, and without even looking her way, Matt tilted his head to rest lightly on top of hers. Maybe that's a stupid thing to notice, but this quiet little gesture of his, especially after what he'd just said, was flipping this entire image I'd had of him in my mind. Maybe there was something behind the ego and self-righteousness after all—something surprisingly genuine.

I shook everyone's hands as they started to leave for their classes, and a few of them gave me these big smiles and told me "Good luck," even though I wasn't really sure what that meant. Maybe they were wishing me luck in trying to figure out who the hell I was supposed to be now, after coming back from the dead and all. Or maybe they were just hoping I'd be able to be brave enough to open all those letters and see what was inside.

The last one to leave was Matt Braynard. He shook my hand really firmly and gripped my left shoulder, looking right into my eyes for a few seconds before speaking.

"Just take one box home," he said. "Just one box. What can it hurt? It could end up changing your life."

When I got home that afternoon, I hid the blue plastic container of letters in the bottom of my closet and had no intention of ever opening it. If taking home a box of letters every week or so would get them to leave me alone, then I could do that. I knew they meant well, after all.

After staring at the phone for a few minutes, I tried giving Cate a call. I still hadn't spoken to her in a while, and I figured she'd be ready to see me again. But no answer. Nothing. It went straight to her voice mail, and I didn't even bother leaving a message. So I called Lawrence Ramsey instead.

"So how do we do this?" I said as soon as he answered.

"What do you mean, Travis?"

"Well, you've been back for what, like, six months longer than I have? So surely you've got some secrets for me. Maybe you know how to deal with all this a little better than I do. Things are getting pretty weird pretty quickly around here."

"Are you okay? What happened?"

"Let's see . . . where to begin. Okay. Turns out my parents are divorced. Yeah, they've been pretending to still be together since October, *for me*, you know. And Dad's got this apartment across town with this creepy Travis shrine in it. I can't even begin to explain how crazy that is. And my girlfriend is getting married to someone who is, well, not me, and everyone expects me to just move on and get over all of these things when it feels like I keep getting pianos dropped on my head over and over and over."

"Yikes," he said.

"You bet your ass, yikes." I laughed. "So tell me how to make this easier."

"Travis, it's always going to be different for us. You and me, we're always a little bit in the past, you know? It's not like that's going to change."

"Then at least tell me what it's like," I said.

"What what's like?"

"What it's like to *know* you're glad to be back. That you're alive again. You call me up and talk about being so relieved to have someone else to talk to and how hard it's been and how strange it is that everyone missed you so much. But I see you on TV and I hear your interviews, and I can tell you're happy. You're so glad to be back. Tell me what that's like."

"Okay. Okay, listen. Yeah, I was happy to wake up. After figuring out what the hell had happened to me, yeah, I was damn happy. Why wouldn't I be? I've got my wife and my kids. But she waited for me, Travis. That whole time. Claire waited all those years for *me*, and I'm still trying, every day now, to be worth it for her. I can't let her down."

"But she waited," I said. "She knew you'd come back even if no one else believed it, right?"

"I guess so," he said. "But it scares me to think that she'd give up a happy life forever just to sit around and wait on the off chance that I'd be back. All those years she raised our girls alone and she didn't know a thing. She had no idea if I'd be back or not. Maybe that's not fair, but it terrifies me."

"Everyone just outgrew me. Now I think I'm just haunting them."

"Give it time. You have to. You and I both know we're just as surprised as they all are. You know how they all must've felt. They had to try to move on because waiting for you might not have worked. We did the easy part, Travis. We took a little nap. They all had to live for five years without us. They had to talk about us and think about us and see the things that reminded them of us. Put yourself in their shoes for a minute, huh? See if you don't stop breathing."

"It was just so much easier before," I said.

"Travis," he said, almost sternly. "Don't you go your whole life comparing everything that happens to the way it was *before*. You know what else happened *before*? You died. Your body gave up on you. Just like mine did. We can't waste our whole lives obsessing over what things were like *before*, or else we'll end up even worse off."

"Maybe you're right. At least my body's better now," I said.

"Yeah. Mine too. I've even been running. I never used to run. I got too winded. Hell, I'm in the best shape of my life, and I'm supposed to be dead. How do you like that?"

"Seems like cheating," I said.

"You and me, Travis, we're the biggest cheaters in the world. You think people don't look at us, don't think about us, and feel sick about all the people they've lost? We cheated the one thing everyone's afraid of. Question is, how do we prove it wasn't wasted on us?"

"I have no idea."

"Me neither. But I'll keep looking. And trying to figure it out. Maybe that's lame and cheesy to someone your age, but I spent too many years the first time feeling sorry for myself and being afraid to do the things that make me happy. Not this time."

Lawrence and I agreed to talk again the following week. When I got off the phone, I felt like chatting with him for fifteen minutes had made me think about everything so much clearer. There was a sick sort of relief in knowing that someone else was out there completely confused and thrown off track like I was. And I thought about all those letters and how those kids at school who I barely knew, and one who I didn't even like, had done this nice thing for me because they thought what happened to me was something special. "Inspiring." And, see, that's just the thing. Up until that point, any time someone said my story "inspired" them, I cringed and I wanted to tell them all the reasons why missing everyone's lives and coming back and being the only one who was the same was the most terrifying thing I could ever imagine. But after that day, after the letters and the phone call, after everything that had happened with my parents, I thought maybe a day was coming when I'd stop constantly worrying about how to live. Maybe at some point I'd just start living, no questions asked.

CHAPTER THIRTY-TWO

NO QUESTIONS
ASKED

When I finally heard from Cate again, it had been a week and a half since we'd followed my dad. I guess Kyle had explained to her everything that went down the day after, because as soon as I answered the phone, she immediately started asking me if I was okay.

"Hey, I get two Christmases next year. I'm fine."

"Travis, you don't have to do that with me. You don't have to make light of it."

"Look, it happened. I think I haven't completely processed it yet. Maybe my head's not screwed on right."

"Travis."

"Get it?"

"Please stop."

"Where've you been, Cate?"

"I can't do this."

"Do what?"

"I can't talk to you if every time we have a conversation, it turns into this long, serious thing about what we are."

"What are we?"

"Friends, Travis."

"Sorry."

"No. I am. You've been through too much."

"When can I meet Turner?" I asked.

"Oh. Umm . . . are you sure?"

"That's only fair, I think. You said he wanted to meet me. If that means I can still see you, then let's set it up."

"Thursday night? You want to come over for dinner?"

"At your place? Your place with him?" I got up and looked in the mirror to make sure my face hadn't exploded.

"Yeah. Or no. Would that be too weird, maybe?"

"I think so."

"Okay. Yeah. You're right. Steak 'n Shake?"

She was taking Jeremy Pratt's heart and scraping it against a cheese grater. She was stomping on it like a pile of grapes. She was running over it with her car, then backing over it to make sure it was dead.

"No. That's a bad idea," she said. "We'll just get coffee. How's that sound?"

"Perfect." I was dead inside.

So the plan was to meet them at the Grindhouse at five thirty Thursday afternoon. I was going to have Kyle take me, but he had class. So I asked Hatton instead, and I knew my mom would let me borrow the car, even if it required another driving test.

"What am I gonna do while you're in there?" Hatton asked.

"I don't know. You can come in if you want."

"No. That's not going to happen. I'm already sort of cringing for you on the inside."

"Yeah. I'm not too excited. But the way I figure, I might as well size up the competition before making my next move."

"And what's your next move?"

"I'm going to ask her to marry me."

"You're shitting me, right?"

"Know that thousand bucks my dad gave me for Christmas?"

"Yeah."

"I'm gonna buy her a ring with it."

"Doesn't she already have an engagement ring?"

"Not the one she's supposed to have," I said. "And I'll ask her soon. Like, maybe this weekend. She'll see how serious I am. She'll see I'm not just a kid pretending to be grown-up to be with her."

"That's kind of exactly what you are, though, Travis."

"Shut up. You know what I mean. This has to work. She keeps telling me we should just stay friends, but then she calls me and she comes over and she wants me in her life."

"Because she cares about you, man."

"She loves me. You don't fall out of the kind of love we had, Hatton. I wish you could've seen us together."

"I think you've gone completely insane."

"You want to help me ring shop this afternoon?"

"You need a ride, don't you?"

"Do you know her ring size, sir?" the salesman at the Zales in the mall asked that afternoon.

"Umm . . . small? Medium, maybe?"

"It's measured in millimeters, sir."

"Oh. Okay. Well, maybe just give me the average size?"

"Fine. Let me show you some of our new collection."

He took us over to a glass case and showed us some rings I was sure I couldn't afford. I started looking around at the other cases, and I could tell he was losing patience with me. Hatton was making sure no one we knew was walking by. I hadn't seen him look this embarrassed before. I think it's because he didn't approve of anything I was doing.

"Do you have something more . . . affordable, maybe?"

"What's your price range?"

"A thousand."

He brought out a small cushioned case holding five rings. They were simple and each had a single, tiny diamond in the center. There were two gold and three silver.

"A silver one, I think." I reached down and felt the diamond on one. I looked over at Hatton and he shrugged. Clearly he hadn't been the best choice for this mission.

"This one. Yeah. I like this one."

"But the question is, will *she* like it?" the man asked me.

"Yeah," Hatton said, rolling his eyes. "Will *she* like it, Travis?"

After Hatton and I got home, I hid the ring under my mattress. This was something, I'm told, that boys used to do before the Internet. They hid things they wanted to keep secret from their parents under their mattresses. I wasn't sure why this ever worked out well for anyone who had clean sheets. But my secret was temporary.

The next day Kyle picked Hatton and me up from school, and I knew immediately that they were about to stage some intervention or something. They had nearly the same expression on their faces, like they were getting ready to tell me really bad news.

"Kyle, do you *ever* have anything better to do than hang out with two teenagers?" I tried to lighten the mood as soon as I got in.

"Shut up," Kyle said. He was angry.

"You told him?" I asked Hatton.

"He told me. Travis, what the hell are you thinking?"

"I'm thinking I want to ask my girlfriend to marry me. I don't see what's wrong with that."

"Okay, well . . . for starters, she's not your girlfriend. And also, she's already getting married."

"Minor technicalities."

"You've completely lost it, you know that?" Kyle pulled into a supermarket parking lot.

"Really, Kyle? I think I'm holding it together pretty well, considering all that's been going on."

"Considering what?" He raised his voice, turning around in his seat to face me. Hatton was terrified and silent. "Oh man, your parents split up. Damn. And they get along so well they were able to pretend to still be married for three months, and you didn't even have a clue! Oh, and you no longer have a body that's literally deteriorating. That must really suck."

"My parents won't even talk. They use me as a carrier pigeon," Hatton said.

"And you know what, Travis? You and Cate were great. You really were. And I wish more than anything that we could all go back to the way it was, that we were all sixteen again and you didn't have to go away. But you know what else? I bet we could walk into that store right over there and ask any stranger we ran into if they wanted the same exact thing, and they'd say yes. Everyone wants to change the past, Travis. But they can't. None of us can."

"Just let me do this," I said. "I know it's crazy and I know I've been acting ridiculous, but I have to do this."

"And then what? What'll you do when she says no, Travis? What'll you do?"

"She won't. You know she won't."

"You're full of shit, you know that?" Kyle practically shouted.

"I have to be back for something, Kyle!" I yelled. "I

can't just be here like this for no reason. Don't you see that?"

"Travis," Kyle said, quietly this time. "If you'd just open your damn eyes for a minute, then maybe you'd see that Cate isn't the only good thing in your life. Just open your eyes."

CHAPTER THIRTY-THREE

OPEN YOUR EYES

I made the mistake of telling Kyle and Hatton about my phone calls with Lawrence Ramsey. They weren't some dark secret or anything, but I knew it would be hard to explain to people what we talked about. When they found out, though, they made me promise to talk to him before Thursday afternoon, before I made my grand gesture to get Cate back. They had a good point. I wanted to know what he'd say too. Maybe he'd have a new perspective on the whole thing. Or maybe he'd tell me I was crazy like they had and I'd ignore him, too.

"Travis! I'm so glad you called."

"Thanks, thanks. I should probably apologize for last time."

"Don't worry about it," he said. "Hey, I have *got* to tell you something crazy. You won't believe it."

"Oh yeah? I've got something for you, too. You go first."

"I talked to his family. It was so wild."

"Whose family?"

"*His*, my body's. Umm . . . my donor's family."

"No way."

"Yeah. Last week I get this call from the Saranson Center, and they ask me if I'd give the family permission to contact me. I figured why not, so I said yeah and about two days later I get a phone call."

"Who was it?" I was half-convinced he was making this all up.

"His wife. How weird is that? She told me all about him. He was a travel agent in Palm Springs. They used to fly around the world together."

"Crazy."

"Yeah. Then one day he has a brain aneurysm and dies. Just like that."

"So she donated his body then?"

"Yeah. Her sister told her about the project in Denver. She'd read about it somewhere. His wife, her name's Jackie, she said she knew immediately that she had to do it. Said he would've loved the idea of it."

"Seems like a cool lady."

"It was so unexpected. I didn't know if I should thank her or what. I could hardly speak."

He told me more about her and about Stanley Baker, the man who was now attached to him. I think Lawrence was having a hard time even talking about it. He might have even been crying a little because he kept pausing midsentence and breathing in really deeply. It was heart-breaking but also sort of annoying because I'd called to talk about proposing to Cate. I'd called to talk about the future, and all he wanted to do was make me think about the past.

"Look, Travis. You have to meet the family. Or at least talk to them. It made me feel so . . . I don't know . . . just so much better about everything. I don't feel as lost."

"Are you gonna talk to them again?"

"Hell yeah, I am. I'm thinking of flying out to California really soon so I can meet them. He had two kids, Travis. I just don't see how I can't go tell them how grateful I am in person."

"That's gonna be so tough, don't you think?"

"I'm sure it'll be tough for all of us. But good for us too, I think. They reached out to me because they wanted me to know what kind of a man he was, and I can't tell you how much of a difference it's made."

He was happier than I'd ever heard him—excited, I'd say. About everything. About the next day and the next week and the week after that. He was ready to fall back in love with life, he said.

And I was jealous of him. Because even though I was about to do this incredibly romantic and drastic and insane thing, I wasn't so much excited as I was completely and devastatingly terrified. But Lawrence, he had been enlightened. The nerve endings and veins and arteries carefully attaching his head to his body were firing and pulsating and pumping with a renewed sense of opportunity and fervor. He had found his answers, and they all added up to one ultimate mission. He just had to keep living.

"So what did you want to tell me, Travis?" Lawrence asked.

"Oh. It's nothing."

"You sure?"

"Yeah, Lawrence. I'll talk to you soon."

Hatton and I sat in my mom's car around the corner from the Grindhouse and let the heat blasting from the dashboard vents make its way onto our faces in silence. I was passing the little felt ring box from one hand to the other, and Hatton was looking over at me from the corner of his eye. I think Kyle had said everything that needed to be said, so Hatton was just going to let this all play out without trying too hard to stop me.

"You're asking her in there?"

"I might. Depends on what happens."

"In front of *him*?"

"I think it would be romantic, maybe."

"Yeah. Or a total train wreck."

"It's almost time. My hands are sweating."

"You don't have to do this, Travis."

"I do, though. Thanks for bringing me."

"I'll be waiting right here, man."

My walk down the sidewalk felt more like a funeral march. Then when I walked inside and saw them sitting in the back corner, I almost turned around. Cate raised one hand up to get my attention, and Turner, who had his back to the door, turned around and smiled. He had sloppy brown hair combed to one side, and his forehead was large and shiny. He had a good smile, an honest one, I think, and it seemed like he probably got a lot of compliments on his teeth. When he stood to shake my hand, I was noticeably taller and it was hard not to show how great this made me feel. Thank you, Jeremy.

"Travis. Nice to meet you, man."

"You too."

He sat down beside Cate, leaving one side of the booth empty for me. I took a seat and nervously looked up at her and smiled.

"So this is nice, huh?" Turner began.

"Yeah," Cate agreed. "How was school?"

"It was fine," I said. "Same as every day, I guess."

"And what grade are you in again, Travis?" Turner asked. I could see how this was going to go down.

"Tenth. Supposed to be a junior, but I didn't have the credits from before."

"Travis missed a lot of class when he was sick," Cate added.

"Oh. Man, that's really too bad," he said with surprising sincerity. "I bet it's weird being back there, huh? After so long?"

"Turner," Cate said. "I told you, for Travis it's not been long at all."

"Oh, right. Right. That's confusing for everyone, I bet."

"It is," I said. "It's confusing for me sometimes too."

"Turner here went to Prentice Academy."

"Oh geez," I said before thinking.

"What?" he asked.

"Nothing. Just used to know a few guys from there."

"Yeah. It can be a pretty lame place sometimes. But I liked it there. I mostly kept to myself, though. I had some trouble fitting in when I was a freshman."

"Fitting in?" I asked.

"You know, those kinds of guys like I'm sure you're talking about. They didn't like the chubby kid with the wiry hair and glasses."

"You'd think bullies would eventually evolve past that, right?" Cate said.

"Seriously," I agreed.

I looked over at Turner and was really impressed by how he talked about the past, even painful things, with confidence and not an ounce of shame. He was older, sure, but even my parents had trouble bringing up past embarrassments. He seemed so levelheaded and calm. It was as intimidating as it was surprising.

"I need a refill. Travis, you want something, man?" Turner shotgunned the rest of his coffee and went to stand up.

"I'm okay, thanks."

"Babe? Refill?"

"No, thanks—I'm good." Cate took a sip from her mug of tea, the little white string hanging down and hitting her hand.

I could see this guy's charm, and it wasn't making me feel any better about things. I'd wanted to hate him, to be repulsed by him. I'd wanted him to be an asshole and threaten me in front of her and make her realize that she was about to ruin her life by spending it with him. So far he was such a disappointment.

"He's nice, right?" she asked me after he'd walked away.

"He is."

"Thank you for doing this."

"You're welcome."

"Are you okay?"

I decided to do it right then, just grab her hand and fall to the floor and take out the ring and re-create every television and movie scene I'd ever watched that played out in that exact same way.

"I need to ask you something," I said. I took the ring box out of my jacket pocket and set it on the table.

"Oh, Travis. What . . . what is that?"

"Cate, I think you know how I feel about you and—"

"No, Travis, you have to stop right now—"

"And I think you feel the same way because all this time we've spent together and the phone calls and the trips to the park. And I thought maybe you hadn't waited on me, but now I realize that you did—you just didn't know it, I think. And I have to do this now so you'll know we can work. We can do this. It doesn't matter how crazy it is or how—"

"So that barista guy just asked me if you're that head kid from TV," Turner interrupted, walking up behind me.

"Jesus," Cate said.

"What's happening?" Turner looked at Cate's face, then the ring box.

"Nothing, we were just playing around." Cate snatched the ring off the table and threw it into the seat beside her.

"Look, Turner, you seem like a nice guy. And I'm sure you are. But I just proposed to Cate, and I think she and I both know it's the right thing to do. It's supposed to happen this way."

He laughed. Turner laughed and sat down, looking behind him to see if anyone else was listening.

"Just now? You just proposed to my fiancée in the Grindhouse Coffee Shop while I was standing ten feet away?"

"Well, I wasn't done. You kind of interrupted us. But yeah."

"Let's see the ring, Cate."

He gestured over toward the seat. She placed the little gray box in the center of the table and when she did, I saw the ring he'd given her months before right there on her finger, and I briefly thought about standing up on the table and leaping through the window. That ring had never looked bigger or shinier than right then.

"What'd you say?" he asked Cate. He opened the box and examined the ring. I'd say he had a slightly amused expression on his face. Not anger. Not yet.

"I didn't say anything."

"Well, you should answer him, Cate. You can't do that to him."

Cate cut Turner a sharp look, one I was all too familiar with, as if to say, *You're being a complete ass right now*. Then she turned back to face me and sighed.

"Travis, I . . . you know that we . . . I can't . . ."

"Hey, everybody!" The voice sounded loudly from speakers all over the room. We turned to see one of the baristas in black skinny jeans and a red T-shirt standing on a tiny stage. He was adjusting the microphone on its stand as he spoke.

"It's Thursday, and you know what that means—open mic night here at the Grindhouse."

"You've got to be kidding me," I said under my breath. Turner was laughing. Cate looked like she'd just witnessed someone being bludgeoned to death. In a sense, she had. It was me . . . I had been bludgeoned to death by this moment.

"Can you even legally get married?" Turner leaned in and whispered.

"Turner, stop," Cate said.

"My birth certificate says I'm twenty-one years old," I whispered back, looking right into his eyes.

"Our first performance tonight is by one of your favorites. Let's give it up for Rodrigo."

Then the room started clapping as Turner and I had sort of a stare-down and Cate looked on in horror. Onstage an overweight blond guy with dreadlocks approached the microphone. He held a single maraca in his hand. He was wearing a poncho.

"Hey, everybody," he began in a nasally voice. "I call this one 'Man.'"

"Do you think we can speak alone, Cate?" I leaned down and asked her.

"Are you crazy?" Turner said.

"Man," Rodrigo said in a monotone from the stage.

"I'm not crazy. I love her. I loved her before you even knew her."

"Man." Rodrigo used a high-pitched tone this time. I was afraid of where this was going.

"You know, Travis, I'm trying to be nice here, but you aren't making it very easy."

"I think we should go. Maybe we should go." Cate stared blankly down at the table.

"Man!" Rodrigo yelled. We all jumped a little in our seats.

"Yeah, Cate, let's go," I said.

"Travis," she whispered. "I'm with Turner. I don't know why you—"

"Man." Maraca shake. "Man." Maraca shake. "Man."

"I'm gonna kill him," Turner said.

"Turner, calm down." Cate put her hand on top of his.

"No, not Travis. This moron hippie on the stage."

"This is the worst moment of my life," I said, setting my head down on the table.

"Which life?" Turner asked, laughing.

"That's not funny," Cate said.

"The one where I kick your ass in this coffee shop," I said, sitting back up.

"MAN! MAN! MAN! MAN! MAN! MAN!"

"Okay, Travis. Chill out, dude."

Then I stood up and punched him right in the face just as Rodrigo held up his maraca and started convulsing on the stage. Turner fell back in the booth and held his hands to his face. There may have been blood, but I didn't get a good look. I thought about grabbing the ring from the table, but instead I just bent down into Cate's ear and said, "You can sell that to pay for the honeymoon." Then I walked out holding Jeremy Pratt's aching fist.

I didn't tell Hatton what had happened, and I ignored the five calls in a row from Cate on the drive home. Once we got to my house, I stormed over to the front door. I wasn't crying. I was too upset to cry. I sat down on the doormat with my knees folded up to my chest. Hatton walked over and sat down beside me.

"What happened?"

"She didn't say yes."

"Shit."

"But she didn't say no, either."

"Oh. Travis . . ."

"I'm not sure I can do this anymore."

"Do what?"

"This. Exist. Be here like this with everything so fucked up."

"Hey, Travis? I don't think it really matters if you know how to exist."

"What do you mean?"

"I don't think any of us do."

"Then what are we doing?"

"I don't know. We're just meandering."

CHAPTER THIRTY-FOUR

JUST ME AND A RING

Let's pretend the whole thing at the coffee shop never happened. Let's pretend Turner never came back to the table and Cate said yes to my proposal and, miraculously, Rodrigo never showed up to perform. Let's pretend it all worked out and everything was okay again. Everything was as close to normal as it ever could be.

It doesn't work, does it? Pretending away something you can't change doesn't work. I thought I was so close, and then I was further away than ever. I was finally forced to face the truth: Cate Conroy was no longer mine. And Turner, who should've beaten me to death with that weirdo's maraca, didn't. And that probably made him the better man. The only man, really.

Two weeks went by after that, and they seemed much longer than all the weeks before. Maybe it was because I stayed pretty zoned out the whole time, at school, at home, even when Kyle and Hatton would drag me out of the house to go see a movie or go eat or just ride around town aimlessly. They tried. I'll give them that. They tried really hard to cheer me up.

I even spent a night at my dad's place, and despite still being pretty disturbed by his secret Travis museum, it was nice being there with all my old stuff. After he'd gone to bed, I went through my clothes and searched all the pockets. And I smelled them, which I know is weird, but you'd have done it too. All these years they'd been in storage and then this apartment, and they still smelled like my house. They smelled like I could open the door and yell for my mom and she'd be just down the hall.

I found an old notebook from school on the shelf in the closet and flipped through it. Aside from algebra notes, each page was covered in sloppy doodles and black-and-white checkerboards of ink. It was something I still did sometimes in class when I was having a hard time listening. I'd draw six vertical lines and intersect them with six horizontal lines, and then I'd fill in every other little square with my pen.

Then I looked through all the books on the bookshelf. I'd read a handful of them, maybe, but Mom had let me sign up for one of those book-of-the-month club things at the book fair when I was in middle school, and I used to get copies of the Boxcar Children or Hardy Boys like clockwork and just add them to the overflowing shelf, promising to read them someday. In one book

I found a leaf pressed between two pages. It was almost falling apart when I lifted it up to look at it. I'd taken it from the park one day when I was a kid. I'd wanted to remember that day for some reason. And even though I was holding the leaf all those years later and I knew it was supposed to remind me of something, it had escaped me completely.

The drawers of my desk were filled with more notebooks and junk that I'd hoarded. There was a Frodo Baggins bobblehead figurine on the desktop that still shook every time I slid open a drawer. In the back of the third drawer down, I found a photograph of Cate and me that I'd stuck under a couple of old yearbooks. We were fourteen and sitting side by side in eighth-grade French class. I was smiling, but I wasn't showing my teeth. I never liked showing my teeth in photos when I was younger. Cate had her hair in a ponytail, and her smile was wide and unattached to any sense of self-consciousness.

I ended up sleeping better that night than any other I could remember, with my old movie posters of *Vertigo* and *Jaws* and *Fear and Loathing in Las Vegas* hanging on the walls around me and my too-long body making my feet stick out over the short wooden railing of the twin bed. On the far wall, just above the TV, there was an empty spot where Cate's painting of the movie theater should've been hanging.

She kept trying to call. For two weeks she called at least twice a day and left messages apologizing and saying she was worried about me. In some of them she was crying. I never thought I could be the kind of person who ignored someone like Cate. But it was too much. I needed more time. Talking to her would make it worse. Seeing her with Turner had changed everything.

Then one day she stopped calling and I found the ring box sitting on the front steps after school. I stood there looking at the tiny silver circle in my hand and wondering what the hell had happened to me.

My parents were worried too. I'd never been the quiet type. Not before and not when I'd come back to them. But now I just sat around listening to music or watching TV and felt like I didn't really have anything to say. I didn't want to talk about the divorce. I didn't want to talk about Cate. And I surely didn't want to talk about the future. The future was something I didn't really care about anymore. It had pretty much been a bitch to me so far, so I think I was allowed to be a little wary of it.

One Saturday at Mom's she came into my room and sat on the edge of my bed. It was around noon, and I hadn't gotten up yet. This would've been normal teenage behavior if I hadn't been in that same spot since four o'clock the afternoon before.

"Travis, you know, you can't stay like this forever."

"Says who?"

"Says me. Now let's get you up. It's a nice day outside. It's warm. The sun's shining."

"Pass. It's a good thought, though. But still. I pass. I'm fine right here."

"You're making it hard to feel sorry for you." She looked down at the half of my face that wasn't smashed into a pillow.

"I'd think it would be pretty easy, actually."

"You want to know what I think?"

"What's that, Mom?"

"I think if the old you were here right now, hooked to IVs and doped up on all kinds of drugs, well, I think he'd probably kick your sorry ass."

With that she put some clean socks she'd been holding into my top dresser drawer and walked out. She had a point, I guess. The old me probably would kick my sorry ass. He'd probably look at me and be embarrassed at what I'd so quickly become—someone healthy who pretends to be dying.

After she left, I rolled over enough to nearly fall out of bed and caught myself before my face hit the floor. When I looked up, I noticed my closet door had been left open just enough to see the bottom edge of the container full of letters from school. I dragged it to the center of my room and tossed the lid aside, then reached in with my eyes closed and grabbed an envelope. I tore it open at one end and started reading.

YOU ARE A SIGN OF THE END
TIMES. REPENT!

I picked another letter.

Dear Travis,

*You are my hero. Do you have any information
on the Saranson Center? I have been diagnosed
with a fatal illness and would love to undergo
the same procedure as you. Does it hurt?
How do you like your new body?*

And then I stopped reading. I dropped the letter, put
the lid on the box, and crawled back into bed. How was I
supposed to respond to any of that? I didn't have answers for
these people. Not the crazy ones or the ones who thought
I'd made the right choice. I was just some dumb kid with a
hell of a lot of good luck. It was hard for me to imagine a day
when I'd be ready for that—when I'd be able to sit down
and listen to all the things these strangers expected of me.

Exactly three weeks after my failed marriage proposal to
Cate, Kyle and Hatton showed up at my door holding a
Ziploc bag full of cremated cat remains.

"Travis, say hello to Binky." Hatton held the bag up to
my face.

"Oh no."

"Oh yes, Travis," Kyle said. "Step aside, there's work
to be done."

Once they were in the house, Kyle and Hatton started looking around. Keep in mind that Hatton was still holding a liter-size plastic bag full of Binky's ashes. They were definitely Binky's, by the way, because it was written in black Sharpie ink on the side.

"Your mom home?" Kyle asked.

"She's at work. We really don't need to do this now, guys."

"But we do, Travis. We've got to bury the past. Or spread it or whatever," Kyle said.

"Or it's not too late to get those tattoos we discussed," Hatton added.

"So where are they, then?" Kyle asked.

"I'll go get them. Hang on."

I found the green tin cookie jar right where I'd left it, in the back corner of the guest room closet, and I brought it out to them. Kyle grabbed it from me and headed toward the kitchen. He set it in the sink and took the lid off.

"What're you doing?" I asked.

"We can't risk spilling any on the floor. Hatton, bring me the cat."

Hatton walked over with Binky's remains and opened up the bag like it had potato chips inside. He handed it to Kyle, who immediately got this confused expression and looked up at us.

"We need like a . . . mixing bowl, maybe."

"What?" I was going back and forth between frustrated and disgusted.

"Well, we need to get you out of the jar and Binky into the jar and then you into the bag. So we need an in-between container." It scared me how serious Kyle was.

I opened the cabinet by the sink and handed him a shiny metal mixing bowl and then stepped back in horror. He slowly and carefully poured the contents of the cookie jar into the bowl, and then Hatton walked over and started pouring Binky into the empty jar. Then Hatton held the bag open as Kyle poured me into the now-empty bag. The whole thing took less than five minutes, but I would be scarred for life.

"There. Perfect. Hatton, this was a grand idea." Kyle patted him on the back.

Hatton held up the bag, which now had all that was left of my body inside, and gave me this dead-serious stare.

"Travis, what do you feel?"

"Nothing. Well, a little nauseous."

"No," Hatton said. "Focus on Binky's Plastic Bag of Raw Emotion and just let it happen, man. Let it all out."

I returned the cookie jar to its hiding place, and when I walked back into the kitchen, Kyle was scrubbing the mixing bowl in the sink. He was whistling. And Hatton? Hatton was sitting at the counter eating a baby carrot.

"What now, weirdos?"

"Now, Travis, now we lay you to rest once and for all."

"Oh boy."

"When's the last time you talked to Cate?" Hatton asked, still chewing a carrot.

"Are you serious right now? *That's* what you want to talk about?"

"It's important."

"Three weeks ago. In the coffee shop."

"She says she's tried to call you a million times," Kyle added. He was using a hand towel to dry the bowl.

"I can't yet. Maybe eventually but not yet."

"But can you see her?" Kyle asked.

"Why do you even ask that? If I can't talk to her, then I don't want to see her either."

"Just hear us out," Kyle began.

"What'd you do?"

"We invited her to go with us," Hatton said.

"To go with us where? What the hell are you guys talking about? Where are we going?"

"Oh. Yeah. We should tell him. Should we tell him yet?" Hatton had a very excited, almost sinister look in his eyes.

"Travis," Kyle said. "Maybe sit down for a second, okay?"

"Okay." I sat down.

"Travis, we found Jeremy Pratt."

CHAPTER THIRTY-FIVE

JEREMY PRATT

Before he died, Jeremy Pratt and his parents signed a waiver stating that the Saranson Center for Life Preservation could transport his corpse from a hospital in Quincy, Illinois, to Denver, Colorado. This was done using an ambulance so a series of machines could keep his heart beating and his lungs pumping air. In Denver he was carefully decapitated and, after the fifty-six-hour surgery to attach his body to my neck was completed, Jeremy Pratt's cremated remains were shipped home to his family and buried in the Pleasant Grove Cemetery on Locust Street.

Which brings us to an unseasonably warm day in February. I was sitting in the backseat of Kyle's truck, and he and Hatton were trying to convince me that everything happens for a reason. They were having a hard time with this. Audrey Hagler was sitting beside me with an enthused expression on her face. I still wasn't sure why she was there with us, but I knew Hatton had something to do with it.

Then we pulled into a driveway I didn't recognize, and as I leaned up to ask where we were, I saw her. Cate was walking toward us with hesitation, no doubt considering turning back and running away. But she opened the door and took a seat on the other side of Audrey. I looked over at her and she half waved, giving me that sad expression of hers. If you're ever dying, which I hope you're not, this is a look you'll get used to. People will try to smile at you and talk to you without thinking about what's happening, but there's always this slight change in their lips and eyes. It'll bother you the first few times, make you feel like no one will ever be sincere with you again, but it's not like that, really. They aren't doing it on purpose. When one of us is dying, they say a part of all of us is. I think that's why it hurts. We go our whole lives losing little chunks until we can't lose any more of them.

"This is so . . . exciting," Audrey said.

Hatton turned around from the front seat and looked at her. It seemed like he wanted to say something but was making sure it came out right. She made him nervous, which was kind of sweet and also pretty obvious to everyone.

"Thanks for coming," he said. "I needed you. No, I mean, *we* needed you."

She laughed at his fumble, along with Kyle, and I looked over to Cate to see that she was smiling pretty big.

"How much longer?" Hatton asked.

"About two hours," Kyle said. "Are you gonna ask every five minutes?"

"Maybe."

We stopped at a convenience store outside of Brookfield. Kyle was pumping gas, and Hatton and Audrey were inside using the restroom and getting some snacks. I was just standing beside the truck stretching my arms above my head as Cate walked up to me.

"How's your hand?" she asked playfully.

"Sorry about that."

"It was definitely surprising."

"I can't believe he didn't hit me back."

"I don't think Turner's ever been in a fight. He cried on the way to the ER."

"The ER?"

"You broke his nose."

"Oh my God."

"He'll be fine," she said. "I think I'm angrier than he is."

"He can't be that nice, can he?"

"Yeah," she said. "He kind of is."

"Look, thanks for coming. I'm not sure why they're making a big deal out of all this."

"Because it is a big deal. I think so, anyway."

"It'll probably just be a letdown to everyone. Sprinkle some ashes, say a few words, then drive home. Done and done."

"You know, for someone who got brought back to life, you sure are pessimistic."

"I guess so," I said.

"You should work on that."

Back on the road no one was really talking, just listening to the barely audible music on the radio. Of the string of weird days that had made up my recent life, this one was shaping up to be the longest and most bizarre. Within a couple of hours we would illegally pour my ashes onto the grave of a stranger whose body happens to be holding up my head.

"I can't believe we're doing this," I said. No one responded.

I must've fallen asleep because the next thing I knew, we were driving really slowly and Hatton was hanging halfway out the window looking at rows of headstones.

"Keep going," he said. "These are all pretty old."

"We should get out and walk," Audrey suggested. "Split up and try to find it."

"Teams. We should go in teams." Hatton looked to Audrey, who rolled her eyes but also smiled.

"There's no directory or anything?" I asked, yawning.

"I don't think so," Kyle said.

So we got out of the truck and split up to search the huge cemetery, hoping we could find the one grave with Jeremy Pratt's name on it. Hatton followed Audrey, and Kyle walked off by himself, leaving Cate and me. We walked slowly down a row of headstones, looking at each one as we passed.

"This is going to take forever," she said.

I nodded my head and kept looking. I was pretty warm in my sweater, so I started rolling up the sleeves haphazardly. Cate stopped in her tracks and watched me.

"Here," she said.

She stepped closer and folded each of my sleeves up the way she always used to.

"So they won't keep falling down. Drives me crazy."

"Thanks."

"You're brave, you know that?" she asked. We continued grave hunting.

"Why's that?"

"You want something, you go after it. It's a little misguided, maybe. But brave."

"Immature, you mean."

"A little. Yeah."

"I'm really sorry. I thought maybe you felt the same way." I didn't look at her, just kept my head hung low.

"It's not all your fault, Travis. It's not."

"Oh yeah?"

"You know, when you died, my mom told me something really important. She said it's too easy to get hung up on people the way we do. I mean, that we all get *one* person to be ours and that's it. We should look at it differently. We all get lots of people. And maybe we don't always get to have them the exact way we want them, but if we can figure out a way to compromise, you know, then we can keep them all."

"I love you so much," I said, stopping in my tracks and turning her way. "I don't know how to let that go."

"We're soul mates," she said. "I know that. And so are Turner and me. And you and Hatton and Kyle. We all get people that help us make sense of the world, right? We just have to figure out how to keep them however we can. You and me, we worked. But you had to leave and I had to let other people in or I'd die too. I knew you didn't want that. Did you?"

"No. Never."

"So let me go, Travis. You're the best friend I ever had, and that's what I need from you now. Let me be your best friend."

"Over here!" Kyle shouted from across the way.

I had to squint in the sunlight to see him, and he was waving us over with both arms. Audrey and Hatton were walking quickly toward him from the far-west side of the cemetery. Cate started walking over to him and I followed after her. She let the tips of her fingers lightly graze the tops of tombstones as we passed.

Kyle, Hatton, and Audrey were standing around the grave forming a broken circle when we walked up to help them complete it. Hatton was holding the plastic bag full of my ashes. It still said "Binky" on the side.

"So how do we do this?" I asked.

"Up to you," Kyle said. "But we were thinking maybe we could all help."

"That would be nice," I said.

I looked down at the inscription etched into the shiny, deep purple–stained concrete headstone. *Jeremy Lee Pratt: Beloved son and brother.*

"Audrey," Hatton said. "Would you maybe say a few words?"

I didn't close my eyes, but I watched Cate as she held hers tightly shut. She was mouthing something as Audrey prayed. Cate said "Amen" with the rest of us, and she looked right at me when we were done. She held her hands clasped, one cupped over the other.

"Who wants to go first?" Kyle asked.

"I'll go," Hatton said.

Hatton held out the bag and looked around at us. He was moving his eyes like he was searching for something appropriate to say. As he let the ash start to trickle out of the top corner of the bag, he just sort of grinned and stared at me. The ashes floated a little in the air as they fell, but there was no wind, so they found the ground and couldn't be seen anymore. Then he passed the bag over to Audrey.

Audrey did the same—only she closed her eyes and let her ashes fall out more slowly. She passed the bag to Kyle, and her now-free hand swung back to rest right against Hatton's. His eyes widened.

"Ashes to ashes?" Kyle said as he let the gray cloud form in front of him.

"My turn?" Cate asked, reaching for the bag. "Okay."

She held the ashes out and didn't take her eyes off me the whole time. She tilted the bag slowly and gently as we all watched until there was only about a handful left inside.

"Thanks for this, guys," I said.

I stepped forward and took the dusty, mostly empty bag from Cate. It was hard not to laugh, but the solemn looks on their faces kept me from it.

"If it weren't for Jeremy Pratt, I guess I wouldn't be here right now," I said. "And I guess that's something to be grateful for."

I started tipping Binky's bag toward the ground.

"I don't really know much about Jeremy. I know he liked to skateboard. And I know he lived here in Quincy, which seems nice enough."

"And he couldn't play video games for shit," Kyle said.

"And he was deceptively strong," Cate added.

"Yeah. All those things. I know he had to leave his family and friends behind, and I think that's probably what we have most in common."

I paused for a second. I let every memory of the last day of my life flood in, and I imagined Jeremy's last day too. I pictured his mother and father crying and his girlfriend kissing him good-bye.

"You okay?" Cate whispered.

"I'm fine."

I finished pouring the ash out, holding the upside-down bag by both its bottom corners. When it was all gone, I folded it up and stuck it in my pocket.

"So, Jeremy. You gave me your body. Now we give you mine. It's not a very good one, but I—"

"What are you doing?"

We all turned around at the same time to see a middle-aged woman and a young girl standing behind us. The girl was wearing a light blue bow in her hair, and she couldn't have been any older than five or six. The woman looked confused and almost angry. Maybe she'd been crying because her eyes were bloodshot. None of us knew what to say.

"I asked you what you're doing," she said.

"Ma'am, we're sorry," Audrey began. "This is gonna sound crazy, but we were just—"

"You're Travis Coates. Oh my God."

"Yes, ma'am."

She paused and looked down at the ground. Her mouth was open a little bit like she had something to say but not enough air to say it.

"This is my son's grave."

"Oh," I said.

"No way," Hatton said slowly, his mouth hanging open.

"This is how we all go to jail," Kyle added under his breath.

"We just thought . . . ," I said. "We found out he was here and it felt like we needed to—"

"That's okay," she said. "You don't have to say anything."

"Hi," the little girl blurted out, looking right at me.

"Hi," I said.

"What's your name?" Cate asked her.

"Julia," she answered, smiling.

Cate walked over and kneeled down beside the little girl, telling her she liked her bow and asking where she got it. Cate was like that with kids, always had been.

"Jeremy gave it to me," Julia said.

"She wears it every time we come see him," her mom said.

"We can go. We should get out of your way." I looked over at my friends.

"Can I see it?" Jeremy's mom asked, stepping closer. "Your neck, can I see it?"

She walked up to me, and her eyes were so red that I was sure she hadn't stopped crying since October, since she lost him. She stood to my side a bit and very carefully leaned in to see the scar. She took one quick deep breath like something had scared her. Everyone was just watching us. Cate was talking to Julia in the grass, but even she had her eyes pointed in our direction.

"You're doing well?" she asked. "You're healthy?"

"Yeah. Uhh . . . yes, ma'am."

"My son never said 'Yes, ma'am' one day of his life." She laughed a little.

"Missouri, I guess," I said to her.

"Can you do something for me?" she asked quietly. She wasn't crying, but I think that's only because she was all tapped out of tears.

"Sure."

"Jeremy, he used to be so protective of his sister. No matter where we went, he was always on guard like something would happen to her. Shopping malls, super-markets. He always had to be holding her hand. Can you just . . ."

"You want me to hold her hand?"

"I don't know. I know that's weird. It's just . . . I was thinking maybe she misses it."

Cate stepped away from Julia as I walked toward her like I was approaching a wild animal. She looked at her mom with her eyes squinting and her nose wrinkled.

"Okay, no. Maybe you don't want to, huh?" I asked.

"Here," Julia said, placing her little hand in mine. "Like this."

Then her mother, Jeremy Pratt's mother, started crying, holding her chin down to her chest, and Audrey walked over and put an arm around her.

And now Julia was looking at our hands with this smile on her face, and I stared down and noticed how hers fit perfectly in the center of mine. I looked over at her and I swear I felt something I've never felt before. I felt like I knew this little kid, like I'd heard her voice before and felt her little hand in mine and seen her smile in the sun-light like that. It was so familiar to me, and despite being completely absurd and illogical, I *knew* in that moment that I was not just Travis Coates who died and came back from the dead. I was the older brother who she lost. I was the past she couldn't ever have back. All that time I'd spent worrying about why I'm here and how I'm supposed to live had kept me from remembering that Jeremy Pratt will never be back. His people will never have him again. He is Jeremy Pratt who died and stayed dead and will never get a second chance. And even though that hand that spent the last five years holding hers was somehow doing it again, it wasn't Jeremy Pratt's anymore.

On our way home I stared down at the backside of a plumber's business card where Mrs. Pratt had written down her phone number. Cate was sitting beside me, and I felt her stare on my face. I put the card in my front pocket and leaned back, closing my eyes.

"That was intense," Hatton said.

"It was beautiful," Audrey added.

We were back in Kansas City much faster than I expected, and as we pulled up to Cate's house, she leaned over and asked if she could drive me home. I hugged Hatton and Kyle, and Audrey gave me a kiss on the cheek before I got out to follow Cate. I turned around to look at the three of them as they pulled out of the driveway and waved to me from the open windows of the truck.

"I just need to grab my other keys," Cate said, unlocking her front door.

"Turner here?" I asked nervously.

"No." She laughed. "He went out with some friends."

She led the way inside, and I stood in the entryway with my hands in my pockets. I heard her fumbling around in some drawers in the kitchen and cursing at herself. Cate always loses her keys. It's the curse of someone who thinks they need to put things in a safe place and then never remembers which safe place they used.

"Ah! Found them!" she yelled, walking back out where I could see her.

"You ready?"

"Is it . . . here?" I asked, looking around. "The painting?"

"Oh yeah. In the bedroom. Wanna see it?"

"Can I?"

"For sure. This way."

It was hanging right in the center of the wall above a bookshelf. I reached out and touched it, remembering the way those brushstrokes felt. I traced them until my finger fell off the edge of the canvas. I looked at us right there in the center of that movie theater and shook my head in amazement.

"Still the best gift I ever got," I said.

"You should have it back, Travis."

"No. I like it right here."

"You sure?"

"I'm sure. It'll remind you of us."

She was driving me home, and it had gotten much darker and colder out since Kyle had dropped us off, so cold that the windows were all fogged over and we were both shivering in our seats. We stopped at a red light on the way, and I swear I could hear both our hearts beating. There are moments when you know something is going to happen and you know that the other person knows it too. These are the moments when you stop thinking and you just go for it.

When I died, I didn't see anything. No bright lights or heavenly bodies or long, dark tunnels. But when I leaned in to kiss Cate Conroy in her freezing car while we were stopped at that red light, I saw every single moment of everything. I felt every single thing I've ever felt and heard every sound I've ever heard. And even when she turned her face so my lips touched her cold cheek in the dark, I knew I'd do it all again. I don't know why, but I would.

"What the hell, Travis?" She pulled the car over onto the side of the road.

"Sorry," I whispered. "I . . ." Then I leaned toward her again.

"You just don't get it, do you?" she yelled, pushing me. "This is never going to work. You can't keep doing this."

She was crying now, and I watched her there with her head turned down a little, with her hands gripping the steering wheel tightly. I tried to touch her shoulder, but she waved me away and started crying even harder.

"You don't get to do this," she said through her tears. "You left."

"Do you remember that snowstorm?" I asked, still watching her.

"What?" She looked up at me.

"That snowstorm. Before I got sick."

"Yeah," she said, wiping her eyes.

"You were at your house and I was at mine, and you called and said you were coming over. You remember that?"

"And you told me not to, yeah."

"Right. They were calling it a blizzard on the news. I thought you'd lost your mind. But you insisted, said you were seeing me that night whether I liked it or not."

"And I made it, didn't I?" she asked, sitting up.

"You did. And do you remember what you said to me when you got there? Do you remember?" And though I was trying not to let it happen, I felt a tear escape from my eye.

"I said it would take a lot more than a little snow to keep me away from you."

"What else did you say?"

"Travis, I can't . . ."

"Please say it, Cate."

"I said one of us would have to die. It would take dying to keep us apart."

"At least you weren't lying," I said, opening my door.

"Where are you going?"

"I'll walk the rest of the way. It's three or four blocks. I'll be fine."

"Travis. Let me drive you. Don't be immature."

"I'm not being immature. I'm *sixteen*, Cate. I'm not

going to stop being sixteen until I grow up, don't you get that?"

"I know, but—"

"And when you were sixteen, when you were like this, you said one of us would have to *die* for this to be over. Die, Cate. You said that. You all got five years that I didn't get. Stop expecting me to be caught up to you. All I did was wake up. That's it."

I got out of the car, shut the door behind me, and then leaned down into the open window. She was still crying, shaking her head from side to side with that bottom lip in between her teeth. She looked over at me, and I looked back at her as I took a deep breath and managed a feeble smile.

"It's okay," I said. "It's okay."

She drove away, and her taillights cast this red glow all over the street and on my arms and legs. I raised one hand up and sort of left it in the air, waving her good-bye. But I hoped she wasn't looking back. I hoped it was like it was in Denver when she just turned away and kept walking. I needed it to be that way because as long as she kept looking back, I'd keep being there. I wouldn't go anywhere else. I'd stay in one spot till she came back to me.

And of course it wasn't okay. But that's what we have to do, right? We have to tell people it's okay even when we know it isn't. That's what we say to people we love when we realize that maybe we can't have them the way we want them. I guess it was kind of like that with everyone. For me, anyway. No one would ever be exactly who they'd been, and I'd never be exactly who I'd been either. I'd always be the miracle boy from Kansas City, wouldn't I? That head kid from the news. Noggin. Travis Coates, who died but isn't dead anymore.

E P I L O G U E

ONE   MONTH   LATER

"Okay," I say aloud to myself. "One game and then home."

I feel a rush of cold air from the AC as I step inside, and even though I know it's not there, I look to that same spot up front. No one's dancing this time. There's just the chaotic pulsating of blue and green and yellow lights accompanying the loud music. I think about stepping up to it and seeing what happens, maybe testing out Jeremy's moves, but then I just laugh and walk past. That's not why I'm here.

I've got a token in my hand. One token for one game, found it in the pocket of my blue jeans this morning at Dad's place—a pair of jeans that haven't been worn in five years. So now I'm here. And why shouldn't I be? It's a Saturday in March, and yesterday I became the first twenty-two-year-old to turn seventeen.

I can already hear the beeps and buzzes as I step

through the purple curtains. It's weird how you can go years and years without hearing them and then as soon as you do, as soon as the familiar tones reach your ears, you feel everything—every awful moment and every great moment of your life—so fast and so heavy that you aren't too sure you can keep moving. But then you do.

I let the token slide out of my hand, and the screen wakes up and shines a bright glow onto my face.

"Hello again," I say.

The music gets louder and louder, and those words are flashing there like they have a million times before, telling me what I should do. So I grip the joystick. I take a deep breath. I nod my head. And I press start.

ACKNOWLEDGMENTS

There are many people who helped make this ridiculous book work, especially when I thought it couldn't.

Those people are, first and foremost, Namrata Tripathi—an editor and friend like no other, who worked tirelessly to help give Travis's story a heartbeat. Thank you for always pushing me to be better than I think I can be.

Stephen Barr, my fearless superhero of an agent, who talked me down from many ledges along the way. And who always answers his text messages. And who never sleeps.

Justin Chanda and everyone at Atheneum and Simon & Schuster for letting me into your very large, hilarious, well-read family.

Ken Wright and Holly Goldberg Sloan, great friends who helped me fall in love with this absurd idea.

Michael McCartney for designing this cover, because—c'mon!

Adam Silvera, who let me read the entire first draft to him in one sitting and whose contagious belief in this story pushed me onward many, many times.

Charissa Sistrunk and Kimberly Powell for collectively being Cate Conroy.

Julie Murphy, whose Skype-calls-turned-author-therapy-sessions saved my life and whose words inspire me to aim higher and higher.

Many thanks to the following friends who helped along the way—who listened to ideas, read pages, inspired with their love for books, and offered welcome distraction:

Melanie Hines, Ben Jenkins, Ashley Bankston, Chase Cummings, Nate and Anna Nelson, Shalanda Stanley, Stephanie Wilkes, Ginger Phillips, Sarah Gundell, Amy Koester, Beth Towle, Mike Dodaro, and Josh Stabinsky.

A special thanks to every librarian, bookseller, fellow author, and reader who I've met over the past couple of years for letting me continue to be a part of this incredible world.

And, lastly, thank you to my big-hearted family (and anyone I forgot to list because, geez, I wrote a whole book so lay off me already) for the constant encouragement, enthusiasm, and love you all so selflessly give. If my head is ever cryogenically frozen, I hope you're all still here when I get back.

Oh . . . and to Madelyn Claire Whaley—thanks for being patient with Uncle Corey while he worked on this book. We can ride bikes now.

Interview with JoHN CoREY WHALEY!

Where did the idea come from, for a transplantation of a full cranial structure onto a donor body?

I thought about why I liked Kurt Vonnegut. What is it about him that I'm able to connect with so much? He's able to take absurd ideas and scenarios, and you can be laughing hysterically on one page, and he'll bring you to tears on the next. Could I take something absurd and ground it in some sort of emotional reality? What about a literal out-of-body experience? That's where it came from.

What was it about the five-year time lapse that was key?

The original lapse was going to be 10 years. Last year was my 10-year high school reunion. I didn't want to go. I thought, "These people won't have changed that much, but just enough to not be the people I knew 10 years ago." I kind of wanted to keep some of them the way I remembered them.

When I decided to do five years, it was first of all supposed to be funny. Travis was expecting to come back 100 years in the future or expecting to never wake up. With the five-year thing, I was able to have him experience a world that was not different, but just one little tiny step ahead of him. That was the most realistic way I could re-create the way people feel their friends and family are growing up a little faster than they are. A lot of life is people moving faster than we are, and us moving faster than others. Being 16, and being only 16, and not being able to not be 16 in the context of this story is what I wanted to explore; you're right there at the cusp of waiting to see what will happen to everyone.

Cate and Travis were inseparable before he was frozen. In the intervening years, Cate decides to move on, but Travis is still in love with her.

The more I got into the story, I didn't want to go the cliché route of Cate having a bad boyfriend; that would take away from Cate's character. She judges people quite well. Even if not for her own good, she's unable to let Travis go. Everyone says Turner [her fiancé] is a really nice guy. That makes Travis even angrier. Turner is Travis—five years older.

Even while the situation with Cate is rife with problems, Travis and Kyle find a way to work things out.

Whereas Cate was able to move on, Kyle was not able to connect with anyone the way he connects to Travis. Kyle didn't have a great time of it when Travis left; he reverted to being secretive. Travis is taking his nap and waking up, but Kyle had to go to bed every night for five years, wondering if he'd ever have someone like Travis that he could be honest with.

I struggled with the fact that Cate and Kyle don't go to Travis immediately [when he comes back]. Kyle was so afraid that if he saw Travis and lost him again, that he'd never be able to recover. He couldn't risk it.

The friendship between Travis and Hatton, and its beginnings, are so terrific. How did Hatton come to you?

I had a lot of fun writing him. I'll be accused of making the best friend the most likable character. It's too fun not to. I think it makes my job a little easier. When I have someone very different from the narrator, he's able to show the flaws. In our lives, there are usually one or two people trying to relieve us of whatever our hardships are. That's what Hatton and Kyle do.

Travis helps Kyle be honest with himself, and then Kyle is able to return the favor when Travis comes back.

It goes back to the thing of Kyle still having trouble liking himself because of his struggle with identity. When Travis died, Kyle didn't get to do these things [that he and Travis and Hatton do together]—because of his secret and because Travis died. Kyle is getting a second chance, too.

What inspired the idea of Travis having someone like himself, a compatriot to talk to, in Lawrence Ramsey?

I thought, "How do I write a book about a situation that's never happened before? How do I know what Travis is going to feel like?" There's no research to do on someone coming back from the dead. I had to put that mindset into Travis's head. The most horrible thing is that you'd be experiencing something no one else had ever experienced. With an adult coming back, he'd [get to] be in the car commercials to benefit his family. Lawrence Ramsey is hassled by the media. I wanted to show that in opposition to Travis, who's still protected, by his parents and the school. In a subtle way, to show that even if Travis feels out of control, he's still in a safe situation.

Lawrence says, "How do I live up to this? How can I be the man that this woman waited for for five years?" Everything he'll do will be a little less than what they thought they were waiting for. It's in juxtaposition to Travis. If Cate had waited, would they still be the same? Would she still be able to love Travis the same way? Would Cate-and-Travis still exist if she'd been a miserable, sad person putting her life on hold? Which would you rather?

In both Where Things Come Back and Noggin, you play with the idea of second chances. What draws you to this theme?

I'm the second-chance guy. Someone tweeted the other day, "I think it's really great that the title for Where Things Come Back could also be the title of Noggin." In my third book, I think it also applies. It's a fascination of mine. With WTCB, I knew they'd all have second chances.

With Noggin it was fueled more by the Vonnegut-esque idea: Can you ground an absurd story in realism and emotion and have a reader connect with something that's impossible?

I think it stems from growing up in a really small town, and you see a lot of people who never went the extra step to do what they wanted to do or to live the life they constantly think they should be living. That affected me when I was younger – a dread of aging, that I'd go right back to that place. Not that it's a horrible place, but it's not a place I wanted to be.

Noggin could be me processing the huge change of life I had going from a teacher to an author. The book thing was what I always wanted to do. That was me waking up from a frozen nap, if you will.

**This interview was originally published in
Kid's Maximum Shelf on Wednesday, March 19, 2014**